THE FINAL
BEAR HUG

THE FINAL BEAR HUG

James D. Navratil and
Sylvia Tascher

Rev. date: 03/25/2019

To order additional copies of this book, contact:
Xlibris
1-888-795-4274
www.Xlibris.com
Orders@Xlibris.com
786184

Contents

Synopsis Of The Bear Hug By Sylvia Tascher vii

Prologue xi

Chapter 1 Return to Colorado 1

Chapter 2 Security Clearance Troubles 37

Chapter 3 Teaching in Australia 45

Chapter 4 California Dreaming 89

Chapter 5 Academic Life at Clemson University 136

Chapter 6 The Final Bear Hug 190

Epilogue 211

Acknowledgments 229

Summary 231

Synopsis Of *The Bear Hug* By Sylvia Tascher

The Final Bear Hug—authored by my husband, James Navratil, and myself—is a continuation of the story in my first book, *The Bear Hug*. The following is a summary of the first book.

The prologue of *The Bear Hug* begins at the new headquarters of the International Atomic Energy Agency (IAEA), where Margrit Czermak is copying for a Russian agent confidential documents belonging to her husband, Dr. John James Czermak, a world-renowned scientist and contributor to the development of the neutron bomb. Subsequently, the Russian security (KGB) agent sexually attacks Margrit; and as she is fleeing, her lover, Andrei Pushkin, intervenes and is shot by the agent.

In chapter 3, a red Mercedes-Benz roadster is seen inching its way around the Gürtel (Vienna's outer perimeter street), the driver eyeing the few scantily clad prostitutes who are soliciting their wares in spite of the heavy snow that has blanketed the city. In the third district, a Ukrainian dance ensemble—sponsored by the United Nations' (UN) Russian Club of Art and Literature—has just finished its performance. During the cocktail party that follows, Andrei Pushkin—suspected by the U.S. Central Intelligence Agency (CIA) of being a covert Russian agent—captivated by a woman's melodious laugh, turns to gaze in her direction. He is immediately enraptured by the beautiful, charming Margrit Czermak, gracing the arm of Boris Mikhailov, a prominent man with the IAEA, as he steers her in the direction of her husband. Meanwhile, two covert agents of the KGB, huddled in the background, are discussing the instructions received from the Kremlin to elicit from the prominent American scientist his knowledge of the neutron bomb by whatever means necessary.

A few months later, on Margrit's return flight from London, where she has been attending her stricken brother, she encounters and is consoled by the compassionate Pushkin. In due course, he invites her to dine with him. As her husband's travel has again necessitated his prolonged absence from the city, in a state of extreme loneliness, she accepts. In the interim, both the KGB and the CIA keep the American woman under surveillance, it being the KGB's intention to instigate an illicit relationship and the CIA's to use her as a means to entrap Pushkin.

At the same time, John Czermak is suffering profound personal problems. While he has been employed in the nuclear weapons field, his scientific endeavors have demanded first priority. As his present position with the IAEA has created substantial leisure time, he is both angered and dismayed to realize his wife's newly found independence. And being a man of high moral values, it has never occurred to him that his wife is to become romantically involved with another man. To compound matters, he has belatedly sought to create an atmosphere of congeniality with his children, only to discover that he has little rapport with them.

With the passing of time, the clandestine liaison between the American and the Russian flourishes, eventually culminating in Paris and again in the Soviet capital. However, realizing the futility of their relationship, they have on several occasions unsuccessfully attempted to terminate it. Meanwhile, the KGB—eager to record on film the boudoir events of the couple—applies pressure to Andrei by kidnapping his younger son. Thus, successful in obtaining the desired photographs, they are able to prevail on Margrit for information relevant to her husband's work at the Colorado nuclear facility. During an assignation, a CIA agent meets his death as he is propelled in front of a high-speed subway train. As Margrit has witnessed the event, an attempt is then made to eliminate her as well.

The relationship with her husband continues to deteriorate, and John makes good his threats to leave her. Therefore, she beseeches Andrei to abandon his family to share a life with her. But Andrei has undergone a substantial ideological transformation during the course of his affair with Margrit and, as a result, suffered agonizing continual self-debasement. Thus, he eventually takes his own life.

Shocked beyond belief by the receipt of her lover's farewell letter, Margrit deliberates between life and death. Her friend the Austrian Anna Winkler, who minutes before has heard of Andrei's suicide on the midmorning news broadcast, drives frantically to reach Margrit in time. And John, unaware of the morning's bizarre events but certain he wants his beloved wife at any cost, rushes to make amends to her from the opposite side of the city.

Prologue

> Men wanted for hazardous journey, small wages, bitter cold, long months of complete darkness, constant danger; safe return doubtful; honor and recognition in case of success.
> —Sir Ernest Shackleton's advertisement for a crew for his Antarctic expedition

It had been a beautiful day in Antarctica, and now the sun was starting to set as Prof. John James Czermak, his graduate student Alex Pushkov, and some of their fellow ship mates prepared their camp spots on Hovgaard Island. They had to dig a level place in the snow to place their sleeping bags, and James had selected a secluded spot near the top of the hill overlooking the entrance to the Lemaire Channel and a glacial mountain range on the mainland that reminded him of the Grand Tetons in Wyoming. The expedition leader had suggested that James put a big rock at the foot of his camping equipment to prevent him from accidentally sliding down the hill. The equipment consisted of a cocoon waterproof outer cover (bivy bag) with inside sleeping bag and foam pad.

After watching a colorful sunset at about ten o'clock over the sea, James turned his attention in the opposite direction toward the red glow on the mountains reflected in the channel, containing numerous ice floats, a few icebergs, and their ship, the *Akademik Abraham*. The stars were starting to come out as James took off his boots, waterproof pants, and jacket and zipped himself into the cocoon outer cover and sleeping bag. As he watched the number of stars increase around the Southern Cross, he spotted a satellite slowly crossing the sky. Then he saw a falling star and made a wish. The last time he had come close to seeing this many stars was camping out at Yellowstone National

Park in Wyoming or perhaps on his property in Nederland, Colorado.

His mind raced back to Nederland and how wonderful it had been to have his Pine Shadows summer home at 86 Doe Trail, bordering Boulder County Open Space, with stellar views of Barker Reservoir, the Continental Divide, and the Eldora Ski Area. They joked about Doe Trail as the Department of Energy (DOE), not a female deer, as it was ironic that '86 was the tragic year that he had lost his DOE security clearance and had ensuing trouble with the Federal Bureau of Investigation (FBI).

Shortly after, he and Margrit had purchased the land in 1993, the Norwegian who had built the home four doors up on Doe Trail had died, and his son had him cryogenically preserved along with his father's deceased friend from California in hopes they could be brought back to life once medical science had advanced to that point. The townspeople—primarily a mixture of old miners, hippies, and New Agers—started to hear stories about the two frozen, dead men and held several town meetings on what they should do about the bodies that were starting to attract national publicity. One weekend at the height of the public attention, Cable News Network (CNN) televised the event, including a sign put out by the local baker that stated "What is the big deal about two Norwegians in the freezer? I have six Danish in the oven." The town finally accepted the bodies and now capitalized on the publicity by having annual Frozen Dead Guy Days. He had missed the event this year, where there were frozen-dead-guy look-alike contests, coffin races, and more.

James's thoughts returned to the Antarctic, and he reflected on the day. Indeed, it had been wonderful. James was an early riser, and with coffee cup in hand, he made his way back to his usual spot, the middle rear of the lower deck near the cargo gate. There, he watched a spectacular sunrise over the mountains between six and seven as the ship made its way to the Yalour Islands after crossing the Antarctic Circle the previous day; it had indeed been a wonderful crossing.

After breakfast, they had Zodiac cruises in the morning along the mountainous coast. The weather had been pleasant as the ship crossed Waddington Bay, passing through lots of brash ice and some beautiful icebergs. They spotted more humpback whales and some crabeater and leopard seals and made a few stops in the Zodiacs to watch Adélie penguins with the icy mountains in the background.

After lunch, they visited Vernadsky Station, a Ukrainian research center once owned by the British and called Faraday Station. They toured the station and were informed that its scientists were mainly performing upper atmosphere studies and were instrumental in discovering the ozone hole. James gave a short talk on his environmental radioactivity studies at Clemson University to a small group of Ukrainian scientists. The station was colorful, with a bar and homemade vodka, pool table, dartboard, and souvenir shop. They also visited Wordie House, a small museum preserving part of the early British base, and ended the visit with a walk to the top of a nearby snow hill to enjoy the view, followed by sledding down on their bottoms.

Then they went back to the ship for dinner. Afterward, they were treated with a superdisplay in the bay by a pod of eight killer whales, including a mother and calf. There were also humpback whale sightings as fifteen campers were being transported to Hovgaard Island for their campout.

James was pleased that he had the night off from his surveillance of the Argentinean nuclear scientists and whoever was suspected of trying to pass nuclear weapons technology to them. James really thought that Brazil, or even Venezuela, would be a more likely country, but of course, Argentina was having economic problems and might be starting down the road to nuclear blackmail like the North Koreans. Only one of the Argentineans had opted for the campout. In spite of terribly missing Ying, James was not going to pass up an experience of a lifetime and stay aboard ship to continue his covert government assignment. At least this way, he would not have to worry about another attempt on his life and could hopefully get a good night's sleep.

But James was mistaken as he was awakened in the middle of the night by a sharp jar to his sleeping bag and found himself sliding fast down the hill, cocooned in his sleep equipment, and heading for a high ledge over the icy channel. As James was frantically trying to unzip the bag and cocoon, all he could think about was *Is this the same feeling Margrit had experienced when she lost control of my car going down Black Canyon in the Santa Susana mountains in California?* Margrit's death was no accident as the brakes of the car she was driving had been tampered with. As James was sliding down the hill, he too knew this was no accident but yet another attempt on his life.

Chapter 1
Return to Colorado

I

John kept a diary most of his adult life. The following was what he wrote on his way home from Vienna:

In late June, I resigned from the IAEA and planned to return to the Rocky Flats Plant (RFP) from my three-year leave of absence. The movers had taken all our household and personal items for shipment to Arvada. Eric, Lorrie, Margrit, and I, along with four suitcases, took an early morning Austrian Airlines flight to East Berlin. Immigration was easy since I still had my UN passport. After a walk around a small part of East Berlin, we crossed over at Checkpoint Charlie into West Berlin. Then we toured the city and spent the night at the Berlin Hotel.

From West Berlin, we flew to Oslo and took a short train ride into the city and then a taxi to the Thon Hotel Bristol. After check-in, we went to our room with two single beds and one double bed. Later, we had a walk around the area and came upon a beautiful church near the train station called Dome Church. Between the church and the hotel is a nice walking mall where some young guys were doing everything from playing music to standing as a statue of someone famous. Of course, they wanted some money. The city has lots of colorful old buildings, and I took lots of pictures.

On Sunday, a tour bus picked us up for our ride to the airport. Our guide told us some facts about Oslo and Norway that were quite interesting. Their taxes are quite high, but they have free medical care and good retirements. They have large oil reserves offshore, and the people are well off. The population is small for the size of the country. The highest mountain is only seven thousand feet, but they do have lots of ski areas, lit up, of course, for the long dark winter days. The high rate of alcoholism is blamed on the winters. Last night between ten and eleven, it was still light outside.

From Oslo to Longyearbyen, I had a window seat. During takeoff, I saw that Oslo is relatively spread out and has many parks and a port full of boats and ships. Outside Oslo, there are some patches of farmland as well as many forests. I told Margrit that I had seen a big cloud that looked like a polar bear. Eric and Lorrie were sitting in front of us, so Eric got to see the cloud as well. The SAS flight was three hours. Our flight had about 140 passengers.

Spitsbergen is the largest and only permanently populated island (about 2,600 people) in Norway. It borders the Barents, Norwegian, and Greenland Seas. Its administrative center is Longyearbyen, the northernmost city in the world. The island was first used as a whaling station and later for coal mining. Now research and tourism have become important supplementary industries, featuring among others the University of Svalbard and the Global Seed Vault. The island has an arctic climate and many glaciers, mountains, and fjords. It also supports polar bears, reindeer, and marine mammals. Its highest elevation is 5,600 feet. There are four months of total darkness and four months of complete sunlight. Last night, we left Spitsbergen on the *Akademik Abraham* to the open waters of the Greenland Sea and started traveling to a large fjord system known as Isfjorden.

The *Akademik Abraham*, designed for polar research, is a modern, comfortable, and ice-strengthened ship. It is a Russian-flagged vessel and has a library, lounge, bar, dining room, conference room, swimming pool, sauna, exercise room, and gift shop. It was built in Finland in 1980. There are sixty-three staff and crew, and our cruise has sixty-one passengers. Eric and I are sharing a cabin that has a bunk bed, and Lorrie and Margrit have the adjoining cabin separated by a small shared bathroom with a toilet and sink and shower that empties onto the floor.

On Monday at about 10:00 a.m., we were in the Isfjorden fjord system and saw a couple of calving events from several glaciers and lots of beautiful snow, ice, and blue ice floats. We then went up the coast north to Krossfjorden, which has glaciers.

On Tuesday, we entered the narrow Sorgattet to cruise and search for wildlife. After breakfast, we anchored off a small island, Amsterdamoya. In the afternoon, we went to Smeerenburgfjorden, which translates into "blubber town." The area is famous from the seventeenth-century whaling period. Instead of a stop, our afternoon consisted of a cruise up the northern waters through lots of ice to try to see polar bears. We did see several seals and a few walrus. In the late afternoon, the ice broke up a lot, and it started to snow. Earlier, the ship had a lot of hard knocks on the ice to break through it. Right after dinner, we finally saw our first polar bear. It was fairly close to the ship at first and then went walking in the direction of a seal. About halfway to the seal, the bear started running, and the seal ducked into the water as the bear got near. We were so far north that there was no darkness.

On Wednesday, we went over the tip of Svalbard, with the ship hitting big chunks of floating ice. At times, it seemed like the ship would split open. We ended up in a fjord called Woodfjorden. There, we saw a couple of polar bears and three walrus lying on separate pieces of floating ice. In the afternoon, there was a Zodiac cruise of the area.

On Thursday, the ship went back the way it came, through packed ice, going south along the area of Spitsbergen known as Albert I Land. We then went into a bay called Kongsforden. After dinner, we docked at Ny-Ålesund, a village where scientific research is being performed by about 150 scientists. The winter population of the village is forty. It has a rich history of coal mining. There is also a gift shop and a place to buy and mail postcards. Margrit sent some to the United States from the northernmost post office in the world. A monument of the famous Norwegian explorer Roald Amundsen is also located there.

Before dinner, there was a call for people who wanted to join an elite group who have jumped into the Arctic Ocean above eighty degrees latitude. I had not used my long red flannel underwear that I got at a surprise birthday party from my nutty brother, so I decided to put the underwear on (as a joke) and go to the place where seven crazy folks were jumping in. Margrit and the kids thought I was nuts to be wearing the underwear. I only wanted to show off and had no intention of jumping into the icy water. At the last minute, after the seven brave souls had jumped and gotten pulled out of the water, I joined the elite group. However, I decided to dive in, whereas the others had just jumped into the sea. My dive was a belly flop. All the onlookers, including Margrit and the kids, had a good laugh as a crew member helped me out of the freezing water a few minutes later.

On Friday, we were at sea all day, sometimes being tossed around by the rough seas. All four of us started the day off at seven thirty with an exercise class led by the professional masseuse Claire. She is from the Philippines, whereas the rest of the staff and crew are all Russian. I had a massage and sauna in the late afternoon. During the trip, all the Russians were very cordial and talked with us. There was one crew member who avoided me. Felex was a rough-looking big guy resembling Jaws from the James Bond movie.

We had another day at sea on Saturday. Margrit and I started the day with half an hour of exercise in the lounge, followed by breakfast with the kids. Later that morning, Ankha—one of the technical staff members—gave an excellent talk on public speaking. Then all of us had a nap before lunch. In the afternoon, we attended a lecture on sea ice and how the environment is affecting it. Ankha thinks one reason sea levels are rising, besides glaciers melting, is the depletion of groundwater sources.

After the talk, we took another nap, followed by dinner. I made a faux pas at our dinner table. I asked Kelly (good-looking blond schoolteacher) if she took the pill. I meant a motion sickness pill since the ship was bouncing along. Everyone at the table, including Kelly and Margrit, looked strangely at me, thinking I meant the birth control pill, and then I said, "Motion sickness pill."

Late that evening, I was alone at my usual place at the stern, next to the cargo gate, watching the stars. All of a sudden, I found myself falling overboard. I managed to grab the bottom of the swinging cargo gate and quickly pulled myself up. I then saw a crew member running off in the distance. He looked like Felex since most of the other crew members were much shorter. In the morning, Margrit urged me to tell the captain. Captain Putan thought the gate must have been unlatched, and as I leaned against it, it opened. I did not see Felex the rest of the voyage.

On Sunday, we visited the isolated island of Jan Mayen, named after the Dutch whaling captain who claimed to have discovered it in 1614. It is an active volcanic island with high mountains and a barren landscape. Through its history, whalers, sealers, and fox hunters have used it as a base. The island is about 270 miles east of Greenland and about 330 miles north of Iceland. It has a distinctive spoon shape, with the glacier covering the 7,470-foot-high volcano Beerenberg in the center. The island is known for its unusual geology.

We had a thirty-minute walk up to the top of a hill overlooking the bay and a beautiful rock formation. The volcano was on the other side, but the top was covered by clouds. After our return to ship and lunch, the captain took the ship around the island. We passed several glaciers and some narrow waterfalls. Then we headed for Greenland. The sea was not too rough during the night.

On Monday, we traveled all day, and there were two lectures in the morning and two in the afternoon. I skipped the last lecture and went to the map room to write. After dinner, we saw lots of ice floats and land to our left. There was a polar bear off in the distance, so the captain plowed through much broken ice, which periodically crashed into the ship. We finally caught up to the bear, but the ship's ice-crashing noise kept the bear about a hundred yards away. Meanwhile, someone spotted another bear way off on port side. Everyone was taking lots of photos until we turned around and headed out to sea.

On Tuesday, we arrived at Scoresby Sund, Greenland, which has the largest fjord in the world. Greenland is the largest island in the world. It is thought to have been named by William Scoresby Jr. for his father. William Scoresby was a noted whaler in Greenland from 1785 to 1823 and possibly entered the fjord during that period. The fjord branches like a tree, with glaciers at the base of its branches. Ice was a determining factor for our entry as, at times, large bergs broke off the glaciers, becoming grounded, in addition to fast ice still blocking most of the passages. Sea ice conditions along the east coast are characterized by being more dynamic than in other parts of the Greenland waters. This is primarily due to the constant ice movement, which is induced by the East Greenland current.

The ice in East Greenland is called "Storisen." Every second, an average of 150,000 square yards of sea ice is transported through the Fram Strait, between Greenland and Svalbard. Typically, the ice going through the Fram Strait has taken five to six years to be formed in the Polar Sea; and because of this, it is often several yards thick. While drifting southward along the coast, the ice breaks up into smaller floes. The size of the floes is therefore decreased from north to south. In wintertime, new ice is rapidly created in between floes. This is the reason why Storisen is composed of both thin new ice and yard-thick multiyear ice. Icebergs are found along the east coast all year round. To put it in perspective, East Greenland is larger than France, Germany, Italy, and the U.K. combined.

We had an early lunch, and our captain, who resembled the movie actor James Cagney, found a cove in the Scoresby Sund to allow Zodiacs to go ashore. Because of the wind and the cold and there was nothing really to see on the shore, the four of us decided to stay on ship to relax. Before dinner, a polar bear was spotted in the distance. The ship finally approached the bear, sitting on a big piece of floating ice. He seemed curious, swam toward the ship, and put on quite a show for all of us—swimming, climbing up on ice floats, and walking around on the ice.

On Wednesday, we spent the morning cruising farther into Scoresby Sund, searching for wildlife. Later, we did spot another polar bear. During the afternoon, we visited the only Greenlandic village in the fjord, Ittoqqortoormiit. All the visitors had a walk around town. The town is small with gravel roads, and there are many all-terrain vehicles in use. They have a tourist shop and a grocery store. We were requested not to buy any food items since they only receive two shipments a year. We saw lots of cute kids, and one small boy in a playground, which seemed to be a day care, was making funny faces at us while waving his hand.

The next day, we entered the Greenland Sea, which is the outlying portion of the Arctic Ocean. It lies south of the Arctic Basin proper and borders Greenland to the west, Svalbard to the east, the main Arctic Ocean to the north, and the Norwegian Sea and Iceland to the south. A line linking northeast Iceland, the isolated island of Jan Mayen, and Bear Island forms the conventional border between the Arctic Greenland Sea and the Norwegian Sea to the southeast.

Today we are on our way to Iceland. There were four presentations on the various things we will see in Iceland. After dinner, there was a blue whale near the ship coming up for air and then diving under the surface. Captain Putan said we were lucky to see so many whales on the voyage.

On Friday, we found ourselves in the northwest corner of Iceland in the large expanse of Ísafjörður. Later, we anchored near Vigur Island, which is only about a mile long and less than half a mile wide. Vigur is one of the few privately owned islands in the country with only a handful of residents but thousands of birds, including eiders and puffins. There are also historic buildings there, including the sole surviving windmill in Iceland

and the smallest post office in Europe. We went ashore at 9:30 a.m. for a short visit. In the afternoon, the ship went across the fjord to a calm location where we went ashore. We ended up docking at the port of Ísafjörður. Ísafjörður is the largest of all the towns in the northern part of the west fjords with about three thousand inhabitants.

The next day started with a sunrise at two fifty-two and ended with a sunset at half an hour after midnight. Before breakfast, we cruised near the cliffs of Latrabjarg, which is one of the largest seabird-nesting colonies in Europe with a spectacular rugged landscape. It is about eight miles long and has sheer cliffs 440 yards high with an east-west direction on the northern coastline of Iceland's second largest bay, Breiðafjörður. It provides nesting sites for millions of birds, including about 40 percent of the world's population of razorbills.

In the afternoon, we sailed farther into Breiðafjörður as the bay contains thousands of small islets and skerries. Our last landing was at one of the largest islands called Flatey. The island played a significant part in trade around Iceland during the Middle Ages. A monastery that was founded during the late twelfth century resulted in the island being the center of culture and education for the country at that time. That evening, there was a captain's dinner; and afterward, we packed our bags and placed them outside our cabin for pickup.

The next morning, we disembarked and boarded buses for a tour of Reykjavik. We stopped at a church with a statue of Leif Eriksson in front and then had a thirty-minute walk in the area. Later, we went to the Blue Lagoon, which has large thermal baths that appear blue. There is a swimming area there, but we just took a walk on a path through lots of volcanic rocks. In the distance are several mountains as well as an inactive volcano. We were told that there are several active volcanoes beyond the mountain range. Iceland sits on the Mid-Atlantic Ridge, and sometime in the future, Iceland is thought to be split in half because of the few periodic earthquakes. I think Greenland should have been named Iceland and Iceland Greenland.

After our lagoon adventure, we were transported to the Reykjavik Airport. It was about an hour drive through an interesting volcanic landscape. The crowded Reykjavik Airport was built by the U.S. military in World War II, and until 2006, there was a strong American presence in the region. After an eight-hour nonstop flight on Icelandic Airlines, we landed in Denver to resume our lives in the United States.

II

Even though his office was behind the thick concrete walls of the plutonium-processing building at Rocky Flats, Dr. John James Czermak was pleased to be back. His new job was manager of Plutonium Chemistry Research and Development. In this position, he reported to the director of R&D, his old position, which was filled during his three-year leave with the IAEA. Aligning the walls of his office were glass-fronted cabinets containing a host of awards, books, manuals, and *Rockwell News*. On the concrete walls, award plaques and safety posters abounded, including a replica of the slogan used by the former management company for the RFP, Dow Chemical, "The life you save may be your own." On a hook beside the door was a white lab coat along with safety glasses and a respirator.

The move back to Denver was good for him and Eric but very difficult for Margrit and Lorrie. Amy had returned earlier to start her university studies. John was reminded of Margrit's difficulties when she copied him on an e-mail to their good friends Jan and Janice Preez; Jan was returning to his position at South Africa's Nuclear Research Center after being at the IAEA for four years in the Technical Assistance Section.

Dear Jan and Janice,

My god, my heart bleeds for you. Where did the years go? You two, the last of the Mohicans, are leaving. We will have no reason to travel to Vienna now that you won't be there. I'm so sad just to think of it. And then there's the added sadness of seeing your children grown and on their own, just you two again. Well, I will say this. Our time in Vienna, brief as it was, changed my life and my outlook completely and for all time. The readjustment to life in the United States was horrible, and my daughter and I still suffer from it. Yes, I've had a wonderful life. Yes, I've seen some of the world and others since we left there. But the impact of having lived in an international community and losing it has left me bereft in my heart and soul. It's just there, and it won't go away. When I left the United Nations Industrial Development Organization, my coworkers were so assured with my knowledge of the German and Russian languages that I would be in such demand. Ha! Nobody wanted to hear, and nobody cared. Nobody understands the sorrow in another's heart, not that I'm unhappy—how could jolly Margrit Czermak be unhappy? In truth, I'm telling you this in case you two should feel terribly misplaced upon your return to South Africa and you get the feeling that nobody cares because John and I care. I send you both my love and best wishes for a happy reunion in South Africa.

Margrit

John was also happy to be back at their home in Arvada, which they had rented during their stay in Vienna, as well as that he and Margrit were resuming a close, loving relationship that had been badly damaged in Vienna. He was also glad to be getting back into his old routine of working out at the gym in the weight room and swimming pool, as well as jogging several miles every morning and doing yoga. John had continued with his gymnastics, where he can easily do backflips—one of his favorite things to show off. He also enjoyed eavesdropping on people speaking French, German, or Spanish.

One time he was boarding a flight in Los Angeles, and there were two Germans in front of him. One asked the other what time it was, and the other said in German he did not know. John piped up and told them the time in German and continued to speak in German, asking where they were from, what they did for a living, and more depending on their replies. In addition, he always enjoyed getting to know the people sitting next to him on flights or people he met at hotels and on tours.

John also resumed his activities with the Rocky Flats Toastmasters and Speakers Club. The latter was an organization whose members went out into the community to give talks at clubs and schools. John's favorite topics were water treatment and taking care of the environment. He talked a lot about what one could do to slow down climate change. One thing he always mentioned was that the wife of his PhD adviser preached that our greatest problem was overpopulation. John would then comment that we all had to train and take a test to get a driver's license, but anyone can have a child without a single course on child-rearing.

John continued to travel a lot, mainly to conferences around the world and to Vienna and Moscow to have meetings with his coauthors, Oleg Yakushin and Dmitri Frolov, on a series of books they were writing for the IAEA. At the conferences, he always presented papers and even organized a few sessions, mainly at American Chemical Society (ACS) meetings. On the trips to Moscow, one of his Russian friends always arranged a dinner at their home.

On one trip with Margrit, a funny thing happened at dinner in Boris's apartment. Margrit asked Boris where the bathroom was, and with a puzzled look on his face, he asked her to follow him. He opened the door, and it was indeed a bathroom minus the toilet. Then she said, "I need the toilet."

Boris said with a laugh, "I did not think you wanted to bathe."

Margrit told Boris she knew that most of the bathrooms and toilets were separated in Europe, but it was a habit to ask for the bathroom.

Boris jokingly said, "Why do you sometimes call it a restroom in the States? You don't go in there to rest."

One important meeting that John had founded and organized concerned actinide separations. Actinides included thorium, uranium, neptunium, plutonium, americium, and curium. Chemical engineers and scientists from all the national laboratories and a couple of universities were in attendance at the first meeting. John introduced the meeting and presented a summary talk on the research of his group related to the separation and purification of plutonium. These meetings continued to be held annually with a different national laboratory hosting the conference each year.

The second time the meeting was held at Rocky Flats, John started an award with plaque for the most outstanding nuclear engineer or scientist to date. Of course, John recruited several colleagues to serve on an awards committee to assist with the selection. John called the award the Seaborg Actinide Separations Award, named in honor of Glenn Seaborg, the codiscoverer of plutonium, who was selected to receive the first award. A few years later, John received the award. He also founded two journals where he served as editor.

John visited his laboratories a couple of times each week and spent time with each member of his group to see how their work was going and if there was anything he could do to assist. The group members were very happy with their work and working conditions. Once a month, John would hold a safety meeting and a few times off site in Boulder at a bar and restaurant called the Dark Horse. The place was unique as there were antiques and junk hanging from the ceiling and hooked to the walls. The group met in an upstairs room that they had to themselves. Of course, most of the group members had a beer with some snacks while discussing the monthly safety inspection of their laboratory as well as general talk on one aspect of safety. These meetings and John's leadership and rapport certainly created dedicated and happy employees.

III

Several months after John and his family returned from Vienna, he received a phone call from a gentleman who introduced himself as Tim Smith of the CIA and asked John to meet with him in Boulder the next day for lunch. At lunch, sitting at a booth in a quiet corner of the restaurant, Tim first showed John his credentials and gave him his business card with only his name on it. John thought that Tim sure looked a lot like the movie actor James Stewart. Tim said, "Of course, that is not my real name on the card."

Tim asked a lot of questions about John's recent trips to Russia. He wanted to know everything John knew about the Russians and his previous contacts with them. He told John that he had read his IAEA trip reports during his tenure in Vienna as the American Embassy always received copies.

John then relayed to Tim information about his first meeting with Boris at a solvent extraction conference in Toronto and that, at the IAEA, it was rumored that he was the head KGB agent. John also told Tim about meetings with other Russians at several IAEA meetings and technical conferences over the years. He explained the series of review books that he and two Russian scientists, Dmitri and Oleg, were authoring for the IAEA and that the agency had paid the expenses for several trips to Vienna and Moscow to work on the books.

Tim then offered to pay John's expenses to go on an expedition on a Russian ship to Greenland and the High Arctic to see if any nuclear materials or radioactive wastes were being smuggled into Canada for use in dirty bombs in the United States. The semiannual trip was sponsored by a Canadian adventure group. John agreed to cooperate and serve his country as best as he can.

Tim said, "Specifically, John, just keep your eyes and ears open and make as many friends as possible, especially of the crew. Also, have a clandestinely look around the ship and use this miniature portable nuclear detector to see if there are any signs of radioactive material on board. Take some water samples of the ship's wastewater that is used to wash the ship, and bring the water samples back for very sensitive radiochemical analysis. But please be careful as the trip could be dangerous, and you could be kidnapped with your knowledge of nuclear weapons."

At the end of the meeting, Tim swore John to secrecy, never to discuss their meetings, CIA assignments, or relationship with him to anyone, including his wife, family, and friends as well as DOE security and the FBI.

Travel funds arrived for John two weeks later from the Penny Group in San Francisco, CIA's financial front. After explaining to Margrit and the kids that he had received funds for travel to Greenland and the High Arctic for an eight-day expedition to sample water, John left Denver two weeks later, using vacation time at Rocky Flats. John loved to use his camera and see new areas of the world; thus, he welcomed this opportunity to see the High Arctic for the first time. He flew to Cartwright, Canada, via Detroit and Quebec, where he boarded the *Akademik Abraham* along with about forty tourists. John was surprised that the ship was the same one he and his family took on their Spitsbergen trip.

IV

Two weeks later, John meets Tim at a different restaurant in Boulder to give him a debriefing of the trip. John told Tim, "The ship's homeport is Kaliningrad, located on the Baltic Sea between Lithuania and Poland. Kaliningrad was formally a Prussian city, but after World War II, it became a part of the Soviet Union. The *Akademik Abraham* and an identical sister ship, both ice strengthened, were built in Finland in 1980. The ships were radar/sonic spy ships during the Cold War, built to follow U.S. submarines. Now they are used to perform acoustic research for the Russian Academy of Science's Institute of Oceanology and to serve part-time tourism. However, it was thought by my cabinmate, Don Cunningham, that the ships are still being used to keep an eye on our submarines. Surprisingly, my family and I were on the same ship on our return to Colorado from Vienna.

"I was lucky to have such a great guy sharing a cabin. Don, tall and Hollywood handsome, was retired from the Canadian government. Later in the cruise, especially after Don had a few drinks at dinner, he would loosen up and start talking about his previous work. He told me that he worked in the intelligence branch. At the end of the trip, I was sure he was a Canadian government contractor trying to get the same information that you sent me to get. That's all I know about Don. Tim, let me continue about the trip itself and about Don and I getting shot at and almost killed."

Tim got a surprised look on his face and said, "What?"

"Well, I will tell you about that in a few minutes. The first day after leaving Canada for Greenland and crossing the Davis Strait, I had a long walk around the ship after a lifeboat drill and lunch. Usually, during the evening happy hour, when everyone was upstairs drinking, I would have another look around at different areas of the ship. A couple of times, Felex—a crew member who was on the ship during my last voyage—reminded me not to go into certain rooms, especially the engine room.

"But I continued to explore, take water samples, and use the miniature portable nuclear detector anyway. I did manage to get water from various places, trying to take as many samples as possible. Probably the best sample was some drain water on the lower deck. Later on the cruise, I took more samples, and they are all in this bag. The sonic equipment is still on board and located in the mudroom, where we would put on heavy coats and boots for landings in the Zodiacs. There are also laboratories on the lower deck, which are inaccessible as most of the rooms in the lower deck are locked.

"By the way, Tim, I had a near-death experience on my first voyage on the ship. I fell overboard at the stern and managed to save my life by quickly grabbing the swinging cargo gate. As I pulled myself up, I saw Felex running off in the distance. I think Felex pushed me, but when I reported the incident to the captain, he said I must have leaned against the gate that was usually latched. I did not see Felex the rest of that trip. I will tell you more about Felex in a couple of minutes.

"I do not require a lot of sleep, so I was awake when we arrived early the next morning at the entrance to Kangerlussuaq Fjord, the longest one in the world, on the way to the Sisimiut coast town of Kangerlussuaq. On a walk outside the town on soft tundra, we spotted an arctic fox and observed some ringed seals sunning themselves on rocks near the shore. After a visit to Kangerlussuaq, we returned to the Sisimiut coast and went north to Itilleq, which has the second largest system of fjords. There are dozens of deep fjords carved into Greenland's west coast. The glaciers are fed by the ice cap, which covers 80 percent of the country. Unfortunately, they are starting to disappear because of global warming.

"The ship maneuvered between the soaring icebergs at the mouth of the Ilulissat Icefjord, a UNESCO World Heritage site. Here, we saw a polar bear floating on an iceberg. The next day, we took a Zodiac cruise among towering icebergs of the Ilulissat Icefjord. We went ashore at Itilleq, a small fishing village that has an interesting museum. Then we went to Sisimiut, a former whaling port, and visited the museum and wandered amid a jumble of eighteenth-century wooden buildings. We also had an exciting walk outside the village on soft tundra to the Sermermiut Valley."

Tim commented, "John, you sure have a remarkable memory, and I appreciate hearing details as I would like to take the same trip someday."

"Thank you. So far, the things that really watered my eyes were seeing the mass of glaciers; different varieties of seals, whales, and other wildlife; and icebergs floating out in the middle of the Davis Strait, hundreds of miles from any shoreline, with polar bears resting on a few of them. It was remarkable to see them, and I wonder how they survive out there. When we climbed a glacier and saw the massive cliffs with waterfalls, it reminded me of Yosemite National Park.

"So far on the trip, I had befriended several of the Russian dining room staff and had an opportunity to practice my Russian. I did not overhear any discussions from any of the Russians concerning nuclear materials.

"The next day, we went across Baffin Bay to Qeqertarsuaq Island and Disko, Nunavut. On the way, we saw a couple of humpback whales. Then we went to Uummannaq and Karrat Fjords, with rocky peaks and lots of icebergs as well as marine life nearby. On the crossing, I had more time to explore the ship but did not find anything new.

"We started our exploration of the Canadian High Arctic the next morning with a visit to the small Inuit community of Pond Inlet, Nunavut. We explored some beautiful bays and inlets along Baffin Island's Lancaster Sound, the eastern gateway to the Arctic Archipelago. The group and I enjoyed seeing the ragged coastline in Zodiacs and spent part of the day looking for ringed seals, arctic foxes, walrus, polar bears, and bowhead whales. We also had a brief visit to Devon Island, the largest uninhabited island on the earth. This was the northernmost part of the trip.

There, we had a long walk with the ship's archaeologist to learn about the Thule people, ancestors of the modern Inuit, who once inhabited this region. Our group got to see the stone dwelling once inhabited by the Thule people. Shortly after leaving the island, the ship got stuck in the ice. Later, a Canadian icebreaker came to our rescue and pulled us about a mile out of the broken ice.

"The next day, we went ashore on the rocky Philpots Island to hike in the tundra. Felex came along with a rifle in case we had an encounter with a polar bear. It was a long walk, and on the way back, Don and I took a lower nearby trail. A little later, we heard a shot and saw a bullet hit a big nearby boulder. Then it happened again, and we ducked and yelled to stop firing. Our fellow passengers ran over to see what had happened. Felex came and said that there was a bear nearby, and he shot at him. However, both Don and I said we did not see any bear in the area. I think Felex was trying to kill me since I was exploring the ship and asking too many questions."

"John, I will try to find out more about Felex in the CIA's database."

"At the end of the trip, we flew out of Arctic Bay on Baffin Island to Quebec. After my goodbyes to Don and a few others, I continued on another flight to Detroit and then Denver. In conclusion, I think that the ship, in addition to being used for scientific expeditions and tours, could easily be used for smuggling nuclear materials. It will be interesting to see what your laboratory finds in the samples I took."

"Well, John, you had quite a trip. I wish I could have been along. Anyway, I will pass these notes onto my superiors. Let's keep in touch. Thanks."

"Tim, I almost forgot to tell you, but next month, Margrit and I are going to Vienna. I will attend another IAEA consultant's meeting on our book. After the meeting, Margrit will stay with friends, and I will fly to Vladivostok via Zurich and Moscow and then take the trans-Siberian train back to Moscow. From Moscow, I will fly to Kaliningrad and stay there for a couple of days and then return to Vienna via Moscow. I have always wanted to take this trip as I love traveling by train. Margrit was not interested in going on the adventure."

"Well, John, let's plan on meeting here shortly after your return from Europe as I am very interested in what you discover in Kaliningrad. Be sure and watch out for kidnappers."

V

A week after John and Margrit returned from Europe, John met Tim at a restaurant in Golden. Tim asked John, "How was the trip?"

"It was educational, interesting, and enjoyable."

"Please give me a detailed account after we order our lunch. I would like to take the trip someday. If you do not object, I want to tape record your story so I will not have to take notes as I did last time."

"Well, Tim, if you really want all the details, I will begin by saying that our meeting in Vienna at the IAEA headquarters was all business without anything to report that would interest you. However, I think what I discovered on my train trip was very surprising since it may be related to the future leadership of Russia. By the way, Tim, did you find anything out about Felex?"

"We got his full name, but unfortunately, he was not in any of our databases. Sorry."

After ordering lunch, John started telling Tim about his trip. "To begin, exactly three weeks ago, I was on an early morning Swissair flight that was about a half hour late leaving Vienna. Coming into Zurich, I could see the snowcapped Alps. On the flight from Zurich to Moscow, a nice young blond Russian was sitting next to me. She was going home for a couple of months to rest in her hometown in western Siberia. She had just quit her job in Boston, where she worked for a small chemical engineering consulting firm. She had chemical engineering training from

Moscow State University and plans to start working on an MBA at Columbia University in the fall.

"I told my new Russian friend, Tanya, the French guillotine joke. I also related to Tanya that Margrit and I had a lot of Russian friends and that Margrit spoke Russian well. She asked if Margrit had once worked for the CIA since she had two good friends who spoke Russian but were laid off from the CIA Translation Section since the downfall of the USSR. Tanya was going to stay in Moscow for a few days to see old friends and was disappointed that I was catching my flight three hours after our arrival in Moscow for Vladivostok."

Tim interrupts John, "Please tell me the French guillotine joke."

"Okay, but it is funnier when I tell it to a mechanical engineer. There were three men sentenced to die on the French guillotine—a chemist, a lawyer, and a mechanical engineer. They lay the chemist down and pull the rope. The blade comes down and stops just short of the chemist's neck. The French say, 'This is an act of God, so you can go free.' Then they lay the lawyer down, and the same thing happens. The French say, 'This is an act of God, but since you are an attorney, you will not die but spend the rest of your life in jail.' They finally lay the mechanical engineer down, and as they get ready to pull the rope, the mechanical engineer says, 'Wait, I think I see the problem.'"

Both Tim and John laugh.

John continues, "We landed at the Sheremetyevo Airport, one of four airports in Moscow. The airport is very nice, but the runway is rough. My contact was waiting at the exit to customs to give me my airline and train tickets. I exchanged some money after she sent me in the direction of check-in. There were five lines for check-in, and it seemed like we had returned to the Dark Ages, with passengers rudely crowding in line. I finally got to the check-in agent to find out that my only small suitcase was over the weight allowance for carry-ons. So I checked the suitcase in and got my boarding pass. Because of the hurry, I stupidly left my kit bag with medicine in the suitcase. I began to worry if the bag would arrive full and nonviolated since everyone seemed to be checking in bags that were wrapped in sheet plastic to prevent anyone from opening them.

"The flight was delayed two hours, but I met one of my fellow passengers, Natia, and we had some interesting conversations during the wait. She was a beautiful model and spoke English well. On the flight, she sat several seats down from me and slept most of the flight, probably because of the three glasses of white wine she had at the airport and more on the plane. There were a couple of cute kids on board the flight. A boy, about five, who was sitting two seats ahead of me started exchanging funny faces with me and later continued to stick his tongue out at me when I would look his way.

"The plane was a Boeing 767 with two-three-two seats, but it seemed old. Both on takeoff and landing, everything would shake because of the bad runways. The flight took about eight hours, and it never got dark outside, but the sun did go down for about an hour. We were apparently flying over the Arctic Circle. The land looked very flat, and I periodically saw lights of remote houses.

"Moscow is two hours ahead of Vienna, and Vladivostok was seven hours ahead of Moscow. During the flight, I discovered that my train tickets from Ulan-Ude to Irkutsk and Irkutsk to Novosibirsk were missing, and I wondered if I dropped them at the chaotic check-in. Upon arrival in Vladivostok at 9:30 a.m., there was no one to greet me. I had already paid for the tour package that included train tickets, hotel transfers, hotel stays, and tours. Natia showed me where to pick up my checked bag, and all was intact. After bidding Natia goodbye, I waited for my host while being hounded by a taxi driver who said he would take me to town for $100. And later, he came down to $50. After waiting about an hour, I walked over to the nearby airport hotel, and the desk clerk kindly ordered a taxi for me that was six hundred rubels, which is about $20. The airport is about twenty-five miles from the city.

"After arrival in Vladivostok, I checked into the classy Versailles Hotel and then took a walk down to the beach. It was Sunday, and the streets were very crowded. Almost everyone was carrying around a beer—maybe the children had beer in their milk bottles."

Tim laughed.

"There were many sailors in town, and most of the women were nicely dressed and beautiful. There were mostly families out, with some swimming, sunbathing, and enjoying the sea and the amusements, such as the Ferris wheel, merry-go-round, horse and reindeer rides, having their pictures taken with monkeys and more—a very nice place for kids."

"Wait, John, our lunch is here. Let's eat, and then you can continue with your detailed narrative."

After lunch, Tim turned the tape recorder back on, and John continued with his story. "My host and tour guide for Monday afternoon did not show, just like at the airport, so I had to give myself a walking tour. A map was a big help in finding all the key sites, so I managed to see most of these places on my own. At the seashore, I tried to take a picture of myself by placing my camera on a fence, but it fell off and broke. Luckily, I found a camera shop where I bought another one. There were many Russian warships in the harbor, and it seemed like they were ready for war."

Tim interjected, "Indeed, Vladivostok is a strategic naval outpost and was closed to most of the world since World War II."

John gave Tim copies of some pictures of the Pacific Navy War Memorial, the steamboat *Krasny Vympel*, and some of the warships as well as a picture of him with a group of Russian sailors. "One of the sailors kindly took the picture, and as you can see, I had his hat on. I managed to talk a little Russian with them, and they enjoyed speaking with an American.

"The next morning, the hotel taxi took me to the brightly painted nearby railway station, where I caught the train to

Ulan-Ude. I had a two-person sleeper carriage all to myself in first class. The first night on the train was rough as the train swung side to side. I had trouble sleeping but did get to see all the stars, including the Milky Way, after we got out of the marine layer. We must have stopped at a dozen towns during the night. I finally managed to get some sleep after the sun rose at six thirty. I woke at nine and had a nice breakfast in the dining car.

"During the day, I saw many Siberian settlements near the tracks, village after village of wooden houses, all with vegetable gardens. Between settlements were rolling hills of wildflowers, green grass, small ponds, and aspen trees. In the evening, the sun was to the left of the train, and we were still heading north. That night, there was an attempt on my life."

Tim interjected, "What?"

John continued, "The adjacent carriage was occupied by a big bald-headed Russian. He had a key to his compartment, unlike me and the other passengers I met, and would lock his compartment upon leaving. During the evening and probably into the night, he kept his door open and was watching people passing by. At about four, I was awakened by someone turning my doorknob from the outside. And before I knew it, the bald Russian had entered and tried to suffocate me with a pillow. I fought him off and then awoke, realizing I had just had a bad nightmare. The next day, I noticed that the bald villain was part of the train staff."

Tim joined John in a good laugh.

"During the morning of the second day on the train, it appeared we were finally heading west. There were lots of small mountains and trees in the area. Some of the trees in the forest had moldy black lower trunks and were sitting in water. We went by an abandoned prison with double outside fencing. Later, the terrain was more rolling hills of grass but no trees.

"We arrived in Ulan-Ude the next morning. Irena and driver met me at the station and took me to their offices where I met Svetlana, the owner. Their offices were in a hotel, and I was thankful Svetlana had my missing train tickets. One was for me to go onto Irkutsk by a later express train, arriving about the same time as the one I was scheduled to ride. Dark-headed and brown-eyed, Irena then took me on a walk in the old city, where we saw lots of beautiful old buildings and a couple of magnificent churches.

"At dinner, overweight Irena told me about how she went to the University of California in San Diego and got a bachelor's degree in finance. She then got a job at an investment firm in Orlando, Florida, and worked there until she was forced to return to Russia. She worked for her dad at his pipe company for a while but found out they could not work together. So then she had various jobs but not using her undergraduate training. She cannot find a finance job in her province and is discriminated against in Moscow and other provinces because of her Mongolian ancestry. Last year, she sank all her money into a tent beer hall in the center of the city, but it went bust after the first year. Now she works as a guide for the tourist company and someday would like to open a hotel near Lake Baikal and offer guided tours.

"Very early the next morning, the train left Ulan-Ude and arrived in Irkutsk a few hours later. Irkutsk is five hours ahead of Moscow time and was an important Siberian outpost established by the Cossacks in 1652. In the early nineteenth century, many Russian artists, officers, and nobles were exiled there for their involvement in the Decembrist revolt. Friday in Irkutsk was spent relaxing in the morning at the Baikal Hotel, charging my camera battery, washing underwear, and having my clothes laundered at the hotel.

"After lunch, my guide, Alex, collected me for a four-hour city tour. We visited several major churches, and I was told about the country's third largest church, which was torn down after thirty years. We visited the house of one of the Decembrists, a prince who was sent to Siberia, losing his son. Alexandre Dumas wrote a novel about this event. We went to the town shopping area, next to Marx and Lenin Streets, where there was a camel used for rides. At six, I returned to the hotel and had soup at an adjoining outdoor restaurant in front of the park and river. The two lovely waitresses thought I must be rich to be on a private trip.

"Tim, please let me know if I am getting too detailed in the account of my trip, especially what I eat."

"No, no, please continue."

"The next morning, Alex, driver Alexander, and I went by van to Lake Baikal. About halfway, we stopped at a village that contained a collection of classic Russian and Siberian cottages, a mill, shops, and a reconstructed church that had been saved from being left underwater after the nearby reservoir was filled. We then went to Lake Baikal that holds about 20 percent of the world's unfrozen fresh water and is the deepest lake in the world. After visiting the visitor center and observing some freshwater seals, Alex and Alexander took me to catch the train to Novosibirsk that was to leave at about 3:30 p.m., which was 11:30 a.m. Moscow time.

"Beautiful and charming Marietta, my carriage companion on the train, was an economist for a big oil company in Irkutsk. I also met a couple in the next carriage, Julius, a Russian, and his Japanese wife, Toschie, who were going directly to Moscow. Julius was a graduate student at Moscow State University, very intelligent, and his English was excellent. He had a lot of interesting things to tell me. One thing was that he was writing his PhD thesis on Kissinger's speech behavior and how Kissinger could win arguments by stating foundation facts first and then driving home his point several times during the second half of his speech. In his sophomore year of high school, Julius got to be an exchange student for a year on a farm in Ohio near Dayton. He did not get along with the family since they had three children who treated him badly and called him a Commie hippie, which indeed he was. The girl always had her boyfriend over, fornicating. He finally arranged to go to another family with the help of his history teacher.

"Julius was very outspoken about his government and the corruption in Russia. He thought the recent school massacre was coordinated by the secret police so that the Moscow government could have the power to appoint governors rather than have them elected. He said the Mafia controls most of the big businesses, from industry to entertainment, and sternly related to me that the Chechnya people have always been fighting and will continue to do so. Julius planned to work as a translator for an oil company near Irkutsk.

"Later on the trip, Julius told me about a Kansas preacher who took his wife and two kids to a remote village in the middle of Siberia because he got a calling from God. Before the trip, the preacher had looked at a map, and it came to him where he should go. He and his family have been there for ten years and had to renew their visas every six months. He usually went to Europe for the renewal, but this time, he went on a ferry to Japan. The preacher told Julius that he had to sleep in a Tokyo park overnight, but none of the homeless bothered him. The return ferry was Russian and loaded to the hilt with tires, all types of consumer goods, and used Japanese cars that several of the Russians aboard were taking back to sell. The ferry was designed for tourists, but they had goods everywhere, including in the aisles, and the cars were in the empty swimming pool. The missionary told Julius that the Russian Orthodox Church was putting political pressure to not have some of the missionaries' visas renewed. So he did not know how long they would be able to stay.

"The other story Julius told was about a retired naval captain who figured out by maps that the Chinese may have discovered America before Columbus. Thus, if the Chinese had colonized America before the Europeans, it would be a much different place—a Ming dynasty. He also stated that the British were about to take Alaska away from the Russians, so that is why they decided to sell it to the Americans.

"I awoke early on Sunday morning to find that we were now on Novosibirsk time, three hours ahead of Moscow. The car stewardess brought cookies and coffee for me and Marietta. She had just awoken. As we ate, we talked a little in English as well as Russian while traveling past some villages and the beautiful countryside of rolling hills covered in forest. An hour later, we stopped in Krasnoyarsk, a major city with a large river flowing through it. Unfortunately, Marietta departed and was replaced by a young man who did not know any English and did not want to talk to me in Russian. I arrived in Novosibirsk late in the evening and was met by Olga and driver Kate, who took me to my hotel.

"On Monday morning, Olga and Kate picked me up after I had a great breakfast. Novosibirsk is Siberia's largest city, very busy with 1.5 million people and broad streets. We saw Lenin Square, the largest opera house in the world, a couple of churches, and a few monuments. We also went to a technical university and then out to the Academic City, about forty minutes from Novosibirsk. We went by the Ob River and drove over the dam of the very large Ob Lake. A village had been submerged in the reservoir when it was filled, just like the village near Lake Baikal.

"We had lunch at the Academic City's conference center, where a meeting was taking place. I ended up paying for all three of us, and Olga spent more time talking to Kate than to me about the Academic City. The tour was rushed at the end since we took so long at lunch. We got to meet a math hydrologist, an academician who first lived in a tent with his family. There were many research institutes there, such as Inorganic Chemistry, Organic Chemistry, Catalytic Chemistry, Physics, and more. A couple of professors in nuclear physics had constructed a new type of linear accelerator, and a chemistry professor and his graduate student had developed a new method to purify gold and tin. Olga had once worked as a translator for the city, so she knew what went on there. She also worked for a while at the brewery that was still in operation, making Pepsi, beer, and champagne.

"Olga seemed very Communistic in nature with her opinions and did not wear a scarf during the church visits. However, she said that the politicians were getting too rich, while pensioners were living in poverty. She and her husband were caring for her mother and sister's daughter, who is an invalid after a car crash that killed her sister and her husband about four years ago. She said life is hard, but she lives each day to the fullest and likes to develop her mind with reading and learning languages. Olga's great-grandfather had a lot of land at one time and was very rich but lost it all when Lenin took power. She thought some of the land should be returned to her. Instead, she had to buy her two-room flat. When Olga and I were walking around the academician's home, she walked through the grass while I took the walkway. I said I wanted to avoid ticks, and then she started to worry about them.

"That evening, I left Novosibirsk for Yekaterinburg. I had a young lawyer, Tanya, as my carriage mate. She was twenty-seven years old and worked for her small city as one of four lawyers. She was going to some other city on business. She tried very hard to express herself in English and did manage to tell me quite a bit. She would like to visit the Canary Islands and has a boyfriend. She also has a brother, mother, and stepfather. Her father died about ten years ago of liver failure. She showed me on a map where she lived and where she was going today.

"The next morning, we continued discussions about our jobs as we were waiting for our breakfast to arrive. Tanya got her breakfast, but mine did not arrive, so I had to go to the dining car. Over breakfast, I was thinking how very hard it must have been for Tanya and her mother after her father died. Everyone is so poor in Siberia. Olga told me that only the strong and fit survive and that, over the generations, many have died who could not stay well. After breakfast, we arrived in a small city where I sadly said my goodbye to Tanya. Again, Tim, I hope I am not getting too detailed about the people I met."

"No, I find it very interesting, and it still amazes me how you can remember all these details."

"Well, Tim, I do keep a diary, and I reviewed it before our meeting today. Maybe in the future you may want me to make a copy of my diary for you." John continued, "We arrived in Yekaterinburg early afternoon of the next day. No one was there to greet me, and after waiting half an hour, I went to an information booth and asked a young lady if she knew where the Red Star Hotel was located. She pointed across the street from the station. I walked through the station parking lot and then through an underground tunnel to a major street and went into a hotel, but it was not the Star. I finally took a taxi to my hotel some distance away. I checked in and, after unpacking and washing my socks and underwear, arranged for a hotel taxi to take me on a drive through the city and to the Asia-Europe dividing line.

"At that point, Anna showed up, apologizing for not meeting me at the train. She thought I was arriving Moscow time, two hours later. Alexander, our driver, took us around the city with its two highest buildings, main streets, Kremlin building, a nice walking street, a dam on a river, an area with ornately decorated wooden houses, and then the cathedral that was only completed a couple of years ago. It stood on the site of the demolished home where the czar Nicholas II and his family were executed and then taken out of town and dumped in a ravine where there is now a monastery. We also went to a place in the Ural Mountains, where the rainwater runs west to Europe and east to Asia. Anna took a picture of me with one foot in Asia and the other foot in Europe.

"With Anna's help, I boarded the train for Moscow the next morning. An elderly gentleman, Oleg, was my cabinmate. He spoke excellent English and is a professor at the Organic Chemistry Institute in Yekaterinburg and a member of the Russian Academy of Sciences. Later in the conversation, I told him the names of the Russians I knew. I realized what a small world it is when Oleg said he knew my Russian friends. In fact, Oleg is a good friend of Boris's and made macromolecules for him to test. Oleg said that Boris will have a conference in his honor at his seventy-fifth birthday party in September in the Black Sea city of Sevastopol.

"During our conversations, I also had time to view the lovely scenery passing by. The Ural Mountains are not too high in this area of the train route but are full of evergreen and juniper trees and lots of wildlife. I joked with Oleg about his dacha, which is about forty kilometers west of Yekaterinburg. I said, 'So you go to Europe every weekend to chop and saw firewood. That is how you stay in shape?' Oleg said, 'I suppose a lot of people live near the dividing line between Europe and Asia and visit each place every workday.'

"He also told me about life in this area during the war. Stalin moved whole industries to the Asian side of the Urals, and there were many hardships. They had no electricity most of the time, and he was always cold and hungry. In grade school, they each received half a piece of bread at lunch. His father tried to enlist in the army but was refused since he worked in a vital food industry supervising only women. He told the story about his uncle who was with a small group of fellow soldiers surrounded by Germans near Moscow. They were in a swamp and fought off the Germans for many days, only eating rats, birds, and insects. Finally, the Germans told his uncle and comrades—Asians—to go home, and the kind German soldiers let them leave for home.

"Tim, I think you will especially take note of what I am going to disclose to you next. Oleg told me in confidence that the Russian Academy of Sciences may run the country soon. Oleg was trained in the military school that is part of the Academy of Sciences. He was a reservist and served every summer for two weeks, learning how to drive and operate a tank that was very hot, crowded, and especially noisy. Oleg said that the academicians run institutes of thousands of professors and scientists, teach, and have students worship them for life. The academicians meet regularly, confer, and represent almost all facets of society. They have the real brain and political power of the country and are highly respected by the average university-educated Russian. Oleg said there may be a coup by the intelligentsia someday soon, especially since our leaders are so corrupt.

"When we arrived in Kazan on Wednesday night, Oleg got off the train as he was to lecture the next morning at a European conference for mainly PhD students. Oleg was met by three colleagues, and they stood outside my car, discussing some things for about fifteen minutes. Then they all shook hands. One of the gentlemen joined me in my compartment. I introduced myself, and he said in halting Russian that he did not speak English. I thought that maybe he was one of a series of train companions there to keep an eye on me during my trip. Anyway, the only question my overweight compartment mate had was, 'Why you are in Russia?'

"The next morning, I woke at about six and was up for an hour before Oleg's friend woke. Then the policeman who had been patrolling the train came and asked for his ID. He seemed very nervous about this. When we arrived in Moscow, another policeman and two plainclothes police were waiting to take him off the train. I thought, 'Did the secret police/local police find out that the academicians were following me and trying to get my support or to kidnap me?'

"The elderly lady that had my airline tickets in Moscow was waiting for me with her driver, and they took me to the Rossiya Hotel. I got lost in the 'world's largest hotel,' trying to find my room. Once in the room, I received a call from Boris, saying he would pick me up in thirty minutes and take me to lunch. Traffic in Moscow was very bad, and we waited and waited to get out of the Red Square area. Finally, Boris's driver started driving down the sidewalk for about half a block.

"We went to see Boris's office at the Academy of Sciences, an old palace next to a park. He has a lovely corner office, and I got my picture taken below a picture of Mendeleyev. Boris showed me their meeting room, where the leaders meet and electronically bring in the Far East, Ural, and other divisions.

Then we went to the Academy of Sciences high-rise building for lunch. Boris mentioned that the Mayak nuclear accident site was south of Yekaterinburg, between another large city and Yekaterinburg. They are studying the site and evaluating water treatment methods. The government had plans to treat all the radioactive water, but after perestroika, the funding stopped.

"After lunch, we took the elevator to the twenty-second floor, where there was a bar under construction. I got some nice pictures of the city there. Then we went to the Vernadsky Institute to see Boris's lab and meet his wife, Tamara, and some of her students. They took me on a tour of the labs. Boris stated that he was responsible for the lab getting its first computers, and I said the most important improvements were the modern toilets with toilet paper. Twenty years ago, I had to use newspaper for toilet paper in dirty old toilets."

Tim laughed.

"Boris then went back to work at about four, and his driver brought me back to the hotel. On Friday, I went for a walk before breakfast. Moscow is very quiet that time of day as most of the shops do not open until eleven. At breakfast, I sat with three young American ladies from San Diego that were professional ballet dancers. They were in Moscow for an international dance contest with their professor from Iowa. One of the young ladies had grown up in Pueblo, Colorado. After the early morning breakfast, I took a taxi to Red Square, had a walk around the Kremlin, and visited St. Basil's Cathedral and the Armory Museum.

"After I returned from Red Square around noon, I checked out of the hotel and took a taxi to the airport for my flight to Kaliningrad. After leaving the hotel, we got off busy Leninsky Prospekt Boulevard and took some back roads through several small villages. There were many housing projects under construction with big homes for the wealthy.

"At my departure gate, I found that it was full of American Baptists working all over Russia with their families. They were going to a conference in Poland, near the coast, for a week. One guy I spoke with lives and works in former Stalingrad. He was traveling with his pregnant wife, their five-year-old daughter, and their two-year-old twin girls. One single gal was from Arkansas and was working in the major city above Vladivostok for about ten years. She goes to Seoul, South Korea, once a year for her visa renewal. Another lady was from a small town near Asheville and really missed North Carolina. Her husband and three boys were with her. The airport almost seemed like a preschool. Everyone thought I was with their group and was anxious to meet me.

"After departing Moscow, the plane got fairly quiet as most of the children had fallen asleep since the plane was warm. I had an aisle, emergency-row seat, but I think the legroom was tighter than the other seats, which is really the tightest I have ever encountered on a plane. Adam, who was sitting next to me, told me they have been in Russia for over five years, the first year in Moscow and now former Stalingrad. He says that the entire family must leave Russia once a year to get their visas renewed. The first year, it was every six months. A fellow across the aisle with an Asian wife (from Oklahoma) and no children runs a parish in the major city south of Yekaterinburg. He said he heard a lot about the contaminated lake and the Mayak accident. These missionaries would make good eyes for the United States on the pulse of the Russian people. Maybe some of them do, but do not worry, Tim, as I will never ask you if they do.

"I really hated to leave all my friendly fellow Americans at the Kaliningrad Airport, especially all the cute kids. At the airport, I was met by Sophia, a nice-looking elderly lady who would be my host and guide. She and a wild-looking young driver, who drove like crazy, took me to the Institute of Oceanography, home of the *Akademik Abraham* and its sister ship, where I gave my lecture. Then we went to one of the outer old fortresses surrounding Kaliningrad for a short walk, followed by seeing the cathedral in town. I was tired, so they left me at the hotel, where I made an early evening of it after dinner.

"After a late breakfast the next morning, Sophia and driver picked me up, and we went through the old part of the city that still has old German villas. Many rich Russians are buying out the two to four families that live together in a villa and restoring them. Sophia referred to them as robbers and crooks. She said that is how many wealthy Russians have made their money. Sophia also said that she usually serves as an interpreter at another oceanography institute and has been on several voyages on the *Abraham*, even once to the port of Boston. She talked about East Prussia belonging to Germany for six hundred years and how their major castle was partly damaged in the war. After the war, Stalin ordered it to be completely destroyed so as to rid the city of German reminders and to make it a Russian city. After the war, all Germans in Kaliningrad were sent back to Germany. Today many come back to see their childhood homes and to talk with the present owners.

"There were many Germans staying at my hotel, and Sophia said they were doing a lot of business investment in Kaliningrad. Sophia and the driver kept debating what will happen to the area since it was really German, but only Russians lived there. Most of them have never been out of Kaliningrad since it takes two visas to go to big Russia and return to Kaliningrad, and ship travel is slow and planes expensive. Sophia thought it may someday become part of Poland or Lithuania with only a Russian port. She was born Russian in Lithuania. The Russians started to build a big Russian-style building at the castle site but ran out of money to finish it. The authorities agreed to restore the damaged cathedral that was bombed by the British during the Second World War.

"We also visited part of the inner fortress where there is an artificial lake and restaurant. I thought, 'Are a group of Germans making a nuclear weapon so they can have their independence from Russia?' Maybe someone in the *Akademik Abraham* crew was smuggling in enriched uranium or plutonium instead of shipping it out.

"The next morning, I went for an hour walk before breakfast. It was nice to see the city with less activity. There were many Russian athletes in the city for some kind of sports competition. One lady told me all types of sports. The breakfast was great, and I heard a lot of German."

"After breakfast and hotel checkout, my driver came and took me to the airport. Check-in was very confusing, but somehow I managed to get to my gate without announcements or signs. All passengers had to walk across the open airport taxiing area to our plane, boarding an hour before departure. We had to wait about ten minutes at the bottom of the stairway before boarding, and a couple of small boys walked over to the grass area next to the runway to pee. People were still boarding forty-five minutes later. At least the air-conditioning was on since it was warm already. The flight left at eleven and seemed to be full of Russians, unlike my arrival flight. There were only four Aeroflot planes at the airport, with one going to Saint Petersburg ahead of us. The flight was one and a half hours, and we landed at Sheremetyevo Airport, north of Moscow. I then went to my hotel by taxi for an uneventful night's sleep.

"In taking a shuttle bus to the airport late the next day, I was reminded of the large number of foreign cars, especially Japanese, in the crowded and congested streets. Ten years ago, there were mostly Russian-made automobiles on the streets with no traffic jams. We drove by lots of new shops with colorful signs and many new buildings. They even have the tallest building in Europe now, an apartment building.

"I arrived in Zurich early on Sunday morning and then caught my flight to Vienna. I had a wonderful reunion with Margrit at the Wandl Hotel, and we spent the day telling each other about our adventures. The next day, we returned to Colorado.

"I would be happy to send you copies of the important pictures I took after leaving Vladivostok."

"John, please do. It appears to me that this was indeed a trip of a lifetime, and I hope I can do it someday but without the interference of Russian security. Anyway, my superiors are going to find my written summary of this tape very interesting, especially the part concerning the Russian Academy of Sciences getting involved in political matters."

Chapter 2
Security Clearance
Troubles

I

During the early 1950s, a Republican United States senator from Wisconsin—Joseph Raymond McCarthy—gained worldwide attention by charging that Communists had infiltrated the government. Such widely scattered fear became known as McCarthyism, and phrases such as "Better dead than Red" and "Don't be caught with a Red under your bed" swept the land. As a result, a goodly number of patriots were accused of disloyalty, even treason, many of whom suffered horrific hardship. One of the best-known casualties of this parody was physicist J. Robert Oppenheimer, the man who designed the atomic bomb.

In 1980, with the inauguration of Ronald Reagan as the fortieth president of the United States, McCarthyism leaped from the grave; for almost immediately after being sworn in, Reagan began to level derogatory charges against the Soviet leaders and their form of government. A witch hunt soon ensued in an attempt to ferret out any American remotely suspected of sympathizing or collaborating with a Communist agent.

Despite the fact that, practically speaking, the Cold War was over and amicable relations currently existed between the United States and the former Soviet Union, no actions had been taken to alleviate the sufferings of those Americans and Russians unjustly accused of treasonous acts during the Reagan era. And without doubt, there were a number of them as there were in the dark days of McCarthyism.

II

In 1983, the Russians shot down a commercial South Korean airliner that had accidentally entered Russian airspace, killing all aboard. At the same time, John was attending an international scientific conference in a Downtown Denver hotel that he had assisted in organizing. At the reception, he got caught up on what his many friends had been doing. Three Russian professors who were good friends of the Czermaks were also attending the meeting. Misha was the chairman of the Nuclear Department of Moscow State University, and Dimitri and Oleg were in the same department. Dimitri and Oleg were also John's coauthors on a series of books they were writing for the IAEA. That evening, a group of close friends, including the Russian scientists, joined John and Margrit for dinner in the Brown Palace Hotel, a Denver landmark.

Halfway through the conference, one day was allotted for tours. John and Margrit took the occasion to entertain their Russian guests by taking them to the mountains, first to Echo Lake and then up Mount Evans, for a walk and to have a grand view of the city. Their final stop was the adjoining old mining towns of Black Hawk and Central City, where they had a bratwurst lunch at the Black Hawk Inn and a walking tour of historic Central City.

Margrit was always looking for fun, so she excused herself and disappeared into a shop that published newspapers with headlines of one's choice. She had one printed that read SOVIET SPIES ARRESTED IN CENTRAL CITY. Luckily, the Russians had a good laugh, and Misha happily accepted the gift.

They ended the day at the Czermaks' home in Arvada for dinner. Before dinner, Misha enjoyed seeing Margrit's vegetable garden. John snapped a photo of him pulling up some carrots for dinner. He also got a nice picture of the group admiring his Ford Model T, which he was restoring.

Before the conference resumed the next day, Misha took John aside in a corner outside the conference room where no one could overhear their conversation. He told John that he thought of him as a very good friend and that he was only delivering a message from the KGB. They wanted information from John on the production of the neutron bomb. Misha brought out a small picture of Svetlana Isenova making love to John, with Vasilenko, a known KGB agent, taking part in the sexual act. Svetlana was also a KGB agent enlisted to blackmail John. This horrific event had been filmed and photographed on the Russian ship during a Russian club dinner on the Danube when the Czermaks resided in Vienna. Of course, John did not recognize the embarrassing event as he had been drugged and had passed out.

Misha said that if John did not cooperate with the KGB, the picture would be sent to the FBI. John flatly refused to cooperate, even though Misha continued to try to convince him that the picture would get him into a lot of trouble, even losing his job. John told Misha that he never wanted to hear from him again on the matter.

Meantime, unbeknownst to John, the FBI had underway an investigation of the Czermaks. The same day that John had been approached by Misha, Margrit was asked to appear at the FBI headquarters in Denver. She told John in the evening, "I had no choice but to comply with the FBI request to submit to the interrogation. Otherwise, I was sure I would have been judged guilty of the charges leveled against me, the charges being that I had been seen passing secret documents to a suspected KGB agent. In the days preceding the interrogation, neither the security officer from Rocky Flats, Meg Showman, nor the FBI agent, Phil Gilbert, had confronted me with the charges. My immediate reaction had been one of disbelief. For this reason, I'm afraid I was initially quite belligerent."

Margrit continued, "Once at the FBI headquarters, John, I was informed that I would be interviewed and given a lie detector test. Leaving my purse in the anteroom, I asked if it would be safe there, which I thought was very funny. Meg, who looked a little like an overweight Marilyn Monroe, greeted me and introduced me to her colleagues, one from the DOE and the other a representative of the FBI, Phil. I was informed that a background investigation had recently been conducted of you to assist the DOE in determining your continued eligibility for a DOE security clearance. Certain matters had been raised as a result of that background investigation.

"The interview began rather comically when I was asked if I was Margrit Czermak. 'No,' I answered. 'My name is Margrit Grayson Czermak.' I was next asked when and why I had gone to Vienna. I told them.

"Then I was asked if I worked while in Vienna. I said I had for the United Nations Industrial Development Organization. I explained that most American wives who wanted to work had to work for a UN agency, and since I wanted to work, I simply applied there. They asked if I had worked for any other agency. I told them I had worked for the United Nations World Refugee Assistance for about four months. I said it was an organization to assist the Palestinian refugees in the Middle East but that conditions there were extremely somber, which didn't suit my personality, and one of my coworkers suggested I try UNIDO, so I did. I said I was only looking for part-time work because I was writing a novel, but I needed to get out and be with people. So when UNIDO called me and asked if I would like to come in for an interview, I did. I was subsequently hired by Taniaka in the Department of Technology Transfer.

"I was next asked about my friendships while working for UNIDO. I replied that they were with Michael Prince, an English Austrian, and Andrei Pushkin, from Estonia. I told them that Prince worked in the IAEA Library and that Pushkin was a staff officer for UNIDO. I said that we were a friendly group and that everyone in our section got to know one another well. 'And how did you and Pushkin become friends?' I was asked. 'He helped me with my Russian,' I answered. It was about now that I noticed Meg had a copy of the last book I had published, *The Bare Essentials*.

"I was asked if I was now or had ever been a member of the Communist Party. That brought a chuckling no from me. I was asked if I was now or had ever been a member of an organization sympathetic to the doctrine of the Communist Party. 'No,' I replied. Then I was asked if I had ever contemplated passing sensitive information to a foreign agent. I told them that I had not myself but that my character in the book I was writing did. And so I went on to explain that the main woman in the book and I were inseparable. Her thoughts were mine, mine were hers, and I spent days thinking of what information she could pass to her lover.

"And then we went through the whole rigmarole again—only yes or no answers this time. I was subsequently asked if I ever meet clandestinely with a Russian national, to which I replied yes and no. I explained that Pushkin was indeed a Soviet national.

"I was then asked if I was aware that the Rocky Flats Plant made triggers for nuclear weapons, to which I responded yes. I was then asked if I was in an intimate relationship with Pushkin, to which I answered yes. That really caught all three of them off guard. I was asked again if I ever passed sensitive information to Pushkin or to any other Soviet national. I paused in my answer. 'I'm sorry, just in case the needle is fluttering, I had better explain that my principal did pass sensitive information to her Russian lover, and—' I was interrupted by a very annoyed FBI agent. 'I'm asking if you, Margrit, ever passed sensitive or classified information to your Soviet lover.'

"'You misunderstood me,' I said. 'He wasn't my lover.'

"'But you just said you were intimate.'

"John, I was really getting exasperated. I replied, 'We were intimate, but we weren't lovers. Can't two people be intimately friendly? I was also intimately friendly with Michael Prince.'

"The apparatus was removed from me, and I was told I could wait in the anteroom. It was some three hours and ten minutes later that I was permitted to leave Denver's FBI headquarters. I had been duly acknowledged for my time and cooperation by the persons briefing me. Agent Gilbert saw me to the door with that same guarded, mistrustful expression that he had betrayed throughout the hearing. Later, I chuckled to myself, considering his short brow and small head. It seemed that, if I could somehow break it open, it would spew forth the entire works of the FBI.

"During the five-hour 'interview,' John, I had not lost my characteristic sense of fun. Never mind that thrice I had been subjected to the polygraph examination. Thrice the same questions had been propounded. For what seemed forever, I was asked to identify photographs of Soviets, most of whom I had never seen before. Each time I did recognize a person, I was asked if I felt that person could be suborned. The entire episode had caused me to feel intimidated and used. I was angry, insulted, and lastly embarrassed by the Neanderthal mentality of my own countrymen."

"John, I am sorry, but they asked me to tell you they want you down at FBI's Denver office at nine tomorrow. The FBI wants you to submit to polygraph tests and answer questions concerning the three visiting Russians."

After the first FBI interrogation, the lie detector testing continued several more times at the FBI headquarters for John, once after returning from a trip to Moscow with a stack of business cards and many photos and notes that he had taken for Tim. John thought that these assignments were the primary thing that contributed to him failing the FBI's polygraph tests. John thought it seemed like Meg was trying to find all the incriminating evidence she could to make herself look good. Of course, she passed all this information onto Phil. After the last polygraph, Phil showed John the incriminating picture that Misha had showed him. John told Phil that he did not remember the sexual entrapment and thought he was drugged.

On Good Friday, Meg came to John's office with a guard and demanded that he give her his security badge as his clearance had been suspended. He was told to remove personal things from his office. Then he was escorted out of the security area and told to go home and that his superior would be in contact with him the next day. That night was one of the worst John had ever endured, especially since he was told that he could be faced with horrendous legal fees if he attempted to exonerate himself. The next morning, his manager told John over the phone to take a few days off and that he could understand how embarrassed and angry he must be.

Several agonizing days later, John went to work in an unclassified area of the plant. The first thing he did was apply for a three-year leave of absence. A few days later, it was approved since Rockwell management was sympathetic to John's troubles. John then accepted an invitation for an academic position at the University of New South Wales (UNSW) in Kensington, a suburb of Sydney, Australia, as head of the Department of Mineral Processing and Extractive Metallurgy.

The last month before the Czermaks left for Australia, they sold their cars and house in Arvada. During this time, the FBI continued to bug their phone and dig through their trash. All of John's mail at the plant was being opened and read. Both John and Margrit agreed it was a dreadful month, but they were excited about a new life in Australia, just like it had been when they went to Austria. The children were already settled in their own lives. Amy was happily married, and both Eric and Lorrie were attending the University of Colorado (CU) and living in dormitories. John and Margrit's plan was to have Eric and Lorrie come down for the summer and Amy to bring Dave for a visit anytime they could come.

Later, John found out that Tim seemed quite pleased by these turn of events since it would be much easier for him to send John on assignments, especially to Russia and Eastern Europe, without the interference of the FBI or DOE security. John would also be asked by Tim to try to take trips to China,

Iran, Libya, North Korea, and South Africa related to nuclear proliferation. They were to communicate mostly by phone. At the time, John wondered if the CIA had any role in turning over the incriminating picture to the FBI.

Chapter 3
Teaching in Australia

I

Tim made his first telephone call to John in Australia. "John, I am sure you have heard of Dr. Khan, father of the Pakistan nuclear program, who has been exporting nuclear technology to Iran, Libya, and North Korea. Everyone knows that terrorist groups would like the bomb or nuclear materials to make one or radioactive materials or waste to make a dirty bomb. Thus, we hope to send you to these countries to find out as much as possible about their nuclear programs. We also hope you can go to South Africa to verify their removal of nuclear weapons. However, I do understand that it will take some time before you feel at home down under."

It was spring, and Sydney was green and lush. It reminded Margrit a great deal of southern California when she was a girl. Sydney put John in mind of Florence, Italy, or San Francisco— Florence because of the red-tiled roofs, San Francisco because of its endless hills and the ocean. From their modest apartment, they could look out on the Tasman Sea with its extraordinary aqua color and see the waves crashing against the rocks. It took about fifteen minutes to walk to the sea from their flat, about the same amount of time John needed to walk to his office. At the seaside, there was a path that wound along the cliffs and provided a wonderful view of the sea, plus gave one an exhilarating climb. In spite of its size, the Czermaks learned that Sydney was a fairly safe city and that most Australians were friendly and pleasant.

John had adjusted to life in Australia much faster than Margrit, probably since he spent most of the day at a job he liked and had use of a university car. He was supervising ten faculty members with the help of a secretary and teaching a mineral separations course. The only thing that initially annoyed him was the large number of students talking while he was lecturing. At first, John stopped his lecture and tried to wait until the chatter stopped. It did quiet down a little but picked up later. After a couple of weeks of this, John gave up as he found out from his first exam that most of the students were indeed learning about the separation of minerals.

John also had time to look after six graduate students and do some consulting and traveling. He had one postdoc, a nuclear scientist from Libya. Ala had his family with him, and during their year's stay in Australia, the Czermaks became such good friends with them that John referred to them as his god family.

Because Margrit had a hard time adjusting to the new life, John became almost desperate in his desire to find diversions to amuse her. One Sunday they rented a two-seater bike (not a bike built for two, mind you—more like a rickshaw) and rode through Centennial Park. Margrit felt so ridiculous pedaling the silly-looking bicycle that she laughed until tears were streaming down her cheeks. Besides doing a lot of fun things with John, she also started working for a temporary agency; she enjoyed the work very much.

Margrit told John one evening about her day at work that included a look at North Sydney during her lunch hour. "I took the train there, disembarked, walked around the block, found absolutely nothing of interest, and went back into the station. 'On what track is the train back to Sydney?' I asked. 'One-oh-two' came the answer from the young clerk. I went back outside and looked at the tracks. There were only two tracks. I went back inside and asked how the train could come on 102 when there are only two tracks. 'Laa-day,' he said, 'I said one or two.' I laughed and laughed about this as I boarded the train back to work."

One of the things John did was take Margrit with him to Melbourne, where he was going to give an invited lecture at the university. The drive down was lovely because they took the Princes Highway along the coast. Because there had been a lot of rain along the coast, everything was very green; and of course, it was great to see the lovely seascapes that appeared from time to time. It took two days driving to Melbourne. They were staying near the university, and Margrit got out and explored the neighborhood while John visited the university. They also had dinner one night with his host and a couple of old friends whom they had not seen since the conference in Denver. Before their return to Sydney, they visited the nearby Twelve Apostles.

John and Margrit's first trip out of the country was to South Africa, where John was to present an invited paper at an international nuclear waste meeting; the conference organizers paid all their travel expenses. John loved train travel, and ever since their arrival in Australia, he wanted to take the Indian Pacific train from Sydney to Perth. Thus, he and Margrit used the occasion of getting to Johannesburg by going first to Perth by train and then flying directly to Johannesburg from Perth. On their return, they would fly from Perth back to Sydney.

They left Sydney on the Indian Pacific train with sixteen single and twenty-five double carriages. The train would cross the vast continent of Australia from one ocean to the other on one of the world's longest and greatest train journeys. The journey from Sydney to Perth covered about 2,600 miles, with the train traveling at an average speed of 50 miles per hour and with three nights aboard the train. There were three tours during scheduled stops at Broken Hill, Adelaide, and Kalgoorlie. Although the origins of the Indian Pacific can be traced back to the early 1900s, it was not until 1970 that the train completed its first unbroken journey from Sydney to Perth.

On the afternoon of the first day, the Czermaks got to see the spectacular Blue Mountains from their small train compartment as the sun was setting. In their car, the upper bunk slid up and down, and it was in the up position during the day. The lower bunk folded down over the two seats facing each other with a fold-down table under the window. There were two narrow closets next to the beds, a fold-down sink that drained the water when one raised it up to put away, and a mirror above the sink. The compartment was in the shape of a triangle. The hallway was very narrow and curved back and forth, and the toilets and showers were located at the end of the carriage. The next car was a lounge with tables and chairs, and the car after that was a restaurant with cooking and seating areas.

On the first morning, the landscape had changed from the tree-covered Blue Mountains to the barren plains with just a few trees. After they arrived in Broken Hill—a colorful old mining town and a major producer of silver, lead, and zinc since 1883—they took a one-hour bus tour. After leaving Broken Hill in the afternoon, the countryside changed to lush green with rolling hills of wheat and hay. In this area, Margrit saw what looked like an ostrich, but John said it was an emu, and there were sheep everywhere, both in the outback and green farm areas.

Their next stop was at four in Adelaide, where they took a one-hour bus tour. Adelaide, known as the Festival City, was first laid out in 1836 by Col. William Light; this elegant city was noted for its superb parklands, galleries, and colonials buildings near beaches and hills. Their tour of the heart of Adelaide included sights of Montefiore Hill, Colonel Light's lookout, Oval Cricket Ground, and Lake Torrens.

The next morning, the Czermaks had great Australian breakfast of eggs, sausage, tomatoes, toast, and hash browns. Now the landscape took on a richer hue as the journey moved through the mallee scrub into the treeless plains of the Nullarbor; here, the train traveled the world's longest straight stretch of railway track (about three hundred miles). The train stopped in Cook, at the middle of the Nullarbor Plain, for a short while to change drivers and take on water. The passengers stretched their legs with a brief visit of Cook. Once a thriving railway settlement, Cook now had only a handful of residents living in lonely buildings straddling the Transcontinental rail line; it was one of the world's most isolated outposts.

A little after noon, the train crossed over to Western Australia from South Australia. Western Australia was a state close to the size of western Europe and had a population of under 2.5 million people; it was the powerhouse of the Australian economy. Famous for its vast reserves of iron ore and unique diamonds, the state also supplied the world with numerous other metals, coal, and other mineral resources and had a fascinating history of mining. With much of an already dry state currently experiencing a drying climate with historically low rainfall or increased rainfall intensity through storm rains, water management had become a significant consideration for all mine operations and developments. The Western Australian mining environment, with a high biodiversity of unique animals and plants, posed great challenges for the mining industry.

The train arrived in Kalgoorlie, Australia's gold capital, at around eight, and most of the passengers received a 1.5-hour bus ride. The tour guide did a good job of telling everyone aboard the bus about the historical aspects of the town as they slowly drove around the city of thirty thousand. There was a lot of fine architecture in the city, which included the magnificent town hall, the heritage buildings, and many pubs. The final viewing was down two blocks of houses of prostitution. The police building was located on the same block. Only two of the brothels were operating today, whereas there were a large number of brothels, pubs, and hotels operating in the past. The adjoining city was called Boulder, and mostly native people lived there.

The gold rush, set off by Paddy Hannan's discovery in 1893, was one of the biggest in Australian history. One hundred years on, the world's largest single opencut mining operation continued to recover the precious metal, and the city had prospered as a result. The bus tour ended at the massive Super Pit gold mine, more than four hundred yards deep and over two miles long, floodlit at night for great viewing by the passengers.

On the final morning of the trip, the countryside was now green farmland, and the train was going through the scenic Avon Valley and into Western Australia's expansive wheat belt. The train arrived in Perth at nine. Perth was a very compact and beautiful city, with the Swan River running through it with wonderful views of the city from Kings Park and Botanic Garden. Kings Park was one of the largest inner city parks in the world. After a tour of the city, the Czermaks caught their flight to Johannesburg.

The following was a letter Margrit wrote to Lorrie:

> Dearest Lorrie,
>
> Please do not throw this letter away. I'm going to tell you all about our trip so far and would like to have this to refresh my memory someday. I thought you would like the lions on the heading of the paper; in fact, that's why I bought the stationery. We first went to Kruger National Park on a flight from Johannesburg and stayed in a hut for three nights. We saw lots of animals on several game drives.
>
> Then we flew to Livingstone, Zambia, via Johannesburg. There, we took some short trips to Victoria Falls National Park and Chobe National Park in Botswana. At Victoria Falls, we were staying at a hotel within walking distance from the falls. The first night at the hotel, the fire alarm went off. Your father walked out into the hallway and saw that no one was leaving the building. He decided that we should also remain put as there might have been some kidnappers outside who were the ones who set off the alarm. The first morning as we were having breakfast at the

restaurant outside, a mother baboon, with her baby hanging on, came running over and jumped on our table, stole some bread, and ran off. Every time we walked to the falls, there would be several baboons blocking the walkway; so in fright, we had to walk around them in the bush.

In Chobe National Park, our tour consisted of a boat ride on the Chobe River between Botswana and the Namibia Caprivi Strip. On the boat ride, we saw some hippopotamuses on the shore and in the river. All of a sudden, a hippo came up under our boat and nearly capsized it. In the afternoon, we had a ride around the park in a safari vehicle and came upon a pride of lions. Chobe has one of the largest concentrations of game in Africa. Later, the skies opened, and we had to find shelter from the terrific rainstorm as the vehicle had open sides.

After we arrived back in Johannesburg, our friends Jan and Janice picked us up at the airport. We went to their home in Hartbeespoort. The next day, we visited the Ann van Dyk Cheetah Center, which was established in 1971. We saw lots of cheetahs that had been saved, as well as falcons, vultures, wild dogs, and a few wildcats. We got our picture taken petting Chaka, one of about twenty king cheetahs at the center. On Sunday, we went to nearby Pilanesberg National Park and saw eleven rhinos, two elephants, many giraffes, warthogs, impalas, wildebeests, ostriches, dung beetles, and a few hippos in the lake but no lions or cheetahs or leopards. Afterward, we went into a gold mine to see how gold is mined; it was very interesting and fun. We also saw Zulus dance, and they were good. Such rhythm!

Jan and Janice are a delightful couple, and it was great to reminisce about our days in Vienna. We had lunch with them at their home. Janice prepared a typical South African meal for us, which was scrumptious. It included mutton pie, chicken of some sort, baked peaches, potatoes, veggies, plus a yummy dessert. Janice's home is very European. You would have loved it. She was a stage actress before marriage and is very striking. We've found the South Africans to be very clannish and friendly. I love to hear Afrikaans sung; it is so soft and calming.

The next day, your father went with Jan to the Pelindaba nuclear site, which means in English "to leave or get out." Your father gave a talk on nuclear waste treatment, and later, he and Jan drove around the site, which by the way is the same place where South African scientists clandestinely constructed several nuclear weapons during the apartheid days.

At noon, they returned to get me and Janice, and we went into Pretoria for lunch. Afterward, we visited the monument to the Boer War and saw how the country was developed (covered wagons like ours). Later, Jan dropped us off at the Protea Hotel Manor in Hatfield. That night, we went to the conference center for the mine water conference reception. Kathy, an old friend, showed up to greet us.

The next day, your father went to the meeting to give his talk and later came back so we could have a walk around the neighborhood. The University of Pretoria is directly across the street from the hotel (about fifty thousand students), and on campus and around town, there were lots of jacaranda trees with their purple blossoms. That night, we attended the conference banquet. The highlight of the banquet was that everyone got to play their own drum along with the band via their instructions—great fun! The next day, we flew to Cape Town.

Now we're at the Inn on the Square, and it's elegant. We've only been in Cape Town a couple of hours and just had time to settle in. Dad has gone to the Cape Sun Hotel, where the conference is being held. He's going to come back soon to give me a report. The reception is being held there tonight, and tomorrow the conference begins.

It's Tuesday morning, and now I'll continue this communication to you. Dad has gone to the conference; he gives his paper this afternoon. Tonight is a reception with the mayor of Cape Town, should be lush. The one last night was first class. One joke that Bret told me was about a mayor giving a talk to his constituents after he won the election; the mayor said, "I thank everyone from the bottom of my heart, and my wife also thanks you from her bottom."

Tomorrow we may go to see Table Mountain as well as the Cape of Good Hope, which is quite near and has lots of baboons in the area. We toured the nuclear facility and a winery. They've had specially labeled wine prepared for the radwaste conference. Thursday, I may take a tour to the botanical gardens. I'm told it's very worthwhile. You can't believe the flowers here, Lorrie; they are so exotic and breathtaking in their beauty.

We had such a good time with Bret and Elda. Your father went to the University of Port Elizabeth during our first day there and met Bret's students. He told me that one of the students name was Pardon. Now if you think Pardon is a curious name, he does too. Asked how it came to pass, he said several stories circulated. One was that the doctor asked his father (who was hard of hearing) what he wished to call the baby. His father replied "Pardon?" "Pardon it is," declared the doctor, and he's been Pardon ever since.

I loved their home in Port Elizabeth, which overlooks a long canyon with a few monkeys about. We then went to Storms River. They told us we would be staying in a hut and have to rough it, so naturally, we assumed it would be a grass hut with no amenities. Lo and behold, it was a modern cabin complete with maid service. Needless to say, we teased them to no end about this. Bret did some fishing and made us South African cheese sandwiches with tomatoes for lunch. There, we took a nature hike. 'Twas fun.

The most fun, though, was our visit to an ostrich farm after our stay at Storms River. We learned a good deal about this fascinating bird; we visited their homes and petted babies. The ostrich egg is so hard it must be opened (by man) with a hammer, yet this tough young critter bursts it open when he/she is ready to be born. (I even stood on an ostrich egg.) Both the father and mother bird sit on them—the mother during the day, the father at night. Ostrich couples mate for life and usually live to be about forty. Ninety-five percent of the world's ostriches live in the area we visited. Each family has its own plot of land. We'll have to revisit with you; you'll love it. Oh, Dad and I got to sit on an ostrich and also watched the ostrich races. They were a riot.

Well, I want to do some stretching and others. I've had little time for any exercise and am so glad to have a day to myself. I also want to go through my karate forms so I don't forget everything. Thank god we have a large room. Take care, my darling daughter. You mean everything to me.

Love and kisses,
Mom

At the end of the conference, the Czermaks flew back to Sydney via Johannesburg and Perth. Shortly after John's return from the African trip, Tim called him and wanted a short report about his visit to South Africa's nuclear research center. John told Tim about his one-day visit, where he toured the laboratories and gave a lecture. "Jan, who manages a chemical research group, was my host. Jan talked about the country destroying its nuclear arsenal and signing the Nuclear Non-Proliferation Treaty. He told me that one nuclear weapon was tested, and six were turned over to the IAEA, France, and the United States. However, Jan said that there was a rumor that an eighth warhead was produced but missing and not destroyed. Jan would like to investigate this more and write a novel about it someday. He thinks the missing bomb might have been clandestinely shipped to Israel for a lot of money for a select few."

II

In the Czermaks' far corner of the globe, they heard about the fall of the stock market in New York, Tokyo, London, Hong Kong, and Sydney; about the hurricane in Britain; about the earthquake in southern California; and about the weather in Moscow, Budapest, Warsaw, and Prague but, of course, nothing about Colorado. In October, about the time of the crash, the Czermaks flew to Auckland, New Zealand, and then relaxed for two days in Papeete, Tahiti, during which the islanders tried to burn down the town. John was to attend a conference in Knoxville, Tennessee, while Margrit stayed in Denver. After the meeting, John flew to Denver to join Margrit for a week with their children. During their visit, John had lunch with several of his Rocky Flats friends and got caught up on their activities and how his former group was doing. He also had lunch with Tim, where they discussed John's future travels, which included an invitation by the Chinese. John and Margrit also planned to meet their adopted family in Libya.

The following was another letter Margrit wrote to Lorrie a few weeks after their return to Australia:

Hello, darling. How do you like my patriotic stationery? This is the last day of November, and I can't believe it. The month has flown by. How has it seemed for you? I talked to Eric earlier today, and he told me he would be going to Fort Collins for the big CU–Colorado State University game this weekend. I hope you will see it and that you will both enjoy it. Eric said he would be staying with Matt for the weekend. I'm glad I called him today. We're going to have to call him one weekend and you the next; our phone bill is astronomical. Have you been following the Olympics? We see the daily news, and that is it. Russia is certainly walking away with the medals. Last night's news reported that there was some political infighting in the Kremlin. I hope nothing happens to upset the Russian applecart because I can't imagine that they would have another go at it for another hundred years if their attempted reforms fail.

We have discovered that kangaroos don't exactly hop around in the streets of Sydney, as many people have suggested to us, but there are many of them in the parts of the country we have yet to explore. Actually, we saw signs along the highway on our trip to Melbourne warning us to look out for kangaroos; and every now and then in the Blue Mountains, we've seen one lying dead by the side of the road. We did see some kangaroos at the Koala Reserve here in Sydney, the mothers with their joeys in their pouches, and they were very tame, like dogs. I don't know what the wild ones are like.

When Harold (as you know, your father's PhD adviser) arrived, we drove up to the Blue Mountains and hiked around Wentworth Falls and Three Sisters. It was a glorious day, and it was wonderful to be out with nature. We stopped in Leura and had lunch in a teahouse. The long ride back was boring, especially since I was riding in the back of the car and couldn't hear the music. Once Harold left, I investigated a French class with Alliance Française because Dad, Harold, and I decided to go to France next year.

We also had good friend George Hitey (from Canada) visiting, who has been in and out of Sydney for the past month and is getting ready to head for China and Japan and then back to Ottawa. We'll miss him as he is lots of fun. But he plans to be back in March—and if we're still here, we'll see him then. At the moment, however, we have no plans to leave Sydney, aside from our visit to Colorado during the holidays because Dad has another year of his three-year leave of absence from Rockwell to go. For the most part, he is happy here with his work and is making a name for himself as a professor and consultant.

And Sydney is a lovely place; there is no two ways about it. And it's quite exciting.

Yesterday culminated weeklong festivities sparked by the Bicentennial Naval Review. Russia wasn't invited to the navy celebration but was here anyway. There is an enormous Russian cruise ship (*Alexander Pushkin*) docked at the harbor; such a coincidence, we think. Of course, we're certain it is here to spy on the other ships. It's so obvious.

We had lunch on the harbor at a restaurant called Phantom of the Opera. The weather was perfect—at seventy-six degrees. The sky was blue as blue could be, without a trace of a cloud. The review, which began at noon and lasted for three hours, included the visiting warships cruising the harbor. There are fifty-three ships from sixteen countries here, including our own battleship *New Jersey*, for a total of seventeen thousand visiting sailors.

Thereafter, there was a flyby from visiting naval aircraft, including jets and helicopters, and then the giant 747 of Qantas and Air Australia's airbus. The entire display was most impressive, and we highly enjoyed seeing it. Australia's biggest ever fireworks display took place last night (which we saw on TV, for we were tired). It was gorgeous. The ships will be sailing out again on Tuesday, for Monday is the Australian Labor Day. We are hoping to get back down to the harbor today to take a cruise around it and view the ships up close.

The Duke and Duchess of York (Andrew and Fergie) were here to accept a salute. Throngs of people (Royalists) gathered to see the young royal couple, who are very popular here. Naturally, this morning's papers are full of them.

Ying Hsu, Dad's graduate student from China, has been trying to teach me a few words of Chinese so I won't be a total loss in China. Ying is very nice, beautiful, and lots of fun and speaks English well. She was telling me about a friend of hers who recently arrived in Sydney and had been talking with an Australian woman while waiting for the bus. The elderly lady had asked her where she was going, and she said to school. Then my friend asked her where she was going, and she said, "I am going to hospital to die." She was aghast and questioned, "You're going to hospital to die?" And she smiled and said, "Yes, I am going to hospital to die." When my friend got to school, she told me about this healthy-looking woman, and I laughed and laughed. Ying told her friend that "to die" is the way Australian's pronounce "today." I really got a chuckle out of this.

I also wanted to tell you that the white flowers are starting to bloom on the funny-looking trees (the ones that look dead for months on end) and that the flies are out, although to date they're not too bad. It's been warm though. What did you think of the election? Did you vote? I simply can't believe the drastic decline our country has experienced in the past two decades. But I shan't go into it, for it is a depressing subject, and neither of us needs it. After I talked to you, we called Eric (maybe you have talked to him since?) and Amy and Dave. I'm going to fix Christmas dinner at Amy's, and she's going to get a tree for us, so we should have a good time.

Enclosed is a check for $1,000 for the balance of your tuition and expenses. Hopefully, this will last until the end of next month. Do not deposit this check until you have made sure Dad's check has been received by the bank. You will have to call Commercial Federal to find out. Dad should be paid by ICI tomorrow for his consulting, and we will get the bank draft off as soon as possible so that you will have your money in time for next month's expenses. Maybe you have heard that the Australian dollar dropped substantially because of the Australian trade deficit (the worst in history), which really hurts us in purchasing U.S. dollars.

Our weather is warm for this time of year, and I'm wondering what it will be like come summer. The beaches are already full of swimmers and sunbathers, and spring is "busting" out all over. I had already been back in Australia two months, and Dad was hearing my typical theme "I want to go home." I sure am hankering for a piece of pumpkin pie. I was wishing I could get together with my mother as we did in days of yore and enjoy her pie and a cup of good coffee. Yesterday for lunch, I had some tasty pumpkin soup, which was probably lower in calories and therefore healthier, but it just didn't satisfy my craving. Dad is keeping very busy as usual.

Love,
Mom

III

The first week in November, Margrit went to the Chinese consulate to collect their visas. The following weekend, the Czermaks left for Beijing. The Chinese covered all their expenses, even the airfare. They had a fantastic time in China. Their hosts in Beijing were extremely kind and courteous, but Margrit became a bit annoyed with one well-meaning woman who accompanied them almost everywhere—even to Shanghai. In fact, she just about drove Margrit mad because she continued talking.

John wrote in his diary that hell would be having to spend a week on a desert island with the Chinese lady. He also wrote that, on the trip, they climbed the Great Wall on Margrit's birthday.

It was cold, as it is in the mountains, but very exciting to be there. One can't believe the depth of the steps until one starts to ascend; you simply think you won't make it. Coming down is even worse because the road is made of marble and extremely slippery in spots; moreover, in sections, the steps go straight down, rather than one in front of the other. It was really scary, but Margrit told me she wouldn't mind at all having another go at it one day.

We only had three hours to see the Forbidden City, and one really needs a full day or even a week. It is enormous, and there is so much to see. We had an adorable guide, one of the English language teachers from the Institute of Atomic Energy. She lives at the institute and shares a room with three other young women, and her husband lives in Beijing. They only see each other on Sundays as, in China, everyone works six days a week. She and her husband were saving every cent they can get their hands on so that they could buy a flat and live together. Because of the critical shortage of homes in China, most people had to share accommodations, that is, the kitchens and baths. All the teachers at the institute had to share their room with three others. The students had to do the same thing, and many of them are married, are from other regions in China, and had to leave their families behind to come to the institute to learn English— usually an eight-month course.

The Cultural Revolution and the Reign of Terror destroyed many people and much of the beauty of the country. One of the young teachers Margrit met (and especially liked, for she had an adorable personality) told her that her parents (both intellectuals) were forced into the fields to work for ten years.

This is where she was raised, in dirt and squalor. Her childhood was total desolation, with no hope for anything better. She was ten years old before she was allowed to go to school. She cried when she told Margrit all this. Margrit and I visited the kindergarten with the teacher and joined in the games with the children. It made the teacher so happy to see these little children so beautifully dressed and having a good time and knowing that they did not have to suffer as much as she had.

One of my colleagues at the institute said he was forcibly separated from his wife and daughter for ten years, being allowed to see them two weeks each year. He worked two years in the field. His wife is a doctor and makes less money than a cabdriver. He detests his government and wants to get his two daughters out of China. At that time, the oldest was twenty-one and a graduate in chemistry. The youngest was only eleven. Dr. Lue was fortunate, however, as he and his wife had been permitted to work in Jülich (Germany) for a year, where they were able to save a great deal of money for their children's future. Having the money to pay for an airline ticket is about the only way one can get out of China, and the entire family is never allowed to leave unless one is fortunate enough to be granted a visa to study in America or Australia. Most of the Chinese who go to America and Australia do not return, which was causing a great problem for those who want to go. Margrit received some beautiful gifts from our hosts, including a jade bracelet from Dr. and Mrs. Lue.

In Beijing, we also visited the awesome Temple of Heaven, where the emperors prayed; the huge and eerie underground Ming Tombs, where the emperors are buried; the beautiful Summer Palace, where the emperors lived; an underground stalagmite cave known as the Grotto of Cave Flowers because so many of the stone formations look like flowers; the Grand View Garden, which was the home eons ago of a rich lord and the setting of the Chinese TV program *The Dream of Red Mansions*, taken from the novel of Cao Xueqin, the classic author of three hundred years ago. Margrit purchased his novel (in three volumes), and the books are gorgeous. At that time, TV in China was great. We watched it just to enjoy the color, even though we could not understand the language.

We also visited the site of Peking Man and the zoo to see the pandas. We did not visit the tomb of Mao Tse-tung but did see the only gigantic picture of him at the entrance to Tiananmen Square, where he is buried, and behind which is the Forbidden City. We were told by almost everyone we came into contact with that Mao is hated by most of the Chinese people. We were also told that discontent runs rampant in China because of the social problems facing the people. For instance, only foreigners and well-placed businesspeople lived well, and only foreigners were allowed private cars.

In Shanghai, we stayed at Fudan University Guest House. The university grounds were beautiful, and we were quite impressed. Here, again, we were beset by people who wanted to get their children out of China. We had a good time in Shanghai. We took a three-hour cruise on the Huangpu River, which runs into the East China Sea. We also saw a world-famous troop of acrobatics, which included Wei Wei, the panda. It was delightful. But what impressed us the most was visiting the magnificent jade Buddhist temple. At that time, religion was allowed in China, and we saw many people, young and old, praying and making sacrifices of flowers and fruit to Buddha. It was quite moving.

Margrit and I met several Americans, also staying at Fudan University, who were in China to teach, and it was interesting to talk to them. One fellow was born in China but escaped with his entire family when he was ten years old. A professor of economics at the University of Florida, he was teaching a class in economics at Fudan University. His wife was also Chinese (born in Hong Kong), but she was disgusted with the way of life in Shanghai and returned to Hong Kong with their two little children to wait for her husband.

I was very impressed with the many changes that had occurred in China since my first visit in 1979, but our hosts told us that life was still very grim for most Chinese, and they could not see the hope for any real changes occurring for another ten or twenty years. Margrit's opinion was that there were just too many ignorant and rude Chinese—pushing, shoving, spitting—and so much filth everywhere. In Beijing, everything appeared brown. There were no lawns, and because it was the fall of the year, nothing was green. People lived in such crowded conditions. Margrit simply could not believe the buses—people were literally jammed into them. She wondered how they manage to get off when they have reached their destination. We also saw the two most advanced cities in China, which made Sydney look like paradise in comparison.

During the trip, I presented six lectures at different institutes, and Margrit presented one about life in America and Australia.

John summarized the trip to Tim in a telephone call after their return to Sydney. He promised to send Tim a trip report.

Margrit thought as she discovered John's China trip report. *Why did he write a report?* She suspected he did the same thing after his trip to the USSR. *Why? Was it for our government? Did John give reports of visits to Communist countries for the CIA?* Margrit concluded that it was not a good idea to broach the subject with him, especially since she should not have been reading his report. Anyway, he would probably deny everything since she was sure he was sworn to secrecy, just like he could not talk about his work at Rocky Flats.

A week after the Czermaks returned home, they attended a reception at the Chinese Embassy in Sydney to celebrate the Chinese Spring Festival. The following Saturday, John spent the better part of the day conducting an experiment along with three of his students, Anthony, John, and Ying. He had on loan six identical cars from the university, and they took temperature readings of the heat buildup in each car under differing conditions. The first car had an expensive sunscreen next to the windshield inside the car, the second an inexpensive cardboard sunscreen on the inside, the third an expensive sunscreen on the outside of the windshield, the fourth an inexpensive cardboard one on the outside, the fifth with no sunshield, and the sixth with no sunscreen but with the windows cracked. Their conclusion was that an expensive sunscreen on the outside of the windshield with the car windows cracked kept the car the coolest. A reporter from the *Sydney Morning Herald* and a photographer saw that the event made the newspaper. The work of John's research group also made the newspapers a couple of other times, which made his superiors very happy.

IV

The Czermaks were caught, as were those around them, in a labyrinth of shoving, tired people who had just disembarked from various transatlantic flights and were waiting to pass through immigration at Milan's airport. John had forgotten, until they now reoccurred, that he had sworn never again to fly through Milan. His travel agent, however, had assured him it would provide the best connection between Sydney and his ultimate destination of Tripoli, Libya.

Now that sanctions against Libya had been reduced, John had been requested by Tim to visit Tripoli at their expense to try to confirm if Gaddhafi had eliminated his nuclear program as claimed. John had hoped that his dear friend Ala, a doctor of nuclear science, could assist him since he was employed at the Libyan Nuclear Research Center. Ala had worked for John as a postdoctoral fellow during John's first year at the UNSW.

In the noisy queue behind the Czermaks, shouting began. John turned his head to look at the throng of newcomers pushing into the airport chamber. Now existed a truly general sense of panic and frustration among those who had arrived on his flight, more than two hundred passengers, as the newly arrived were being ushered into yet another opening queue that clearly had the advantage over those who arrived earlier. John noted that both before and behind him, infants and toddlers, as well as their overwrought parents, in a variety of languages, were loudly voicing their complaints about being pushed and shoved. Now the disorder became even more intense as those first in the queue vied to hold their precious place or to inch forward as space was freed. Clearly, without the aid of more officials and some order, this throng of humankind was going nowhere. John and Margrit had been scheduled three hours between flights. They had already been waiting almost an hour to pass through immigration. Glancing at his watch to note the time, John was beginning to wonder if they would make their connection to Tripoli.

"God be praised!" exclaimed a young mother behind him as she and her infant in arms and three small children were conducted through the disorder. Very shortly, all parents with small children were being shepherded through the same cavity; and within several minutes, more attendants had arrived so that, within the next thirty minutes or so, the Czermaks were able to pass through the howling, thrusting multitude.

Although tired after the overnight flight from Sydney, John read some information about Libya during the three-hour flight to the Libyan capital while Margrit slept just like on the earlier flight. John read that the name "Libya" was probably derived from "Libu," one of the ancient tribes, but the Great Socialist People's Libyan Arab Jamahiriya, as it was now known, was the modern name for a country as old as human history. Tripoli, which sat on the North African coast, was Libya's largest city and was known locally as "the queen of the seas."

Tripoli was founded in the first millennium BC. First settled by the Phoenicians, the city had been occupied through the centuries by the Romans, Vandals, Byzantines, Arabs, Sicilian Normans, Spanish, Turks, and finally the Italians and British in the twentieth century. The historic city had a wealth of old and new monuments and was an important site of Islamic civilization. The basic street plan was laid down during the

Roman period, when the walls were constructed. The high walls survived many invasions, and in the eighth century, a fourth wall was built facing the sea. Libya's strategic geographical position and profound history made it a vital link between the eastern and western parts of the Arab world and between Europe and Africa. Its importance was ensured through the centuries by its fertile hinterland of irrigated fields and olive groves, whose grain and oil were exported throughout the Mediterranean by ships that crowded its port.

Upon arrival at the Tripoli Airport, the Czermaks were immediately ushered through passport control and customs and directed to baggage claim to be greeted by the joyous faces of Ala's wife, Mimara, and their three children, Abdul, Salan, and Mary. The older boy, soon-to-be eleven-year-old Abdul, was truly overcome as he exclaimed again and again, "Uncle John, is it really you? Are you really here? Oh, I'm so glad to see you!" While waiting in the shadows, equally boisterous was his younger brother, Salan, who quickly clasped his godmother's hand and was not to be released. Two-year-old Mary, who was born in Australia and initially (thanks to Margrit) spoke only English, was now chattering away in Arabic, one minute coyly flirting with John, the next shyly hiding behind her mother. The boys looked magnificent in matching outfits, which their parents had purchased for the festival after Ramadan. Little Mary was in a multicolored dress with lace at the sleeves and throat, which Margrit had purchased for her the previous year. They could see how much she had grown since that time. Mimara, glancing about for Ala, was modestly attired, her head covered with a colorful shawl.

When Ala and his family arrived in Sydney more than two years ago, neither of his sons could speak English. Neither could his wife. Before the term was out, both boys were on the honor roll at Kensington Elementary School. English became their first language. For the next year, the Czermaks shared not only

Christmas but also Easter, Thanksgiving, Ramadan, and other holidays, both Christian and Muslim, with Ala's family.

After John claimed their two large suitcases, one filled with gifts for their god family and the other with clothes to tide them over for five days, Ala took the Czermaks to their hotel in the heart of the city. After check-in and getting settled in their room, they made an early night of it after supper.

On Christmas Eve morning, John and Margrit took a walk near the hotel. On the walk, they stopped to peek inside St. Francis Catholic Church. There was joyous music coming from the front of the church. They had not intended to participate in the Mass but rather just take a look at the interior, but lo and behold, they were propelled in by loving hands and ushered to the first pew of the overflowing church. The ceremony was the most moving they had ever experienced. A bishop from Rome said Mass in English and was assisted by priests from India, Korea, Africa, and Sri Lanka. Beautiful hymns were sung in cadence in native tongues by the many Africans, Indians, and Asians.

On Christmas, the Czermaks went to their host's home and celebrated joyously. Everyone exchanged gifts after a wonderful meal that Mimara had fixed. After spending the day at their home, John and Margrit returned to the hotel for some rest.

The next day, the Czermaks and their host family visited the other two cities that formed the African Tripolis. Sabratha, the smallest of the three, was founded by the Canaanites in the sixth century BC and ruled by Carthage, Phoenicia, Numidia, and then Rome in 46 BC. Today it was the second largest archaeological site of Tripolitania. Its well-preserved theater is its most archaeological attraction. Built in AD 161–192, it continues to be used as an arena for performances and concerts.

The group also visited the renowned World Heritage site of Leptis Magna, the best-preserved and most extensive Roman city in the Mediterranean. Originally a Berber settlement and then made into a trading port by the Phoenicians, it was conquered in the sixth century BC under the aegis of Carthage. The port city grew wealthy from slaves, gold, ivory, and precious metals, as well as by the rich agricultural land surrounding it. After the end of the Severan dynasty in AD 235, the city fell into decline. When the Vandals conquered Tripolitania in the mid-fifth century AD, it fell on the emperor Justinian to reclaim the land for Byzantium. In the seventh century, the Arabs conquered Leptis Magna, and it never regained its former glory.

By the eleventh century, the city was abandoned to the encroaching sand dunes. In the twentieth century, when serious excavations began, archaeologists found that the sand dunes had preserved the ruins remarkably well. The group saw the Severan Arch, erected in honor of the emperor's visit; the marble-and-granite-paneled Hadrian Baths, the largest outside Rome; the partially covered nymphaeum, a shrine dedicated to the worship of nymphs; the palaestra or sports ground; and a pair of massive forums. They also saw the amazingly detailed Severan Basilica, the theater, and the circus and amphitheater, where spectacles were held for the amusement of the populace. At the height of the North Africa campaign in World War II, British and Canadian soldiers under Field Marshal Montgomery and German troops under Rommel swept back and forth along the coastal road right outside the gate at Leptis Magna.

On the next to the last day of their visit, Ala took John to the Libyan Nuclear Research Center for a tour and for him to give a talk to a group of nuclear scientists. The day was very interesting, especially what Ala told John in his office about their nuclear weapons program. That evening over dinner, Ala asked John to tell everyone about other trips he had taken to Africa.

"Well, my first trip to Africa was to Ghana, directing an IAEA training course on nuclear analytical techniques and their applications for African scientists at their nuclear research center. I gave a series of lectures on the topic. After my arrival at the Accra Airport and going through immigration and customs, two husky guys came, grabbed my two big bags, and started to leave the baggage area. I followed and kept asking them if they were from the institute. They did not reply but went to a waiting car. Just then, my host came and stopped them. He told me later that they would have probably taken me out in the jungle and robbed me or, worst, killed me.

"I had another scare the first night in the log-and-straw guest hut. I was lying in bed and saw a big green lizard running up the wall and across the ceiling. The next day after a sleepless night, my host told me each hut has a lizard to keep the insects under control.

"During my stay, we visited Akosombo Dam and saw the world's largest reservoir. The car ride was along a remote road that our driver thought was a racetrack. Later, I asked him to slow down so I could enjoy the scenery. The weather was good, and the people were very friendly. The main food we got was rice. Before the trip, I was informed to bring a lot of old clothes to trade for their handicrafts. I got a wooden African drum and some wooden masks in exchange for some shirts and pants. At the airport after my visit, I was very relieved to see our Lufthansa plane land. I was ready to return to Vienna. After they refueled our plane, we were on our way via a short stop in Abidjan, Ivory Coast.

Abdul said, "Please tell us about some of the other countries you have visited in Africa."

"On one trip, I got to visit several African countries. The first country was Tanzania to see some of the places my grandfather had seen when he was a German soldier marching across German East Africa to Lake Victoria. As you might know, Dar es Salaam is Tanzania's largest city. Dodoma is the capital. Lake Victoria, Africa's largest lake, and Lake Tanganyika, Africa's deepest lake, are located in Tanzania as well as Mount Kilimanjaro and Serengeti National Park. It is home to both the highest and lowest points on the continent. Kalambo Falls, the second highest waterfall in Africa, is located near the southern tip of Lake Tanganyika.

"Upon arrival in Dar es Salaam, I got a taxi ride to a new Holiday Inn. The first night, I had a very realistic dream about a terrorist rolling a bomb from a vehicle into the crowd of people I was with. I grabbed the bomb and rolled it back at the bomber. Then the bomber rolled the bomb back at the crowd again as it was ticking and about to go off. I then picked up the bomb and ran it over to the bomber, who was getting into his vehicle, but then I woke up.

"I spent the first day touring the city, and that night, I had dinner on the rooftop restaurant that overlooks the city. I met two nurses from Sweden who were sitting at the adjacent table. They were very pleasant, and one of them had been a nanny in San Francisco. The next day, I went to the airport after saying goodbye to the Swedish nurses at breakfast (they were off on a safari) and caught my twenty-minute flight to Zanzibar in a small plane. The pilot was a good-looking blonde from South Africa who had been flying for seventeen years. The plane seated thirteen passengers, and she let me sit up in the copilot's seat. On the flight over, I was fascinated by the beautiful blue and green coastal waters below us.

"I found the island very interesting and took a tour of the old city and the slave prisons. The Arabs sold slaves that were confined in very small basement cells. Whoever survived were sold after being tied to a tree and whipped. The ones who did not cry were sold at a higher price. Now an Anglo church stands there and has a monument on its floor where the tree once stood. Next door is a mosque. I had lunch at a restaurant on the beach, and there was a monkey running around inside, entertaining everyone. Later, I returned to Dar es Salaam but with a different plane and pilot.

"The next day, I left Dar es Salaam for Nairobi and experienced a great thrill at seeing Mount Kilimanjaro right outside the window of the plane. I continued on the same flight to Entebbe, Uganda, to have my first look at Lake Victoria, as well as the headwaters of the Nile River. Lake Victoria is indeed a very big lake with beautiful islands and shoreline. I returned to Nairobi later that day and checked into a beautiful hotel with a balcony overlooking the city. Nairobi is much nicer than Dar es Salaam, with good sidewalks, parks, lots of jacaranda trees in bloom, and newer buildings. The people seem very friendly, and the city is clean.

"After a couple of days in Nairobi, which included visiting Nairobi National Park, where I saw many animals, including giraffes, lions, and zebras, I took an early morning flight to Bujumbura, Burundi, to again see Lake Victoria but to also see for the first time the world's longest and second deepest freshwater lake, Lake Tanganyika. To my surprise, the plane stopped in Kigali, Rwanda, which was surrounded by very green hills and mountains. The stewardess said it was a very beautiful place where she would like to spend more time someday. There were also many large lakes nearby.

"I was sitting next to a young German who was working for the German Development Agency in Bujumbura. He had spent a year in the United States and was very interested in the story of my grandfather serving in the German Army in East Africa. He had never met anyone who had a friend or relative there during those times.

"I left Bujumbura for Johannesburg, stayed there one night, and flew to the mountain kingdom of Lesotho. After a short visit, I had my last stop in the beautiful kingdom of Swaziland, surrounded by mountains. I stayed at a hotel on the Royal Swazi Golf Course but did not play. I returned to the good old USA after a long flight from Johannesburg via a fuel stop at Sal Island in Cape Verde."

"Uncle John, please tell us more."

"Okay, but this is the last one, Abdul, as Auntie and I must return to the hotel and get ready for our early departure. This story is about my visits to Brazzaville and Kinshasa. Abdul, do you know what countries these two cities are in?"

"Yes, the Republic of the Congo and the Democratic Republic of the Congo."

"Very good. Do you know why a river is so rich?"

"No."

"It is because it has two banks."

Everyone laughed.

"The Brazzaville Airport is very beautiful, modern, and good sized. I stayed at the Olympic Palace Hotel, a nice five-star hotel with three restaurants. I had a great room overlooking the pool, and I could see, through the fog/haze across the Congo River, some high-rise buildings in Kinshasa. Later, I took a walk around the neighborhood and saw some beautiful buildings with unique architecture, including the university hospital. That night, there was a lot of music from a wedding party below my room that kept me up until midnight.

"On Sunday morning, the gal at the reception arranged a tour for me with her brother. The bad thing was that his English was not good, but he took me around town for about four hours and only charged me $30. On the tour, we first went to the Congo River, where six young boys where doing some diving into the rapids. The kids were also burning a pile of rubbish. From this point, I could look over the Congo River and clearly see Kinshasa. We continued the drive and saw lots of areas with well-kept buildings and houses and new streets and sidewalks and other areas with small homes and dirt streets with no sidewalks. On the drive, I saw a lot of Toyotas, all yellow with black tops. The people were well dressed, and no one was begging for money, just trying to sell a variety of goods.

"When we returned from the tour, there were many soldiers and police at the hotel, and my driver/guide was not allowed into the hotel. I was searched and was told that the president of the country was coming to the hotel. Later, I peeked through a banquet hall window and saw that there were about two hundred people having a fancy dinner with lots of beer, wine, and champagne and having a good time. I found out later that the event was the president giving the vice president a birthday party. After breakfast the next day, I flew from Brazzaville to Kinshasa."

"John, it is amazing how well you remember all these places you visit."

"Thank you, Ala. Indeed, these trips are very memorable." "Along the main road from the airport to the city were many vendor shacks containing everything one would want, from clothing to food. Many vendors just had their goods lying on the ground. I wondered how anyone had any sales as most of the vendors were selling the same things. At stoplights in the city, various vendors were carrying their wares and trying to sell them as they went from one car to the next. The items included water, snacks, candy, smartphones, CDs, kitchen utensils, sunglasses, and other small items. It took at least an hour to get to the hotel since there was much stop-and-go traffic.

"The Hotel Memling is five-star with six floors of luxurious rooms. My room was on the fifth floor with a spectacular view of half the city, looking toward the airport. There are several buildings higher than the hotel as well as many two- to four-story apartments with shops on the ground floor.

"After a delicious breakfast the next morning, I arranged for a tour of the city. My driver was Braise Pascal, about my age, who had a Renault sedan. The city streets were very crowded with vendors outside buildings and many shoppers sharing the streets with cars. There was everything for sale. In one area, only food was being sold. Traffic came to a halt there, and I got a look at some steaks displayed covered with flies, and loafs of bread were transported in baskets perched on sellers' heads.

"Our first stop was the Nautic Club of Kinshasa. The clubhouse is located on the broad Congo River. Across the river is, of course, Brazzaville. The drive continued through another part of the city to a small village where we stopped at a riverside villa to get another glimpse of the river. The villa had a couple of goats running around as well as two big pheasantlike birds in a cage.

On the way back to Kinshasa, we hit heavy traffic. And at one point, it took about thirty minutes to go just a few blocks. The entire tour was about three hours, and I only had to pay $60.

"The next morning, Braise was waiting to take me to the airport. On the way, I continued to take pictures of the crowds of people walking in the streets, most of them shopping in the small shops on the ground floor of various buildings, some sellers in shacks, and others with their goods displayed on the ground. On the drive, we passed several Christian churches but only one mosque. It amazed me that they have solar-powered streetlights where the United States has none to my knowledge. Most people were colorfully dressed in new clothes.

"A frightening thing happened about fifteen minutes from the airport on the six-lane major road. Periodically, we had passed several police checkpoints. This time, an officer stopped us and asked for Braise's license and car registration. Then the two got in some type of argument concerning Braise cutting off another car. Then the officer got into the back seat along with another policeman, and they told Braise to drive. Braise drove about fifty feet and then stopped and argued more with the cops. This stop-and-go drive was repeated a couple of times, with the three of them continuing to argue. I pleaded, saying, 'Mercy, airport,' and pointed to my wrist, where a watch would be worn. Braise offered them some of their country's currency, but the arguing continued. Finally, Braise asked me for $10, and he gave his and my money to the crooked cops. Then they got out and let us continue to the airport.

"Well, I just thought of another interesting trip I took to the Western Sahara. I flew from Casablanca to Laayoune on Air Maroc. After a short taxi ride, I checked into the two-star hotel La Grande Gare. The young lady at the front desk spoke good English. She told me that they had no restaurant and suggested that I go to the main shopping street to have dinner at the new Al Massira Hotel, a twenty-minute walk. She also arranged a tour of the city and a trip to the Sahara Desert for the next morning.

"Later, I took a walk to the shopping street. The sidewalks were in good shape, and I passed a nice park on the way that had a track for small electric cars for kids to drive around. There were three hotels in the area and a few restaurants, cafés, and shops. I went inside the new Al Massira Hotel, had dinner, and made a reservation to come the next day and check in for a night's stay. I was tired of the crummy two-star Gare Hotel already.

"The next morning, I packed, checked out, and met my tour driver. Abdullah was driving an old four-wheel-drive Santana, much like a Jeep coupe. As we left the hotel, we went by a group of one-story homes that looked like half a ball and then past the airport that was on the edge of the city. The highway was a nice four-lane asphalt road that had direction signs to the port. In a few places, sand had blown over part of the highway, and there were bulldozers clearing the road. We went past many hills of sand, and about halfway to the port, Abdullah turned onto a one-lane rock-covered path. He spoke no English, so I did not have a clue what was going on except I envisioned a kidnapping, killing, or robbery. We kept going down this rocky path through many sand dunes, where Abdullah had to put the Santana into four-wheel drive. I thought for sure the car would get stuck in the sand, or we would get a flat tire from hitting all the sharp rocks.

"After about a mile of this scary ride, we reached the beautiful shores of the Atlantic. As far as one could see, there were sand hills to the left and right—the western end of the Sahara Desert. After I took a few pictures, we headed down another rocky path with even more and bigger sand hills. At one point, Abdullah put the old car in four-wheel drive again, hit the gas, and plowed through the sand to the top of a very large sand hill. There, he stopped so I could take a few pictures. The ride down the sand hill was even scarier than going up, but we made it to another sharp rock path and, after about mile, got back on the highway and eventually to the major seaport.

"After leaving the fenced-in port area, we took a drive around the small port town and then returned to Laayoune for a drive around the city. The city is quite large, spread out, and has a valley on one side with a small river running through it. There are at least three mosques and one large Catholic church in the city. After the three-hour tour, Abdullah dropped me off at the hotel. I left the next morning on Air Maroc for Casablanca.

"Well, Ala, we had better return to the hotel and get ready for our departure in the morning. Thank you all for your kind hospitality, and it was wonderful to spend this week with you all." After emotional goodbyes by all, Ala took his guests to the hotel. Since Ala had to work in the morning, John and Margrit took a taxi to the airport to catch their flight home via Milan.

V

After their return from a wonderful time in Libya, John phoned Tim and gave him a report on what he had found out during his visit to the Libyan Nuclear Research Center. It seemed like Gaddhafi had fooled the world into thinking they had developed nuclear weapons, but according to Ala, he only had a nuclear power program underway.

John also told Tim about his next trip to attend an IAEA-coordinated research program meeting in Kiev, Ukraine. All expenses for the trip would be paid by the IAEA. At the end of the meeting, the attendees would visit Chernobyl and observe the progress of the decontamination of the nuclear reactor facility. After that meeting, John would travel to Baku, Azerbaijan, to give an invited lecture at Baku University.

Several months later, John started making arrangements to return to Rockwell since his three-year leave of absence would end. One of the professors in the department would take over his management duties as well as continue to supervise his remaining graduate students. Before leaving Sydney, John and Margrit arranged to have their personal items shipped, sold their furniture, and checked out of their apartment. They stayed in a hotel before catching their flights two days later. John wanted to take the Ghan train, from Adelaide to Darwin, before he headed back to the United States, but Margrit preferred to fly directly from Sydney via Los Angeles to Denver.

After John escorted Margrit to her gate at the international terminal for her flight back to the United States, John took the train to the domestic terminal to catch an early morning flight to Adelaide. He needed to arrive at the train station in time to catch the Ghan leaving at one. Shortly after departure, he saw a kangaroo under a tree as the train went through many wheat fields with some small hills and periodic farmhouses. Later, the train passed by a herd of sheep.

As with the Indian Pacific, the Ghan train had just as many cars. John's car, the last on the train, had a few empty seats, and he was in the front row, with the seat next to him vacant. This time, unlike the Indian Pacific ride, he was not in a private cabin but in a car full of reclining seats, like on an airplane.

The first major facility that the train passed was the Snowtown Wind Farm, which was located along the Hummock and Barunga Ranges. The wind farm consisted of 47 turbines. By the end of construction, some 150 turbines would have been built. As it stood now, the output from this wind farm generated enough electricity to power sixty thousand homes. Each turbine consisted of a seventy-yard-high tower and forty-yard-long blades.

Then the train passed Crystal Brook, originally named Chrystal Brook by the explorer Edward John Eyre (who was a notoriously bad speller). Crystal Brook was where the Ghan and Indian Pacific trains parted company, the Indian Pacific heading east to Sydney or west to Perth. Claimed by locals to be "where the Flinders Ranges begin," Crystal Brook was a lovely town that serviced South Australia's productive sheep and wheat country.

The train then went through Port Pirie, South Australia's first provincial city, which was founded in 1845. The city was named after the ship *John Pirie*, which had delivered settlers there in 1842. There was a twenty-yard-high smokestack at Port Pirie that marked the site of a lead and zinc refinery. Beginning as a small settlement, it was today a major port and important commercial and industrial center.

After Port Pirie was Port Germein. Its original site was chosen as a major port in the Spencer Gulf, but it was so shallow that ships could not get close to shore. Rather than relocating the site, they built the longest wooden jetty in the Southern Hemisphere. The length of the jetty in 1883 was a mile, and even at that distance, sailing ships had to get the tide just right to dock.

The train stopped at Port Augusta, but no one got off. It was situated on the quiet waterways at the head of the Spencer Gulf and in proximity to the spectacular Flinders Ranges. It was a natural harbor that was settled in May 1852 by Alexander Elder and John Grainger. The port was named after Augusta Sophia, the wife of Sir Henry Edward Fox Young, the governor of South Australia at that time.

Then the train passed by Woomera, a rocket-testing range that was set up in the 1940s and was still in use today. Woomera was actually the Aboriginal name for throwing stick, a kind of lever used to increase the range and speed of a thrown spear. Rocket scientists worldwide found the isolation of this remote site ideal for testing conventional rockets and fuel sources. Woomera was administered by the Australian Department of Defense.

Tarcoola was next and was proclaimed on February 1901. Its name was taken from the nearby goldfields, which in turn had been named after Tarcoola, the winner of the 1893 Melbourne Cup horse race who had been raised in the town. Tarcoola, in the local Aboriginal language, meant "river bend."

The next major town passed was Coober Pedy, which produced between 85 and 90 percent of the world's opals. Opals were discovered in 1915 by a fourteen-year-old boy. After the completion of the first Australian transcontinental railway in 1917, from Sydney to Perth, many of the rail construction workers went to the opal fields to find their fortune.

Later, the train went through Kulgera, the closest point on the rail line to Ayers Rock (Uluru). This was Pitjantjatjara country. The Aboriginal word for "Kulgera" was "place of weeping eye," after a forty-five-yard-high rock with a continuous trickle of water running down its side.

Situated in the geographic center of Australia near the southern border of the Northern Territory was Alice Springs. The site was known as Mparntwe to its traditional inhabitants, the Arunta, who lived in the central Australian desert in and around Alice Springs for more than fifty thousand years. The town was surrounded by mountains and was nearly equidistant from Adelaide and Darwin. Alice Springs had its start from the telegraph line; a telegraph repeater station was built at a water hole named Alice's Spring to honor the wife of the telegraph builder, Charles Todd. Most of the passengers took a bus tour of the town of twenty-eight thousand during the long stop.

The next morning, the train reached Katherine, a town of ten thousand that lived off livestock, tourism, mango trees, and mining. Katherine, situated about two hundred miles southeast of Darwin, was among a beautiful landscape of ancient limestone formations and subterranean caves. It was the home of Katherine River and Katherine Gorge.

Next was Adelaide River, settled by the telegraph workers who arrived in the area to construct the Overland Telegraph Line. The discovery of gold at Pine Creek in 1892 had a major impact on the settlement. In 1886, a contract was signed to build a railway between Palmerston (Darwin) and the goldfields at Pine Creek, Northern Territory. By April 1888, the railway had reached Adelaide River. During World War II, there were up to thirty thousand Australian Army and United States soldiers based near the town.

Of course, the final stop was Darwin, the capital of the Northern Territory. The telegraph line to Adelaide started the town of Darwin. It was a pioneering outpost and small port, but it was now a modern, multicultural city with a population of over 120,000 people. Darwin had to be rebuilt twice, once after the devastating bombing during World War II and again in 1974 when Cyclone Tracy flattened the town. Being in the tropics, Darwin had two seasons, wet and dry. The dry season ran from April to October, during which days were warm and sunny. The wet season brought monsoonal rains, cyclones, and one of the most spectacular sights of Darwin, the thunderstorms.

John was staying at Palms City Resort. After check-in, he took a long walk around the inner city and along the esplanade next to the harbor. There was a beautiful American memorial near the hotel overlooking the harbor in honor of the American soldiers who fought there during the Second World War.

The next day, John took a day tour of Litchfield National Park along with six other tourists. The driver was a very personable young lady. Katie did a wonderful job of telling stories as she drove about an hour and a half to the park on the Stuart Highway.

Mr. Stuart was famous for being able to map the land from Adelaide to Darwin for installation of the telegraph. He was in a race with another fellow who was well liked, whereas Stewart was friendless and a drunk. Another story Katie told the group was about a crew of men on camels that was installing telegraph poles in an area where Aborigines had never seen a white man before. The only white men they had seen were their own fellow men who had been dead for over a week. After a week, the skin of the Aboriginal lost its black pigment, and the black skin turned white. So they thought the white men who had arrived on camels were dead men with four long legs. And they also could not understand why they were cutting trees down and then replanting them.

The first stop in the national park was to look at some termite mounds. Katie told the group an excellent story about them. These were the kind of termites that did not eat wood, such as in South Carolina, but the workers tunneled out below the mound to get grass. Another group of termites were the guards, and they made the mounds out of soil and their excrement.

The second stop was Florence Falls, where everyone saw the spectacular waterfall from a high vantage point and was given the opportunity for a scenic and interpretive bush and monsoon vine forest walk. They also had a swim after making their way down the stairs, which were surrounded by lush forest with sightings of a variety of bird species and wildlife.

The final stop was for lunch, which was followed by a visit to Buley Rockhole and another swim. Then the group moved onto Tolmer Falls for a magnificent view of the water cascading down to the deep water hole at the base of the falls.

The following morning, John packed his bag, checked out, and took a shuttle bus to the airport for the flight to Nauru. Nauru, called the Pleasant Island one hundred to two hundred years ago, was located about halfway between Australia and Hawaii. It was the smallest republic in the world, only eight square miles and ten thousand people. (Vatican City and Monaco were smaller, but they were not republics.) It was also the one least visited by tourists, only about two hundred a year.

Upon arrival at the tiny Nauru Airport, John met the only tourists. They were a Jewish couple from Omaha, Rich and Fran. Rich was retired and had several grocery stores in Omaha. Now he rented the stores out to his son. They were world travelers and had visited every country except about thirty of them. John, Fran, and Rich had to pay $50 for visas. Then they collected their luggage and went outside to look for the Hotel Menen van. It was nowhere to be seen. A local person called the hotel for them, but there was no answer. Finally, a battered old minivan taxi appeared, so they all shared it.

At the hotel, the young desk clerk greeted the three but didn't apologize for missing their pickup. Generally, the people in Nauru were not unfriendly, but neither were they warm and welcoming. Perhaps that was from their Micronesian, rather than Polynesian, heritage.

After the nasty things John had read from previous guests about the Hotel Menen on Trip Advisor, the Internet tourism website, he was prepared for the worst. Actually, it wasn't terrible, but John rated it two stars. Here were the good and the bad: His room was toward the end of the long strip of two-story buildings, so he had to walk through the offensive odor coming from a septic tank. The air-conditioning was a basic box but worked okay if he kept it operating twenty-four hours. The bathroom fixtures were fine, but there was never any hot water. There were a few ants and other insects but no vermin. There was no water in the pool. There was a nice ocean view, but the window was broken and taped up. You couldn't swim or even walk on the beach because it was covered with tall sharp black coral rocks. There was no Wi-Fi, but there were two computers in the lobby with slow connections that one could use for $5 an hour. The restaurant was fair at best, and breakfast was extra. Yet John felt the $95 per night rate that he had been quoted was reasonable, especially considering this hotel was the only one the island, and it was usually full of Australian workers.

When Nauru became independent in the 1968, it may have had the highest per capita income in the world. Huge almost pure phosphate deposits had been discovered earlier, and the island had huge industries mining and exporting it as fertilizer. Whether the phosphate was caused by natural formation, ancient coral containing organic marine life being pushed up volcanically in the middle of the island, or the result of thousands of years of bird excrement (guano) had not been definitively answered. John liked the bird shit theory.

It was during those boom times that the Menen was built as a luxury hotel. Unfortunately, at the same time that the phosphate deposits were being used up, agricultural companies developed synthetic fertilizers that dropped the price of phosphate. Today there was still phosphate mining in Nauru, but it was nothing like what it was. Money and jobs were lost, and now Nauru reportedly had a 90 percent unemployment rate. Nauru didn't even have a capital. The parliament building was in one district and some government offices in another, and the inhabitants lived spread out alongside the coast.

Meantime, the Menen Hotel also fell on bad times. Anything that broke was not repaired, and remodeling and renovation of rooms and facilities were unknown. So the place was over forty years old and in a deteriorated, crumbling condition. Now that Australia had set up refugee camps on Nauru and the camp staff needed a place to stay, it had become hard to get a reservation. But the Australian government was fed up with paying up to $300/night for their officials, so new facilities were being built. Pretty soon, it would be easy again to get a room at Nauru's "Grand Hotel."

Later, the group of three hired a taxi to take them around the island. Their driver was a nice young lady named Katerina. She had three children—five years, four years, and six months. Katerina made stops at the main grocery store, which had about anything one would want, and then the post office, where John bought forty prepaid-postage postcards for $1 each to send to Margrit, the kids, relatives, and friends. Then they went to parliament and the immigration office to pick up their passports with visas in them. Then the group continued around the rest of the island until lunch. Without the stops, they could have circled the island in thirty minutes. One did not have to worry about getting lost as the only paved road went along the coastal shore.

In the afternoon, they took another drive and stopped at several locations for pictures and went to see the Buada Lagoon in the middle of the island. It was a small lake surrounded by very green foliage. It could be a really beautiful tropical setting were it not for the low metal fences, trash, and debris that transformed the scenic lagoon into a five-minute stop. There were some nice homes around the lagoon, but elsewhere on the island, most of the housing was run down. There were many abandoned houses and stores, including a couple of gas stations.

The next day, John told Fran and Rich, "Let's see the other half of Nauru."

Rich said, "But we already drove around it."

John's reply was "Today we'll drive counterclockwise instead of clockwise." Rich and Fran couldn't argue with that logic, but Rich requested that they try to see the refugee camps. The group got a taxi whose driver was a young woman, Eva, who had only driven once across the high plateau that covered much of the island. Called the Topside, the desolate area consisted of low hills covered with sparse vegetation dotted with empty plastic bottles, phosphate pits, rusting mining machines, and garbage dumps. No locals lived there. The rutted gravel road was uncomfortable for the passengers and hard on the old car, but Eva pressed on.

There were several narrow roads crisscrossing the Topside, and the foursome soon realized they were lost. It was such a small island that they thought being lost was funnier than a reason for concern. It took another thirty minutes of wrong turns, dead ends, and U-turns before the group spotted a big gate with fences and armed guards. One could see several large prefab white buildings inside the camp. Eva drove up and stopped, and one of the guards walked over and asked in a broad Australian accent, "Can I help you?"

John replied, "We came for lunch in the restaurant."

The guard didn't seem amused. "Do you have a written pass or other documents?"

"No, but can we just drive in and look around?"

"Sorry, mate, you can't."

"Can we take pictures from the car?"

"No, mate."

With that, Eva backed up twenty feet, and John took some pictures as they drove away.

The refugee camps were set up in 2001 when boatloads of desperate people from East Africa, the Middle East, and South Asia tried to sail to Australia to start a new life. Many died when their overcrowded boats sank. Australia had signed a UN pact agreeing to take refugees from other countries who were seeking asylum based on political or religious persecution. However, there was no acceptance of those merely seeking a good job or a better life. The Australian government did not welcome everyone who showed up on its shores and now had camps on the isolated islands of Nauru and Papua New Guinea to house the refugees while they were being investigated about whether they should be admitted or not.

Most of the refugees didn't have passports, money, or anything else. Processing the information was a long and difficult, if not an impossible, task. The refugees in Nauru were put in either a family camp (if they arrived as a family) or single-sex camps. There were well over one thousand people just in the Nauru camps. They lived in basic tents. Meals, some English instruction, and social skills were provided by Australian workers, but it was a boring, prisonlike hot life for those unfortunate souls.

John spoke with several Australians who worked at the camps. They rotated in and out for two weeks up to three months. The consensus was that it was a good-paying job but with lousy working conditions. For example, John chatted with Babek, an Iranian Australian who worked as a Persian translator at the camps. He said the staff lived in large prefab buildings. They were air conditioned, but the workers had to live two to a small room, so there was neither privacy nor amenities. Some of the workers were lucky enough to stay at the Menen. It was much worse for the refugees. They had nothing to do but wait in the heat for their application to be processed. Some of the refugees had given up and wanted to return to their native country. However, without passports or other documents, they usually can't go back. They had become people without a country.

The final irony was that even if a refugee was approved for immigration, he or she was just released to live in Nauru, where the unemployment rate was sky high. The Australian government was spending millions of dollars every year to house, feed, and acclimate the refugees to Western customs and to pay and accommodate Australian camp workers. Very few refugees were approved for immigration or even to be returned to their home country. More refugees were continuing to arrive by boat as crooked people smugglers told the poor refugees that they would be welcomed into Australia. It was a terrible situation and getting worse, with no solution in sight.

On John's return flight to Australia, all the other passengers were camp workers. After arrival in Brisbane, John took a Qantas flight to Los Angeles and then a United Airlines flight to Denver for a wonderful reunion with Margrit and the family.

VI

Long before the Czermaks' return, the FBI had been investigating Rocky Flats about unsafe conditions at the site because of disinformation Phil Gilbert had received from a couple of disgruntled employees. The continued search for information at the time was related to Phil's further investigation of John. Because of Phil's reporting, the FBI started clandestinely flying light aircraft over the area and noticed that the incinerator, which was not permitted to be operating, was apparently being used late in the night. After several months of collecting evidence both from workers and by direct measurements, they informed the DOE that they wanted to meet about a potential terrorist threat. When the FBI agents arrived at the plant, the DOE manager was served with a search warrant.

The FBI then raided the facilities and ordered everyone out. They found numerous violations of federal antipollution laws, including massive contamination of water and soil, though none of the original charges that led to the raid were substantiated. Rockwell was charged with minor environmental crimes and had to pay an $18.5 million fine. Rockwell was then replaced by EG&G to operate the plant. EG&G started an aggressive work safety program and cleanup plan for the site, which included construction of a system to remove contamination from the groundwater at the site.

Thereafter, a new name was assigned for the plant, the Rocky Flats Environmental Technology Site, reflecting the changed nature of the facility from weapon production to environmental cleanup and restoration. The cleanup effort was contracted to the Kaiser-Hill Company, which proposed release of 4,100 acres of the buffer zone for public access. The cleanup of contaminated sites and dismantling of contaminated buildings continued with waste materials being shipped to the Nevada Test Site, the Waste Isolation Pilot Plant in New Mexico, and the Envirocare Company in Utah. After all the weapons-grade plutonium was shipped out and the last contaminated building removed, the cleanup was declared complete but remained under DOE control for ongoing environmental monitoring. Two years later, the EPA announced it had certified the cleanup, which started the conversion of the site to a wildlife refuge.

Chapter 4
California Dreaming

I

When John returned from his leave of absence to Australia, he reported to another DOE laboratory in the Santa Susana mountains north of Los Angeles that was managed by Rockwell International. Although John's title was chief scientist and he supervised the research of only three technicians and two chemists, he readily accepted the position to resume his years of service to the company. John did not need a security clearance at this DOE laboratory.

The Czermaks moved into a town house on the west end of Simi Valley after temporarily staying at a hotel in Chatsworth. One of Margrit's letters to Eric and Lorrie described some of their first activities in California:

> Dear Eric and Lorrie,
>
> Dad and I are getting our town house in order, and it looks pretty good. One more Saturday, and it should be there. Since we work all week, we don't get much done around here, and it all falls on the weekend. But Sundays, we play. Today we drove up to the ski area in the Angeles National Forest, and what a joke that was—the skiing, that is. There's absolutely no snow. They make snow at night, but all we saw was one area open, and it had one patch of snow. There were quite a few Japanese skiers, however. We took along our warm jackets because we expected to find cold weather, and I was too warm in a sweater. Anyway, the

mountains are absolutely gorgeous, and the views are breathtaking. The highest point we reached was 7,900 feet, and the air was wonderful.

We stopped for brunch in a little place that is quite like Nederland, where I bought three votive candles—cinnamon, cranberry, and strawberry. Yummy! So the minute we got home, I had to light them to see if they would smell as delicious as the ones in the shop, which they didn't, of course, because there were dozens there and only my three little ones here. Coming back, we drove through Palmdale, which is a desert country to the east, and is it ever! Cacti everywhere. Of course, some people find this sort of terrain enticing, but I prefer the mountains.

Friday night after work, we drove along the Coast Highway to Santa Monica, and then we got onto Wilshire Boulevard. Dad thought we were driving to Hollywood, but we ended up in Downtown Los Angeles. As the neighborhood appeared to be getting seedier and seedier, I begged him to turn around, which he did, and we headed out.

Well, we ran into a drug bust. I couldn't believe my eyes—Dad said it looked like something out of Saigon. There were about fifteen gang members on their knees, hands behind their heads, being handcuffed by police officers. We kept driving, and all we saw were all kinds of prostitutes—male and female—and another drug bust. We finally hit Beverly Hills and got lost again and thought we'd never get home, but we finally did, thanking God and every angel in heaven that we live out here in the boonies.

Dad is busy with his work and happy to be back with Rockwell. He has a lovely work location, atop a mountain between the Santa Susana mountains and the Simi Hills. Many animals—such as bobcats, deer, raccoons, and rabbits—are in the area. We have also sighted the tracks of a mountain lion here in Simi Valley and, on occasion, can hear the coyotes.

One evening Dad and I were riding our bikes in a desolate area near the Simi Hills, and we heard nearby the noise of a mountain lion. He had obviously come down from the hills to find dinner, and he must have been warning us away. You can believe that we road our bikes as fast as we could to get away. Dad rode so fast that he didn't even look back to make certain I was behind him and not being eaten alive by the mountain lion. Once we got home, we took the car out to see if we could actually see the lion; but because of the darkness, all we could see was his shadow. It was rather exciting—and a bit scary.

Today we're having rain again—another deluge! Believe me, when it rains in California, it pours. It's supposed to keep up until Wednesday. Only five days until Amy's birthday. Wow, I'll bet she's excited. Seriously (and I'm too serious of late), it's hard to believe that my adorable little girl is going to be twenty-three. I'm becoming my mother, I tell you. I remember when (each year as she turned one year older) I would say the same thing. "I can't believe my little girl is such and such this year."

Love,
Mom

The Czermaks took a trip back to Colorado to join Amy's birthday celebration and to see her and Dave's new baby son. On the way to Colorado, they did a bit of sightseeing in southern Utah, which was, without doubt, one of the most beautiful spots on the face of the planet. They stopped in five state parks: Zion, Bryce, Capitol Reef, Canyonlands, and Arches. This was their first visit to any of these parks, and they were amazed at their magnificence. Bryce was their favorite, followed by Arches. As the temperature hovered around 106 degrees, they were not able to enjoy the parks as they should have, however.

After arrival in Colorado, they had a cookout at the house of John's brother, and most of the family was there. John also had a meal with his Rocky Flats friends. The Czermaks spent four days in Colorado and then headed to Texas to see Margrit's sister.

On their way to Texas, they had a fun visit with John's younger brother at his cabin in West Cliff. They really enjoyed seeing his latest artwork, which they thought was wonderful. They also had a great visit with Margrit's sister and her family in Wichita Falls. The Waltons had a contract on their beautiful home and were buying a townhome where they would live until Sam retired; then they planned on moving to Yelm, Washington.

On the Czermaks' return from Texas, they drove through Arizona, where they visited the Painted Desert/Petrified Forest and saw the cliff dwellings at Walnut Canyon National Monument and the Meteor Crater, caused by a giant meteor that struck the earth about fifty thousand years ago.

The Czermaks' next vacation was to Europe. A few weeks after their return, Margrit wrote the following letter to her eldest daughter, Amy:

> Dear Amy,
>   We were able to handle the ten-hour flight to Frankfurt with little difficulty and arrived the next morning. From Frankfurt, we took the new InterCity Express Train (ICE)—a beautiful

train that has the most up-to-date appointments, including sucking toilets, such as those on the Boeing 747s—to Stuttgart and then the train to Nürtingen to see cousins Setra and Petr. Somehow we managed to hang in there until the end of the day and then, much to Setra's astonishment, slept for thirteen hours straight; as a result, we experienced no jet lag.

The third was a holiday (Reunification Day), so Petr and Setra had the day free. Petr invited us to visit the fairy-tale Lichtenstein Castle (not to be confused with the country of Liechtenstein), and off we went. The beautiful and romantic castle, which sits high on the side of a hill overlooking the valley below, belongs to the Württemberg family. The original walls were built in 1388; the tower and the rest of the castle were added in the nineteenth century by the grandfather of the present owners. The castle, which has never been besieged, was wonderful to behold.

The evening of the third, the four of us took the train to Bad Cannstatt for the Oktoberfest. This was our second German Oktoberfest, the first being in Munich. The Cannstatter Fest was not nearly as large as that in Munich, but as the evening progressed, we discovered it was certainly as much fun. Dad and Petr enjoyed the beer (Petr drank more than he normally does), and somehow as the evening wore on, we persuaded Setra to ride a dilapidated-looking ride (similar to the log ride at Knott's). It was good fun, and we all got wet; much to Setra's surprise, she survived. Later, we oohed and aahed over the gigantic fireworks display heralding the fest.

The next morning, we had to get up early to catch the six o'clock train for Karlsruhe, where your father was lecturing. Poor Setra, she was the only one who didn't drink, but she awoke with such a headache—and she had to drive us the short distance to the train station. It was raining a little, and she had the windshield wipers on. Still, she couldn't see. She was frantically wiping off the inside window when suddenly it dawned on her that the reason she couldn't see was that she had forgotten her glasses. (It runs in the family.)

In Karlsruhe, which was designed at the architectural whim of a margrave of Baden (in the center of the city is the palace—built in 1752—from which all roads lead), we stayed at the Hotel Greif. I spent the day with my dear friend Monique, and that evening, Dad and I dined with her and her husband, Claude, at the Restaurant Michaelsklause, where we enjoyed the excellent culinary delights and the panoramic view of the Rhine Valley below. Unfortunately, the evening ended early because our dinner companions had to leave first thing in the morning for their home in Belgium.

Before leaving Karlsruhe, we had late morning coffee at the home of Dad's former agency colleague Heinz Undermann. We hadn't seen Heinz and Elisa and their two strapping sons, Karsten and Haiko, since our days in Vienna, so it was quite a treat to visit with them and to learn of their latest adventures. Heinz, who is a retired physicist, recently completed his family tree. He also made an assessment of the greenhouse effect, which he claims is all bunk. (Heinz learned English as a prisoner of war in England.)

From Karlsruhe, we took the train to the university town of Freiburg—the capital of the Black Forest, where we had a pizza lunch and retraced our former steps in the beautiful little city, where the market hall dates back to 1525. Two hours later, we regretfully (all along the way, we regretfully left one city after another) hopped to another train (Rätia) for the Alpine village (population 35,000) of Chur, Switzerland, arriving there that evening to spend the weekend with cousins Fritz and Annie. That night, since we wished to stretch our legs, Annie led us along a scary unlit path to a local Italian restaurant where Dad and Fritz had a beer and smoked foot-long, corncob cigars. (Honest!)

The next morning, we awoke to find the mountains that encircle the town completely hidden in clouds. After our superlative Swiss breakfast, your father and I trekked about the town to enjoy its beauty. That evening, the four of us rode bikes along the Rhine. Upon returning home, we talked by phone with their son whom we missed seeing because, with his girlfriend, he had been in Munich for the Oktoberfest.

Monday morning, we were off for incomparable Innsbruck, the capital of the Austrian province of Tyrol and home to many Hapsburg rulers in the fourteenth and fifteenth centuries. There, we enjoyed coffee mélange in an open-air café on the plaza and then trekked about, enjoying the city's breathtakingly beautiful architecture.

Before boarding the next train, we tossed a coin to see if we would head for Graz (I wanted to see Mürzzuschlag, where we learned to ski) or Vienna; Graz won. Consequently, the ride on the Karl Schönherr provided us one spectacular view after another as the train wound through the Central Alps. It was dark when we passed through Bruck An Der Mur, so we decided to forgo Mürzzuschlag and transfer to the Vienna-bound train.

Since we arrived at the Sudbahnhof at around nine, we decided to spend the night at the historic Hotel Wandl, adjacent to Saint Peter's Church in the first district. As always, it was a pleasure to be in Vienna, the City of Song, to see once again majestic Stephansdom, the splendid Rathaus, the Parliament, and on and on. For the next couple of hours, we lumbered along the Graben and Kärnter Strasse and warmed our hands with hot *Maronis* (toasted chestnuts).

The next day, we treated ourselves and our dear friend Hungarian-born Eona Prince to lunch and then headed for the nineteenth district to visit briefly and enjoy a kind of Austrian *Jause* (Moët champagne and chocolates!) with other dear friends, Anna and Ernst Winkler. Everyone sends their regards. From there, we took the autobus down Krottenbachstrasse (saw our old home at 180) to Peter-Jordan-Strasse and then walked to nearby Hofzeile, where we also used to live (as you know). Our visit was too short, for we had to head to Figlmüller's in Grinzing to meet the Princes for the biggest and best Wiener schnitzel in the world. We then collected our luggage from the Wandl and spent the night at the Princes' home in the seventeenth district.

On Thursday, while I tooled around the enchanting city, your father met with former colleagues at the IAEA. He also met briefly with his former boss, who is now back at the agency as deputy director, the highest-ranking Japanese. That evening, we headed back to the Princes', where we enjoyed one of Eona's superlative dinners.

On Friday, we headed back into the city's first district for lunch at the other Figlmüller's. That afternoon, the chemistry section hosted a farewell party for Rick Muraka, who is retiring after many years. There, we met a Russian who informed us that our friend Misha, minister of education for the Soviet Union, is very popular because of his youthful vision; further, he is wholeheartedly backed because of his reforms and appears often on TV. I was also informed that a friend from Egypt was one of the safeguards inspectors held by the Iraqis at the time of the recent investigation into their nuclear weapons buildup.

That night, your father and I stayed at the Pension Lerner in the first district and, the next morning, caught the Béla Bartók for Budapest, where we would be spending the weekend. "Shocked" isn't the word to describe the conditions at the railway station in Budapest. Because of the number of transients from the former Eastern bloc, the station was dirty and overrun with many desperate people, including several Gypsies, who either were begging or immediately approached newly arrived passengers to change money or steal ladies' purses. Our hotel (the Palace, built in 1911) was within walking distance of the train station. The hotel was in bad shape, and we found out that renovation would begin on the Monday of our departure from Hungary.

The first night in Budapest, we discovered a Czech restaurant (the Pragai Vencel) up the street from our hotel. The food was so excellent (our favorite being the Hungarian dish *Hortobagyi palacsinta*) that we ate all our dinners there. We also learned how to say "cheers" in Hungarian, which is *egészségére*. (But be careful; if you mispronounce it, you're saying something obscene.)

We were reminded that it's always a joy to visit Budapest. Formerly part of the Austro-Hungarian Empire, it is, in my opinion, the world's second most beautiful city (Prague being first). The Hungarian capital (composed of Buda, Pest, Obuda, and Margaret Island) lies on both banks of the Danube. Many historic churches and beautiful old houses cover its steep wooded hills. The Royal Palace stands proudly on a hill overlooking the city center. Saturday night, we rode the metro and then wandered around the city. To our surprise, mysteriously and seemingly out of nowhere, vendors (notably Russian and mostly old women) would unfurl from their bags, their coats, or whatever an array of beautiful handworked items. When Dad captured this on film, the items and vendors quickly and mysteriously disappeared. Later on, finding ourselves at the plush Casino Schönbrunn, a beautiful yacht on the Danube, we did a bit of gambling, including our first try at roulette.

Sunday morning, as we were having breakfast in the restaurant overlooking the street, Dad spotted a man exposing himself to a group of women waiting for the bus. Hearing his exclamations, I jumped up to see what was going on as did the waiters. After breakfast, we picked up our rental car and, with map in hand, headed east toward Gyöngyös to see a few historic villages. Little did we know we would fall in love with the enchanting eight-hundred-year-old cathedral town of Eger, which lies in the Mátra and Bükk Mountains in the Valley of the Beautiful Woman and the Bull's Blood. The Castle of Eger, which overlooks the city, survived the Turkish onslaughts. Ninety-seven steps wind up to the top of the town's exquisite Turkish minaret.

Eger is also world famous for its wines. In fact, we discovered in Eger the Dorner Konditorei, which has a picture-perfect display of pastries in the outer windows and inner casings. Not only is the pastry as good as it looks but the coffee also is superb. The Germans have also discovered (rediscovered?) the city; as a result, basic German will help one there. Before returning to Budapest, we drove to Miskolc, the country's second largest city; walked around the newly renovated streets; and had a cup of coffee. Before this trip, we had only trekked around in cities west of Budapest, so this was really an interesting experience.

Monday morning, we boarded the train to Bratislava via Vienna. As you know, when Dad, I, Eric, and Lorrie made our first trip to the east when we were living in Vienna, we were held at the border three hours while German shepherds and no-nonsense soldiers searched and researched the train. We were scared to death and wondered why we had decided to make the trip. Last year, we saw that all the barbed wire, soldier's posts, and others were gone, and we breezed through with no visas; it is curious to see that the former no-man's-land between Austria and the old Czechoslovakian border is now being developed. More curious still was to see banished from the buildings the multitude of red streamers proclaiming the virtues of Communism.

In Bratislava, we stayed with our dear friends Tibor and Lillya Maksek. That night, she had a dinner party, which included their son and daughter and her husband. Lillya is a wonderful cook, and it's a wonder we didn't gain at least ten pounds while we were with them. The following night, we attended an organ recital at historic Blumental Church. The next morning, your father and I visited the Red Crayfish Pharmaceutical Museum, which contains 2,500 artifacts dating back to the fourteenth century—a fascinating adventure.

Tibor had arranged for Dad to give a lecture (which I attended) on Wednesday at the university, which is housed in several buildings, including the tallest one in Bratislava, where Lillya works. That evening, Dad, I, and the Makseks had dinner in a historic wine cellar. The food was terrible, but the wine was great as was the Gypsy music. We stayed far too long, but we had one heck of a good time. The Gypsies played such pieces for us as the Second World War songs "Lili Marlene" and "Katyusha." Unfortunately, because I requested so much Russian music, the adjoining tables thought we were Bolsheviks, and we almost had a fight on our hands.

Also, unfortunately, we had to catch the early morning bus to Prague; and because of the late night (two hours' sleep), we were in no shape to do so. We were met in the incomparably beautiful city by Miroslav Curie, who had arranged for Dad to lecture at the Nuclear Research Institute (NRI), where he works. What a delight and brilliant fellow Miroslav is and fluent in a host of languages. As we traveled across the city on the underground, he entertained us with many stories about his colleagues, the history of the Czechs, current events about mutual friends in Moscow, and so on. Dad and I stayed at the Hotel International (a Stalinist structure built by the Russians in the 1950s), where each day we enjoyed a superlative breakfast and had lunch in a marvelous French restaurant. Friday night, we enjoyed an excellent dinner prepared by Miroslav's lovely wife, Vlasta.

One can never get enough of Prague, a city of seven hills, rich in mythology, and I cannot praise it enough. In fact, so awed am I by Prague's beauty and mystic that, on the one hand, I would like to keep it a deep dark secret and tourists out while, on the other, I like to herald it for the entire world to enjoy. Visits to this city of cities are never long enough. One has only to stand in the middle of magnificent Charles Bridge spanning the mighty Vltava River to appreciate something of the special atmosphere of the place or to be in Old Town at night and witness the majestic spires of the Church of Our Lady before Týn, looming mightily toward the heavens; it simply takes one's breath away. At any time of day or night, to stand before renowned Astronomical Clock on the Old Town Hall, one feels blessed indeed, and one's mouth seems to remain shamelessly agape in trying to capture for all time the intricately carved, ornamental centuries-old sculptures on the windows and doors, the richly decorated facades that adorn the buildings, or the stucco and fresco work inside. One can glory again and again in seeing stunningly beautiful Hradčany Castle, which hovers like a gigantic bird on the west bank of the Vltava. Ah, yes, whichever direction one casts one's eyes, there is extraordinary beauty to behold; and each time I see it, my eyes mist, taking in the grandeur of it all. And as I am aware of the romantic history of this most magnificent city, it seems to me appropriate for the former Czechoslovakia to have had a playwright as president.

We left Prague with heavy hearts. Traveling northwest out of the city, we were enchanted to discover the train wound through a lovely green valley (the Bohemian Basin) similar to the Rhine Valley in Germany. Your father and I had been laboring with the fact that we only had three days left on our passes and four days of travel. The East German conductor, who obviously had never seen a Eurail pass, unknowingly solved our problem; he repunched a prior day, thereby saving us at least $100.

Before the Second World War, Dresden was one of the most beautiful cities in Europe, the pearl of Saxony, the Florence on the Elbe. Today it breaks one's heart. I was ill prepared for the still existing devastation. As a result, I was shocked. And it must have been heartbreaking for those West Germans who first discovered the city's state of disrepair. The shells of many former structures remain but only in their blackened, burned-out form. Hopefully, enough remain so that restoration will someday be complete. At present, the eighteenth-century baroque Sachsen Palace is being restored as is the Zwinger, a museum complex that houses many porcelain artworks, priceless jewels, and paintings by famous old masters. We noticed that many "Eastern" advertisements remain atop ugly modern buildings in Dresden (and Leipzig, which we visited next), but Russians are not popular in East Germany these days.

Leipzig was founded in 1165, its university in 1409. The composers Johann Sebastian Bach and Felix Mendelssohn-Bartholdy both lived in Leipzig for some years, and there is a statue of Bach erected in front of magnificent St. Thomas Church, where he was cantor from 1723 to 1750. In spite of the war's devastation, much remains of the Old Town, including the majestic Old Town Hall. After dinner, we walked the streets. Although it was Saturday night, there was scarcely a soul about, a far cry from Berlin on Sunday.

It was interesting to be on a train traveling through the former eastern zone, a land from which, more than forty years, many people actually lost their lives in an attempt to escape and one in which, until recently, was considered dangerous for a Westerner to travel (if one could get a visa). How different dull, tired, poor East Germany is compared with vibrant, rich, beautiful West Germany!

I have to admit that, initially, we weren't too excited about being back in Berlin. As you know, when I, Dad, Eric, and Lorrie were there several years ago, we walked the Kurfürstendamm (now overburdened with Eastern bloc vendors) with its restaurants, cafés, shops, and international flair and visited the Kaiser-Wilhelm Gedächtniskirche, Checkpoint Charlie, and so on. But how exciting it was to see more of the eastern sector of Berlin for the first time! To actually stand on the *other* side of the Brandenburger Tor again! To our surprise, in the eastern sector are housed most of the city's historic buildings, including many splendid cathedrals, the magnificent university, and the Rathaus.

We left Berlin on Monday, bound for Frankfurt and the States the following morning. We had no idea where we would spend the night but hoped to find a picturesque city somewhere along the way. In that we were again traveling via the ICE (Franz Kruckenberg) and there was only a minute or two between the times the train arrived and departed, it was quite difficult to get an overview of each little town. But when we arrived in Fulda, the last stop before Frankfurt, from the magnificent steeples that met our eyes, we knew we were at the right place.

Grabbing our bags, one now brimful of gifts and Christmas presents, to the astonishment of our fellow passengers who didn't know we had understood their chastisement of our pronunciation of their German cities, we made a dash for the door. After registering at the hotel near the Bahnhof (Hessischer Hof), we traipsed about the cobbled streets, enjoying the baroque palace and many other historical buildings, including Fulda Cathedral (rebuilt between 1704–12), which was the last resting place of St. Boniface, the apostle of the Germans. What a delight this picturesque village, with its half-timbered houses, is! At nightfall, we had a romantic dinner in the Gondolier, an Italian restaurant in the heart of town.

After breakfast and a short train trip to Frankfurt Airport the next morning, we caught our Lufthansa eleven-hour return flight to LAX. At home, I unpacked the three bags and put them away for our next adventure. The gifts received adorn our shelves, and the Christmas presents are stashed away for the holiday season. How empty I feel to be once again in generic Simi Valley!

Love,

Mom

II

Monday, November 4, 1991, began as any other perfectly glorious day in Simi Valley—with one exception. Today, the day of the Ronald Reagan Presidential Library dedication, would be the largest gathering of presidents and presidential families ever to be assembled; and John and Margrit, who were to be part of it, were excited.

The Czermaks were both up before six. An hour later, they arrived at the press parking lot, a stone's throw from their town house in Simi's Wood Ranch, to catch the shuttle to the library (known as 40 Presidential Drive), which was located atop the mountain directly north and opposite Wood Ranch on Madera Road. There, along with the other members of the press, cameras, purses, and other paraphernalia were subjected to a brief airport-type security before everyone could enter the grounds. Almost at once, John began to shoot a few pictures of the three flags (United States, California, and presidential) unfurled to full advantage by the brisk Santa Ana winds and of the dais and the library in the background.

After everyone found their way to the press section, where countless other photographers were jammed in, they were lucky as they got a place in the first row of the press photographers' section next to the main aisle and about one hundred feet from the red-white-and-blue-bannered stage. A chest-high metal railing separated them from the section in front, in which celebrities would be seated. Also, members of the library staff were positioned in the aisle at their left to prevent members of the press from crossing the imaginary line established by the railing. To the right of the Czermaks were photographers from the Catholic News Service, Ventura County Star Free Press, Simi Valley Comcast, and the Santa Paula News. Directly behind the Czermaks on a raised platform, getting their monstrous cameras in place, were the privileged photographers from the presidential news staff, *Newsweek*, *Time*, Reuters, and so on.

The center aisle separated the press on the left from honored guests. The section ahead of them was reserved for the VIPs, who upon arriving were hustled through the growing (and somewhat unwieldy) crowds. Even though the press was crammed together, they did not have to worry about pickpockets. Regarding security, when the Czermaks went to collect their credentials the Saturday before, they were amazed that no identification was required. They could have been anyone.

As the crowd waited for the festivities to begin, they were entertained by the combined bands of the United States Air Force and Marines and the United States Army Chorus, playing and singing favorites of the five presidents, including the theme from *Beaches*—Bette Midler's "Wind Beneath My Wings"—as well as "Stout-Hearted Men" from *The Student Prince*, "God Bless America," "America the Beautiful," "Old Man River," "Battle Hymn of the Republic," "Bridge over Troubled Water," and the songs of the armed services: the coast guard, air force, and navy's "Anchors Away"; the marines' from the *Halls of Montezuma*; and the army's.

In spite of all the shoving as newly arrived photographers tried to find a spot, the Czermaks managed to retain their spots on the aisle. They had an excellent opportunity to see celebrities entering the arena. Event director and former deputy chief of staff Mike Deaver, busying himself next to the stage, was one of the first VIPs everyone recognized. Once Margrit spotted Caspar

Weinberger, former secretary of defense, she asked him to say a few words to scientists around the world for her tabloid the *Professional Blabbermouth*. He said, "I think a great deal has been done to advance science during the eight years of the president's administration, and I think that will be reflected in the library. I think that the Strategic Defense Initiative is one of the major advances that draws upon science and calls upon science to reach the frontiers, and I think it will be demonstrated that we can do that. Also, many of our weapon systems that worked so well in the Gulf were scientific achievements of the first order."

When Charlton Heston arrived, cameras worked overtime, including John's. The arrival of Arnold Schwarzenegger, who looked terrific, caused even more of a stir, especially among the ladies. Calls of "Arnold, Arnold," including Margrit's—who was hoping to get an interview—rang through the air. He took a seat in the row in front of the photographers' platform. Wheelchair-bound James Brady, former press secretary who was crippled by a would-be assassin's bullet meant for Reagan, received a round of applause as he came down the aisle.

John was astounded to see arriving so many truly beautiful, fashionably dressed, silicon-enhanced young women gathering in one arena. Many of these lassies, especially the blondes— some of whom had glorious locks flowing to their waists—were assumed to be aspiring actresses.

Although he looked familiar, John and Margrit did not recognize movie star Fess Parker, who was with his wife; when he was leaving, they realized who he was. Many of the people in attendance were surprised to see Secretary of State James Baker, who just returned from the Middle East peace talks in Spain. Also in attendance were James Watt, who resigned as Reagan's secretary of the interior; singer turned politician and now mayor of Palm Springs Sonny Bono; somewhat overweight Merv Griffin with his beautiful wife, Zsa Zsa Gabor; Steven Spielberg; and more. Bob Hope's arrival caused quite a stir; Margrit commented that he still looked good in spite of his advanced age. Next to arrive was Edwin Meese, former attorney general. Arriving at almost the last minute was the Japanese contingent, who was escorted by a bevy of beautiful aspiring actresses.

Just before the official ceremonies began, Meese, along with the other honored guests, were escorted to the right side of the stage. Other dignitaries—including John Kennedy Jr., Caroline Kennedy Schlossberg, and Colin Powell, who received a loud round of applause—were escorted to the left side of the dais. A few minutes later, also to a loud round of applause, the First Ladies entered in a group, causing quite a stir. Then shortly thereafter, to the music "Hail to the Chief," the five presidents emerged, followed by a thunderous applause. It was a most impressive sight to see standing before everyone these five distinguished men, who as if by magic appeared larger than life.

Charlton Heston opened the ceremonies by speaking of the presidential office, of the men who had held the highest position in the land, and of this great land of freedom. Summarizing the words of Martin Luther King, F. Scott Fitzgerald, Thomas Paine, Samuel Eliot Morison, William Faulkner, Thomas Wolfe, and Abraham Lincoln, he said about Americans, "I have a dream. I refuse to accept the end of man. I believe he will endure. He will prevail and is immortal not because alone of God's creatures he has a voice but because he has a soul, a spirit, and is capable of compassion, sacrifice, and endurance. America is where miracles not only happen but also happen all the time."

Thereafter, Lodwrick Cook—chairman of the board of trustees—extended a welcome to all. This was followed by the invocation, given by Rev. Donn D. Moomaw, senior pastor of Bel Air Presbyterian Church and personal friend of the Reagans. To the music of the combined bands, the colors were presented by the Joint Armed Services Color Guard. The Pledge of Allegiance was led by Gen. Colin Powell, chairman of the Joint Chiefs of Staff. The U.S. Army's sergeant first class Alvey Powell led everyone in the national anthem, after which the colors again passed in review. Lodwrick Cook then asked the board of trustees and their spouses to stand for a round of applause. Pete Wilson, the governor of California, began the introductions of the dignitaries: Mrs. Anwar Sadat, Lady Bird Johnson, Pat Nixon, Betty Ford, Rosalynn Carter, Barbara Bush, and Nancy Reagan, each of whom was greeted with a round of applause. Wilson stated that this was a historic event, the first time four presidents had come together to honor one.

Former president Richard Nixon was the first speaker to honor Reagan. Still looking good, albeit somewhat aged, he joked, "Speaking as a politician, I think you should know that I am much more impressed by the fact that there are four people here who served and were elected to governors of their particular states. Over the past forty-five years, I have been elected to the House, I have been elected to the Senate, I have been elected as vice president, I have been elected as president. I never made it for governor."

He also spoke of his meeting with Nikita Khrushchev in Moscow thirty-two years ago, at which time Khrushchev jabbed his finger into Nixon's chest and said, "Your grandchildren will live under Communism."

Nixon responded, "Your grandchildren will live in freedom."

Nixon drew a chuckle from the crowd with "At that time, I was sure Khrushchev was wrong, but I wasn't sure I was right." His concluding statement was "Khrushchev's grandchildren now live in freedom." This brought hefty applause.

Gerald Ford remembered an old line from Gen. Douglas MacArthur in his farewell address to the Congress. "He may have been right about old soldiers, but you can be sure that old presidents don't just fade away."

Of the presidents, only Carter was a Democrat. "The Republican side of the program has four times as much time as the Democratic," said he, who arrived in California last night from Zambia after monitoring that country's first free elections. "You all have another advantage over me. At least all of you have met a Democratic president. I've never had that honor yet."

Carter also paid tribute to James Baker for his efforts to obtain peace in the Middle East.

President Bush, who complimented all the former presidents, was most adroit in his tribute to Reagan. "He may have been born February 6, but his heart was born July 4. He was a politician who was funny on purpose." He reminded us of Reagan's unfailing sense of humor of that day in March 1981, when he looked at the doctors in the emergency room and said, "I hope you're all Republicans."

The old Gipper, who despite his eighty years still looked like Peck's Bad Boy, could not forbear such quips as "Although we presidents don't get together very often, when we do—well, as you can see, it generates quite a bit of interest. At one time or another, I've run against most of these gentlemen, and they've run against me. Yet here we are.

"It is said that after leaving the White House, Harry Truman once came into his living room to discover his wife, Bess, tossing their old love letters into the fireplace. 'Think of history,' said a horrified Mr. Truman. 'I have,' said Bess.

"In my eighty years . . . what I prefer to consider the forty-first anniversary of my thirty-ninth year . . ." At the conclusion of his speech, Reagan presented the key to the library to Don Wilson, archivist of the National Archives, as a symbolic gesture of turning the Ronald Reagan Presidential Library over to the American people.

The program was concluded by singer Lee Greenwood, who brought a tear to many an eye and caused a lump in many a throat and many a heart to swell with pride with his beautiful "God Bless the USA." "And I'm proud to be an American where at least I know I'm free. And I won't forget the men who died, who gave that right to me. And I'll gladly stand up . . . 'cause there ain't no doubt I love this land. God bless the USA."

One of the most captivating moments of the day occurred in the next instant, when there was a flyover of four U.S. fighter jets in formation. The dignitaries then slowly left the stands while

John Philip Sousa's "Three Cheers for the Red, White, and Blue" was played.

John and Margrit made their way toward the stands, where lunch was being served. They chose two kinds of salad, some hot pasta, and a slice of sausage pizza. Taking their plates to a nearby tent, they joined members of the Secret Service, members of the press corps from around the world, and other guests to enjoy the delicious fare. Thereafter, they drifted toward tents where vendors were selling souvenir golf caps and commemorative T-shirts.

After another photography session on John's part, at which time they oohed and aahed over the magnificent view afforded them and commented that Mounties were patrolling the grounds on horseback, they avoided the horrendously long line waiting to get into the library and sneaked into the back door for a brief tour. Most impressive, erected in the rear courtyard was a large brightly graffitied slab of the Berlin Wall. Inspecting it, the Czermaks noted it was similar to what they recently saw in Berlin, except that the pieces in Berlin had been graffitied on both sides.

By the time John and Margrit left the grounds that afternoon, they realized that being a member of the press was no picnic but hard work. In spite of it, they were keenly aware that they were most fortunate not only to have been granted the privilege of attending the dedication but to have been part of a good, patriotic rally. They also knew this was a day they would long remember and often think about.

Once again, Simi Valley was in the news with the arrival of former Soviet president Mikhail Gorbachev and his wife, Raisa, who visited former adversary Ronald Reagan. Gorby's visit officially opened the Reagan Center for Public Affairs, an international center that focused on the study of individual freedom and promotion of global democracy and foreign affairs. After a day spent at the Reagan ranch in Santa Barbara, our past president presented his fellow past president with the first Ronald Reagan Award for Freedom. How the world turned!

Terrible riots and burning took place in Los Angeles early in May partly as a result of the verdict given in the trial of Los Angeles police officers accused of beating Rodney King. Unfortunately, Ventura County in general and Simi Valley in particular received a lot of bad publicity because of these events. A large contingent from this area not only went into the devastated area to help clean up but sizable contributions also were made by the community to assist the innocent riot victims. "Can't we all get along?" would forever be associated with Rodney King.

Margrit was currently writing a series of mystery stories about a forensic scientist here in Simi Valley. "It's good fun, it keeps me out of the male brothels, and I'm happiest when I'm writing," she told John after he had arrived home from the office.

He told Margrit about his day. "My group at the lab is making good progress on our projects. The most interesting one is trying to use electrolysis to make oxygen and water from simulated moon rocks for future long-term explorations on the moon. Once the process is perfected, we will be receiving a small amount of actual moon rock that was brought back from the moon during the Apollo mission. It is nice that Rockwell has some connections with NASA. As I told you, there is rocket testing for NASA on the site. I will never forget the ground shaking during my first day on the job when I did not know about the rocket testing. The ground shook, and I first thought it was an earthquake, but minutes later, my coworkers told me about the rocket testing.

"We are also making progress on the project using molten salt oxidation to destroy nuclear waste. The Department of Energy is very pleased with what we have reported so far, and they want to fund a pilot plant demonstration. They also want to fund me to spend three months at the Czech Nuclear Research Institute to learn about their new solvent extraction process to separate the fission products cesium and strontium from spent nuclear fuel. Once the fission products are removed, uranium and plutonium would be purified and recycled to make new nuclear fuel. The fission product waste would then only have to be stored hundreds of years instead of thousands of years."

"John, I hope you accept that assignment since you know how much I love living in Europe. I would, of course, accompany you. I also wish I understood more chemistry so I could ask more questions about your work."

III

Since first getting a glimpse of the Czech countryside while living in Vienna, John and Margrit had long dreamed of a day when they could tool around the country to view its magnificence. That was the main reason John had accepted DOE's offer to send him to Prague to work with the Czech scientists at the NRI, near Prague, for three months. All expenses would be paid by the DOE. Tim was also pleased with John working there. He told John that they needed verification that their two research reactors were only being used to develop the Czech nuclear power reactor program and not nuclear bomb material.

The institute adjoined Řež, a small village next to the Vltava River. The train tracks between Prague and Dresden paralleled the river most of the way and passed by Řež, about twenty miles from Prague. Řež was about a thirty-minute drive from Prague and a little longer when going by train. Workers getting off the train to the institute must cross over the Vltava River on a pedestrian bridge to get to work. The institute was surrounded by a high fence with barbed wire on top, and the cafeteria was outside the fence near the entrance, where guards checked workers' badges.

John had the pleasure of working with Miroslav Curie and his small group of chemists and technicians. As John assisted in the research, he acquired detailed knowledge of the new solvent extraction process, from laboratory scale to pilot plant operation. Discussions with site workers and visiting the reactor areas during his tenure at the NRI provided John with the information that Tim wanted. Some of the workers first spoke with John in Czech, only to find out he did not understand them. They assumed that he was Czech since he had a Czech name. John also interacted with Vera Jedakova at the Technical University and gave several lectures there.

During the three months spent in Prague, Margrit kept a journal of their weekend travels for the kids and some relatives to read if they wished. Thus, John took a vacation from his daily diary writing and just concentrated on his research at Rez and traveled with Margrit on weekends. The following was Margrit's diary:

We arrived in Prague on Tuesday via a Delta Air Line flight from Frankfurt. Miroslav picked us up at the metro station, and we came to our new home at Na Vinicnich Horach 22 in Prague's sixth district, Dejvice. After signing the contract for renting the flat, we shopped for a few groceries and unpacked our bags. We went to bed fairly early as we were suffering from jet lag.

Late in the afternoon on Friday, we visited the Technical University, not far from our house, leaving a copy of the *Blabbermouth* for Vera, and then went into the city, where we arranged to rent a car. Dinner was in Old Town, where we talked with some visiting Israelis. Oh, it was good to be back in this fairyland of a city. I bought a book and cassette, *Czech for Foreigners*, determined to learn a bit of Czech.

The next day, we drove to Slaný and then to Mělník, directly north of Prague, where there is an old and beautiful monastery. There, we ate in the famous Vine restaurant, whose terrace offered a breathtaking panorama of the Labé Valley. The town center is very picturesque. The marketplace, with its fountain commemorating the grape harvest, is framed by arcaded town houses. The clock tower on the town hall and the church of the Fourteen Auxiliary Saints complete the harmonious ensemble. On the far side of the square, we followed the busy street down to the Prague Gate to see the impressive remains of the town fortifications. The countryside is lovely—rolling hills and farmlands. Leaving the city, we bought fruit and veggies from roadside vendors.

As to Mělník Castle, during the ninth century, it was constructed by the Psovan dynasty upon the hill overlooking the juncture where the Vltava flows into the Labé. At that time, there was a feud between the Psovans and the Premyslids of Prague. The marriage of the heiress Ludmila Psovan with the Premyslid prince Borivoj joined the twin territories. From that point onward, the castle, now rebuilt, served as a dowager residence for the princesses of Bohemia. The settlement itself grew into a flourishing trading center. In 1274, Otakar II granted it royal privileges in accordance with the decree of Magdeburg.

Off the main road to Slaný is the site of a massacre wrought by the SS during World War II on the inhabitants of the little village of Lidice. It was in retaliation for the assassination of the *Reichsprotektor* Reinhard Heydrich by members of the Czech underground on June 4, 1942; the SS had received the false information that Lidice had harbored the assassins. Five nights later, the SS commander Karl Hermann Frank had all ninety-five houses in Lidice burned to the ground. All 192 adult male occupants were shot on the spot; the women were taken to the Ravensbrück concentration camp in Mecklenburg, where 60 were tortured to death. The 105 children were transported to Lodz, and 82 of them subsequently died in the gas chambers. After the war, a new village was built next to the ruins of the old. A rose garden was planted, and the site was transformed into a memorial to the dead. The little museum to the left of the entrance shows films of the destruction and reconstruction of Lidice.

On Sunday, we drove to Řež looking for an easy way for John to get to work, and then to Kralupy and had breakfast in a roadside restaurant that left a lot to be desired. Nearby was the town of Ústí nad Labem, the economic center of the region, where Richard Wagner composed his opera *Tannhäuser*. We drove along the Labé River to Děčín (also north but much farther, near the East German border), which is on the Elbe River just before the German border. Děčín was occupied until recently by the Soviet Army; after the 1968 invasion of the Czech Republic, they established a permanent garrison at Děčín Castle. This beautiful area, dubbed "Bohemia's Switzerland," abounds with picturesque rocky cliffs, deep ravines, and narrow defiles. In one of the open-air restaurants (on the river, naturally), we ate, among other things, palatschinken. When we returned to Prague that evening, I fixed macaroni and cheese Czech-style.

On Friday, we had a visit to Bratislava. Once there, we set out with the Makseks to a place called Piešt'any, a famous spa resort where people have been going since Roman times to take the waters and bathe in the therapeutic mud. In our bathing suits, we ventured into the hot spring water, much like Glenwood Springs, Colorado. That night, we had a barbecued chicken dinner in the mountains outside Bratislava. The next day, on the way back to Prague, we stopped at historic Telč, a picturesque town from the Middle Ages, which is lined with mostly Gothic and Renaissance houses of a variety of colors and designs.

By the way, our rented car has a most unusual alarm system. At least we think that's what it is. We don't know how to use it (the alarm system), but John figured out in a hurry how to turn on the alarm that makes a variety of "noises" that are great fun. The noises are, to name a few, a police siren, a machine gun's rat-a-tat, an ambulance, and a variety of animal sounds, such as the moo of a cow, the cock-a-doodle-doo of a rooster, and the braying of a donkey. When we were with Tibor and Lillya, we drove around the country roads tooting whatever noise John or Tibor chose at whomever, and the expressions of surprise on the faces were worth every minute of our nonsense. It was funny to see the hens scatter when we put on the rooster's crow. Tibor is just as bad as John (they are like two peas in a pod), and he got the biggest kick out of turning the police siren on when a taxi came speeding by us. The driver slowed down so quickly and dropped so far behind us (and Tibor laughed so hard) that we honestly think the driver will never speed again. And here we were, riding around in a Czech car in the Slovak Republic, giving the Czechs a bad name, and there wasn't one of us Czech. Ah well.

The next Friday, we headed up to the Krkonoše (Giant) Mountains (the highest in the Czech Republic), which have been a nature reserve and national park since 1963. We drove through Mladá Boleslav (meaning "young Boleslav"), Jičín, and around the Prachovské skály rock formations (but didn't see a lot; we need to return), which contain sandstone rock eroded into a host of weird and wonderful shapes, to Vrchlabí. Outside Jičín, we spotted in the tall pines a marvelous Gothic castle—like something out of a fairy tale. That afternoon, we checked in at the Sami Hotel in Vrchlabí and then drove up to the ski area, Špindlerův Mlýn (it's like the Alps), where we hiked around. It is truly a beautiful country, gigantic pines everywhere, and the air was wonderful. We ate a marvelous dinner in Vrchlabí.

The next morning, we drove from Vrchlabí to Pec pod Sněžkou (which means "the furnace below the Sněžka Mountain"). Dotting the rolling countryside in this entire area are adorable little colorful timber-framed houses from the eighteenth and nineteenth centuries. From there, we went to Harrachov, which was interesting but not too exciting, and meandered along Highway 290 (mountain road) through communities in northern Bohemia (saw some of the damage caused by acid rain) to Frydlant, where stands a marvelous castle. The castle was built in 1241 on a rock above the Smědá by a knight named Ronovec; later, owners had it converted into a Renaissance castle.

Then we spent the night in Liberec. Famous for its cloth production, which was begun in the Middle Ages by Flemish weavers, Liberec enjoyed tremendous prosperity in the middle of the last century. The mostly renovated square there is outstanding—the town drunk (John teased me about picking up men in typical fashion) told me the beautiful Rathaus was designed by the same architect, Franz von Neumann, who had designed Vienna's Rathaus, and it definitely has very striking similarities, although on a smaller scale. Liberec (Reichenberg as it was called between 1938 and 1945) was the largest town in the so-called Sudetenland. It was the home of Konrad Henlein, the Sudeten German leader who demanded the Anschluss with the Reich and subsequently became the gauleiter of Sudetenland and civil commissioner for Bohemia.

It was in Liberec that we met Lucie, a charming young lady (she works at the terrace bar on the sixth floor of the hotel where we stayed) who is studying French and English and saving her money to go to France and the United States. She is only seventeen but so mature. She wants to become a journalist. I was so taken with her that I gave her fifty marks, and John left her a sizable tip. We wanted to take her with us and protect her.

From Liberec, we drove to Hrádek on Nisou (the Polish border) for breakfast but could find nothing; then we drove all the way back to Děčín, trying to find a restaurant. We finally ate at the Czech Crown Hotel, where we surprised the desk clerk. He acted like we had parachuted in, asking in German if we were auslanders. We then drove alongside the Elbe (Labe) River to Hřensko, which houses the biggest natural bridge in Europe (Pravčická brána [Pravčice Gateway]). It is the sandstone region near Hřensko that has earned this area the designation of "Bohemia's Switzerland." The Sandstone Mountains were formed 130 million years ago; unfortunately, the region is in grave danger from today's air pollution. One crumbling sandstone block weighing about eight hundred tons is poised threateningly above the main road from Hřensko. It will probably have to be blown up to avoid the risk of a major catastrophe.

From Hřensko, we drove up to the German border, where we turned around. Thereafter, we left the mountains (much to my consternation) because John wanted to see western Bohemia (Teplice, the oldest spa town in Bohemia, and Most, a medieval mining town lying on the trading route from Bohemia to Saxony), which is really a terrible area—so much industry and smog. But we did see another lovely castle at Žatec, a small town badly in need of restoration but which will be a showplace when it has been restored. The environs surrounding the town of Žatec have fertile soil and a climate favorable to guaranteeing the supremacy of hops from this region; in fact, hops from Žatec give Czech beers their special flavor. Before our return to Prague, we visited Louny, which has a most unusually designed cathedral.

On the following Friday, we headed south to Český Krumlov. On the way, we drove through the beautiful Šumava Mountains (Bohemian Forest), stopping in Strakonice with its thirteenth-century water castle; Vimperk (Winterberg), a picturesque city built on hills and is the gateway to the Bohemian Forest; Prachatice, a walled city (the marvelous Pícká Gate still remains from this period) where Jan Hus (founder of the Hussite revolutionary movement) was educated; Husinec, where Jan Hus was said to have been born; Netolice, once the site of a tenth-century castle of the Vítkovci tribe, where we visited the museum that houses a fascinating collection of national costumes and folk embroidery. We drove through České Budějovice (the home of Budweiser beer) but weren't too impressed with what little we were able to see in passing (we're spoiled already!) aside from the famous Samson's Fountain.

At Český Krumlov, a medieval center barely changed since the eighteenth century (except for the Communist-inspired concrete dwellings on the outskirts), we found lodgings at the Pension Falko on Roosevelt Street, which was lucky since it is just up the way from the town square, where we discovered an excellent pizza place. There, we saw at a neighboring table the exact living replica of Jesus. We were flabbergasted. The next morning (it was raining) after a breakfast of hot dogs and bananas sprinkled with coconut (which I didn't eat), we returned to the pizza restaurant for coffee and yummy sweets. Český Krumlov is a real pearl. (And my pronunciation of these difficult Czech names gets better as we travel along.)

The next morning, we drove back to Budějovice, stopping in the town square to again see Samson's Fountain (1727) and the baroque town hall (1727–1730). Then we were off to enchanting Třeboň, where we came upon a traditional Czech wedding, after which there was another. (The first bride was a brunette, the second a blonde.) While driving toward Tábor, we passed through the picturesque village of Soběslav.

The Byzantine-appearing town of Tábor, founded by Jan Žižka and his Hussite "warriors of God" in 1420, was built as a fortress on a hill overlooking the Lužnice River. Double fortification walls are still preserved in parts of the city. The city's narrow, irregular streets were designed to slow down the enemy, and belowground, there are nine miles of catacombs that were built to hide and protect the defenders. We had a wonderful Chinese dinner in the town square; the Chinese owner is from Shanghai. I spoke so long with her while John ran around, taking video, that he thought he had lost me. We returned to Prague in the evening.

We were off again on the following Saturday. We had planned to be away for two days, so at eight thirty, we headed for Jáchymov, a lovely mountain area near the German border, in hopes of finding something spectacular about Marie Curie or the dollar, in that the uranium Marie used in her experiments came from this area as did the name for the dollar. There was a building of sorts with the name "Curie" on it, but we haven't a clue about what it was. What we did see was probably the mine where the uranium was found. As to the dollar, nothing. However, this is the fascinating story of how it got its name: After the discovery of rich silver deposits, the town acquired a royal charter. The founder of Jáchymov, imperial baron Schlick, was granted the privilege of mining the famous Joachimsthaler guilders. The latter were soon recognized as an international currency, giving their name to the thaler—the silver coin formerly used in Germany and Austria—and ultimately to the leading monetary unit of the modern world, the dollar.

Leaving Jáchymov, we drove to Karlovy Vary, where we had lunch (omelets) in the American Steak House. Then we went to Cheb to see the town square. We then headed south to Mariánské Lázně, which is truly a beautiful spot; we would like to return for a relaxing weekend in a five-star hotel.

On Monday, I received a phone call from Boris, who—with a contingent of Russians—was visiting Řež. Prof. Bob Beld from Clemson University also arrived to take a look at the facilities at Řež. Bob had been participating in a DOE-sponsored program along with John's group. John told me that evening that Bob had mentioned to him that they had received funding from the DOE for a new professor position. Bob told John that he would be perfect for it.

On Saturday, we stayed in the city for a change, visiting the Santa Maria abbey in the sixth district (not far from here), where the local people were cleaning and trying to restore the decrepit structure. Inside the church, we saw the corpse of Santa Maria—kind of thrilling. Then we went to Bílá hora (White Mountain), where a decisive battle was lost (by the Czechs to the Austrians) in 1620, followed by going to the TV tower (similar to the Eiffel Tower), where John climbed up about two-thirds of the way to "shoot" Prague.

On Sunday, we traveled to the Karlštejn and Křivoklát Castles—in fact, we just tooled around the beautiful autumnal countryside. We had a sort of brunch (omelets) in Karlštejn (the town). All through the hills, the colors were magnificent. In the late afternoon, we went into the city to "Franks" and had beer and (very spicy) Mexican chips and cheese. Then we had a kind of Italian chicken with spaghetti (which I fixed) when we got home.

The next day, I was off to Vienna via the 1:10 p.m. train to visit with Anna for a couple of days. The train ride was hardly uneventful. Just as the train was about to pull out of the station at Holešovice, two men appeared—one dark and menacing looking, the other young and pale. The dark one said "Bienna?"

I answered in English that the train was going to Vienna.

He thrust the pale young fellow into the car with me and said several times more in a menacing voice, while pointing in the direction of the young man, who said nothing, "Bienna! Bienna! Bienna!" and off he went.

Once the train departed the station, the young man questioned, "Bienna?"

I thought he was speaking Spanish, so I tried a little Spanish with him, but he didn't seem to understand.

He just kept saying over and over, "Bienna? Bienna?"

Finally, I made it understood that I wanted to look at his ticket. When he gave it to me, I showed him that he was going to Vienna and from there to Venetia, which is what he wanted. He also showed me his passport, which was Colombian, and he was from Medellín. So while the train tooted along, he managed to catch up on some sleep while I studied him. I noticed he had only a small bag and was wearing a rather light jacket for such cold weather and sandals with socks. When the conductor came in for tickets, the young man looked terribly frightened, which only aroused my suspicions more, especially when we were both told we had to pay a supplement to our tickets and the difference between first class and second class. The young man pulled out his wallet, which was filled with American dollars— he must have $10,000 in $100 bills, plus a lot of euros and Czech crowns. Anyway, the conductor took what he needed and left. Then passport control came in, looked at our passports, and left.

Meantime, my gray matter was working overtime. I decided this guy must be a drug peddler. Every time the train would stop, he would wake up and ask excitedly, "Bienna?" Finally, I made him understand just how long it would be to Vienna and that I would tell him when we arrived. I decided that when we did arrive in Vienna, there would be a gang awaiting him who would mow us both down as we got off the train, grab his billfold, and run, so I decided to inform the Austrian conductor (who luckily spoke English well) of my suspicions. He said he would inform the authorities and have the man stopped. Well, when we got to Vienna, I had a puppy dog at my heel, so (feeling sorry for the Colombian) I directed him to information. God only knows what happened from there. When I got to Anna's, she told me that an older couple (farmers from Colombia) had recently been arrested in Vienna for drug smuggling. They had been hired in Colombia, paid $5,000 to deliver drugs to Prague, and caught in Vienna.

The next morning, while Anna ran errands, I walked up to the American International School and briefly visited a couple of the kids' old teachers. I also walked past our old house at Krottenbachstrasse (memories, memories) and down to Julius Meinl. There were many changes in the old neighborhood. I bought John some cookies and then walked back. After *mittagessen* (lunch)—Anna made yummy schnitzel—he and I went to Mariahilfer Strasse (Gerngross and Herzmansky) to shop and then back to Salmannsdorf so that she could look in on the ailing Ernst (who had the grippe).

On Wednesday, I returned to Prague on an uneventful train ride. John met me at the station. On the way to our flat, he told me he had received a letter from Clemson University about his interest in a professorship there.

We decided to horse around in the Czech Republic on our last weekend. We drove west on Highway 8 with the idea of going to Dresden, but it was so frosty in the mountains that we deemed it foolish to go on and turned back. So instead, we tooled around the Czech border, through the mountains (glorious fall colors!) toward Nová Ves, but we really had no idea where we were going. As we drove along, John noted that the road running parallel was much nicer and wider, and it appeared to be a *Zoll* crossing. He was right, as we found out when we reached Nová Ves, and there were the customary Asian vendors with their junk for sale. In spite of the cold, we crossed over to the German side. (It was an open border, no guards on the German side and plenty of Germans walking to the poor Czech side.) We were in Deutsch Neustadt, according to a little old lady. She was totally astounded when we told her we were Americans; apparently, no Americans had ever been in Deutsch Neustadt in her lifetime. From Nová Ves, we continued along the parallel border road to Hora Svaté Kateřiny, which looked like it had been under siege during the last war and where the road dead-ended. So we had to double back to Nová Ves and catch the road back to Litvinov. From there, we drove to Chomutov and through the giant open mining coal pit (horribly gruesome). We had lunch of excellent venison schnitzel in a little mountain community and then came back on Highway 7.

On Sunday, John and I tooled around the countryside (one last time), heading north past Mělník, traveling in the same area we sought out at the time of our first weekend adventure way back in August. Early the next day, we filled our suitcases, turned in the house keys, returned the rental car, and went to the airport to board our Delta Air Lines flight to the States via Frankfurt. It was a long day and so sad to leave Bohemia.

IV

A couple of days after the Czermaks returned from Prague, John got a call from Tim about his stay in the Czech Republic. John told Tim that he had learned all about their new solvent extraction process and that he would send him a copy of his trip report that he had submitted to the DOE concerning his research at Řež. He told Tim that he toured the site several times and spoke with many workers during his three months' stay; thus, John was confident that the Czech nuclear program was only for nuclear power and not weapons.

John also received a call from the head of the Department of Environmental Engineering and Science at Clemson University, asking him to fly down to the university for an interview the following week. The department would pay his and Margrit's expenses. On the flight back to California after the interview, Margrit and John discussed the interview trip.

"John, I was very impressed by the university and the nearby towns. I especially liked Pendleton. I also had a good time at the dinner hosted by the dean of engineering and science and the department head. It was nice to talk with Bob about his activities since his visit to Prague. I sincerely hope you get the job as I am tired of generic Simi Valley, being stuck out in suburbia and not having a house with a big yard. If you get the offer, please call the realtor that showed us the lovely new home on Golden Pond in Pendleton and tell him we will take it."

"I also had a good time at the dinner and finding out a lot more about the position I might be offered. I would start in about two months and would not have to start teaching until the fall semester. I would have three graduate students who are ready to start their research. From Ying's last e-mail from Australia, I know she is looking for a postdoc position in the United States, so maybe I could also get her in my group as I would start with enough funding to financially support her and a couple of other students for at least two years. I got a good laugh out of the dean when he started talking about the Clemson Tigers. I piped up and said, 'Clemson has a football team?'

"By the way, Margrit, I arranged for an appointment for your car to be serviced and worked on tomorrow, so you will have to accompany me to work and use my car to run your errands. After you pick me up in the late afternoon, we can stop on the way back and get your car. Hopefully, Mike can complete the work in one day."

A little after they arrived back at the town house, John told Margrit, "I just received a call from the head of the department, and I have the job. Let's celebrate."

After opening a bottle of Cold Duck and toasting, Margrit asked John, "Are we going to ship our cars or drive mine to South Carolina?"

"Well, Margrit, I am sorry, but I want to sell your car. I will also have to spoil my surprise and tell you that I bought that Smart car you looked at when we were in Clemson. After I accepted the job at Clemson, I phoned our realtor that we wanted the house on Golden Pond in Pendleton. I also asked our realtor to contact the car salesman and have the car waiting in the garage for you."

"Oh, John, what a lovely present." She thanked him with a romantic long kiss.

About noon the next day, Margrit received a very puzzling phone call. The caller said in a Russian accent, "Hello, is this Margrit Czermak?"

"Yes" was her reply with a puzzled look on her face. "Who is this?"

"Please do not be too shocked or offended, but this is Andrei Pushkin."

"What?" she said in a strained voice. "You can't be Andrei as he died over six years ago."

"Yes, it is me, Margrit. And if possible, I would like to meet you this afternoon and explain what happened to me and where I live and work now."

Margrit did not believe that this caller was really Andrei, but she agreed to meet him at a local restaurant mainly because she was curious about who this man was. As Margrit arrived at the almost vacant restaurant, she went to a table in the corner of the room where a man was seated with his back to the entrance. Margrit said, "Andrei?"

He stood up and faced her with tears in his eyes. As she recognized Andrei, Margrit started to hysterically weep and cried out, "It is you!" After several minutes of trying to get over the shock, Andrei helped her sit down.

Margrit was still weeping as she quietly asked in a shaking voice, "Andrei, I am so happy that you are alive. Please tell me what happened and why you are here."

After the two calmed down from their emotional reunion and ordered coffee, Andrei began to tell Margrit his story.

"Margrit, I am so sorry I put you through so much sadness and heartbreak. Just before my faked suicide, I realized the futility of our relationship and the times we unsuccessfully attempted to terminate it. I continued to suffer self-debasement, realizing I was destroying our families. In this state, I seriously considered suicide, but my good Russian friend Mikhail Romanov talked me out of it. He then somehow got a dead body to use as a decoy for the car crash and fire. He also arranged a new life for me in Canada with passport and job. I now work for an aircraft parts manufacturer in Toronto. I am here on business with Rockwell and have been at their Santa Susana site, where your husband works, for the past two days. I return to Canada tomorrow. I followed your lives over the years on Facebook since your husband accepted me as a former friend at the IAEA, where I used my friend's identity.

"I also found out that my wife married someone else and that my elder son works in Moscow. I did contact him and Alexander, but only Alex wanted to join me in Canada. The boys agreed never to tell anyone about my faked death and where I am. Alex has finished his master's degree in chemistry at the University of Toronto and plans to go to graduate school in the United States for his PhD. He will return to Moscow in two weeks. Since that time, I continued to love and miss you dearly. I had hoped someday to start a new life with you, and that is the only reason I go on living."

A shocked Margrit told Andrei that she continued to think about him over the years and, every once in a while, about how she suffered for many months after she received the terrible news of his death. "It would be different if I was divorced or a widow. Then indeed I would consider a new life with you, Andrei. However, I am very happy with my life now. John and I have reconciled our past problems and have a very amicable relationship and a wonderful life together. We have so many memories of traveling together, attending events in California, making new friends, and having wonderful visits with family.

I do not want to jeopardize my marriage, my relationship with my children and friends. I am also very excited about John and my future. We will move to South Carolina in a couple of months, where John will teach at Clemson University, and I can enjoy the academic environment and help students. Andrei, you will always have a place in my heart."

After their conversation and coffee, Margrit told Andrei that she must go as she had John's MR2 and must pick him up at the site. Andrei accompanied Margrit to the car, and they said their very emotional goodbyes with a long embrace.

After picking up John and driving to Mike's car service, Mike apologized to John that Margrit's car was not ready but would be completed by the next afternoon. Since Margrit had a doctor's appointment the next day, she planned to accompany John to work and use his car again.

As they were driving up the narrow, steep, and winding Black Canyon Road the next morning, Margrit asked John, "Do you ever get tired of driving up and down this dangerous road every workday?"

"I seldom see another car, and almost all the workers come up at other times or drive up from the San Fernando Valley on a much better road. I also enjoy pretending to be a race car driver and sometimes time myself. The first hairpin curve at the top is known as Dead Man's Curve. Our secretary describes it as when you turn on that sharp curve, the back of the car kisses the front."

"Do you still see lots of wildlife on the site, John?"

"I do see some wildlife early in the morning, especially deer and raccoons. One morning I even saw a bobcat. About the same time, I witness a beautiful sunrise. As you know, we need some rain, Margrit, but not by the bucketful as happened last month. Because of the flooding, this road was quite literally washed away in places, and a newly formed 'river' ran at the bottom, making it perilous for me to get to work. Nor were most parts of Ventura and the San Fernando Valley spared as raging waters created chaos and destruction throughout the Southland. Of course, as you know, since that time, we've had forest fires, a hurricane, and several major earthquakes—the mightiest, registering 7.4, which occurred near Joshua Tree National Park. Remember, it jolted us from our beds."

After arrival at the outside parking lot and parking the MR2 in his usual place near the road, John and Margrit went through the guard station to the nearby plant cafeteria. Over a late breakfast, Margrit told John that she was so happy with her life with him, loved him more than any other time in their marriage, and looked forward to moving to South Carolina. After finishing their coffee, John took a five-minute walk to his office, and Margrit went through the guard station to the car.

A few minutes later, the guard saw lots of smoke coming from the Black Canyon Road and called the site's fire department. They found a red MR2 upside down and on fire in a steep ravine below Dead Man's Curve. After putting out the fire, they discovered Margrit's dead body nearby.

V

Dear family and friends,

Thank you so much for your thoughtful cards and e-mails on the passing of Margrit as well as coming to her memorial party in Colorado. I received almost two hundred e-mails and cards of condolences from loved ones and friends, and over eighty people attended her party. Your cards and presence at the party gave me much comfort. The surprise guests at the party were Margrit's cousin and her daughter who came all the way from California. Margrit was loved by so many people. Her memorial letter is attached.

Love and best wishes,

John Czermak

Memorial Letter

Margrit Czermak was a wonderful wife, mother, grandmother, humanitarian, secretary, teacher, and writer. Margrit visited almost one hundred countries and saw most of the natural and man-made wonders of the world. She snorkeled in the Great Barrier Reef; saw reindeer above the Arctic Circle; walked on the Great Wall of China on her birthday; traversed the headwaters of the Amazon; took boat rides on many other rivers, including the Danube, Rhine, Mississippi, Nile, Paraná, Volga, and Yangtze; and did much, much more. Margrit was loved by everyone who knew her and had friends all over the world. She was always ready to help anyone in need, from world-renowned scientists to local grocery clerks. It cannot be repeated enough that she loved life, was not afraid to live, and would be sorely missed by many, many loved ones and friends the world over.

I first met Margrit on a blind date. Arlyn Springer and Ron Jones were my roommates, helping me with my $119 monthly house payments. Arlyn's girlfriend Clare had Margrit as a roommate, so they brought Margrit over one night for dinner. Since I was always short on money, I naturally bought the cheapest steaks I could find for dinner. The steaks were tough, and Margrit's steak dropped on her lap as she was trying to cut it. She promptly put the steak back on her plate and continued with the conversation at hand. This incident, her warm handshake, and sparkling personality won me over that night. Perhaps love at first sight, "to be touched by

Margrit is to know what happiness is." On our next date, Margrit offered to cook steaks and wanted to go to the store to pick them out. She selected the most expensive steaks in the store, and the next day, I had to take out a loan to cover our dinner expenses. Margrit was a high-class lady, and I should have realized it then that I would always have to work hard to support us.

At this time, I had completed almost two years of part-time college at the University of Colorado's Denver Center; and after I started dating Margrit that fall, my grades suffered. So we decided to kick Arlyn and Ron out of the house and get married. Margrit promised me at the time that there would never be a dull moment in our marriage, and she was right. For our honeymoon, we went to Sears and purchased a washer and dryer. My Laundromat days were finally over.

Margrit was very supportive of my education but welcomed my receiving the Dow Chemical scholarship the following year so that I would not have to work full time and attend school in the evenings. For two years, I went to Boulder full time and had more time with my new and growing family. The downside was that I only received $333 a month, so Margrit would go out with baby Amy and sell Avon products part time to make ends meet. She made many sacrifices and continued to be supportive of my continuing as a full-time graduate student and returning to full-time employment at Rocky Flats.

My darling, wonderful wife always gave me encouragement and even some homeschooling on many things, including manners, thus cultivating me and smoothing out some of my rough edges. My

English and writing improved with her around, and my perspective of the world was broadened. She was always very thoughtful and kind and had a calming effect on me; she did not realize I was a stutterer well over a year after we were married.

The years with small children in our home were the best of our lives, with us always laughing at the antics of Eric and Lorrie. About once every year or two, Margrit would say she could smell the ocean. She was a California girl, so we would load up the car with the children, clothes, and credit cards and head for the beach and Disneyland. Over the years, she brought so much warmth, love, and happiness into our family, always celebrating the birthdays and holidays to the fullest and never missing an opportunity to have a party. Her family was the most important thing in her life.

Margrit was always agreeable to changes, new challenges, and opportunities, such as going to Vienna to live for three years. Vienna certainly changed our lives, and she never got over having to leave Vienna, always wanting to return to Europe. Indeed, we made many return trips. Prague was another of our favorite cities, and we were so fortunate to have spent three months there. During that time, we would take long weekend trips to various parts of Europe, including Vienna.

Margrit's love of travel started at any early age. She suffered from asthma and had to spend a lot of time in bed as a child. She loved to read about the children in faraway places like China, Japan, India, Lapland, and others. So later in life, she had a strong desire to visit the places she read about as a child; and indeed, she got to see many of these faraway lands.

Margrit had a remarkable memory, spoke several languages, loved history, and was an insatiable reader and an excellent writer. She wrote several articles and books under a pen name, including musical scores, poems, and several manuscripts still in progress, one of which was her autobiography. She also edited several scientific books for my colleagues and edited all my writings.

Margrit loved life and people, and she especially loved my mom, perhaps more so because they both lost their mothers during childhood. Margrit was always helping someone. For many years, she sponsored a girl in India, and she helped many of my students while we were in Australia. In fact, she was so determined to get Ala and his family to Sydney that she spent a good deal of time having the university arrange a student visa for him. After their arrival in Sydney, they became our god family. Their daughter, Mary, was born in Australia before they had to return to Libya.

Everyone who knows Margrit knows of her wonderful sense of humor and great crackling laugh. She was teased for her outlook on life, that she always wore rose-colored glasses, yet she herself took great pride in this aspect of her character. Margrit forever saw the best in all of us and would always lend an ear or give aid. Sometimes we would make a quick stop at a convenience store, and she would run in to buy one or two items; ten to fifteen minutes later, she would come out and say she met the nicest people and learned some of their life story. I think she was late in arriving at her scheduled appointment with God as she spent too much time talking with St. Peter and his helpers at the gates of heaven.

Margrit was not afraid to live or die. I am sure now she is having a wonderful time in heaven with our parents, grandparents, cousins, aunts, uncles, and other departed relatives as well as with many of our departed friends.

The sun has set on the life of a wonderful, wonderful lady. I have never met a more beautiful, charming, classy, gracious, intelligent, interesting, "wanting to be around" lady in my life. I love her so much. She will be sorely missed by me and all our loved ones and friends around the world.

Thank you kindly and best wishes,

John Czermak

After John's return from a very nice but sad memorial for Margrit in Colorado, the Simi Valley Police summoned him to headquarters. They again questioned him about Margrit's death. The police captain told John after his questioning, "You are not a suspect because of information from the front gate guard observing both you and Margrit leaving the car together to come on site and her leaving alone. We also have confirmation from a fellow worker that you left Margrit in the plant cafeteria and went to your office. The guard had also observed a black car leaving the parking lot and going down the other way into the San Fernando Valley just before Margrit came back to the car and drove down the Black Canyon Road. Following our investigation after the fire was put out and Margrit's body removed, we found that there was a trail of brake fluid from the parking lot to the wrecked car and that the brake line had been cut. Thus, we concluded that the person in the black car had cut the brake line, resulting in the murder of your wife. Since that person did not know that Margrit would be driving the car, we assume that person was trying to kill you. John, do you know anyone who has a grudge strong enough to try and kill you?"

John was flabbergasted as he slowly thought about the question. "Well, I did hear from one of my friends at Rocky Flats that FBI agent Phil Gilbert, who was investigating me for disclosing classified information to the Russians, was later fired for providing false information to his superiors about me. Meg Showman was also fired by the DOE for her mishandling of the investigation of me and that I should have never lost my security clearance. Meg let me know about this in an apologetic letter."

Two weeks after Andrei returned to Toronto, he was devastated to find out about Margrit's death via John's Facebook posting. He had cut the brake line, and the car crash was meant for John and not Margrit. He was beside himself with grief and kept saying, "My life is over with no hope for a life with my beloved Margrit. I have no reason to live."

At that point, he started drinking glass after glass of vodka and then pulled out a revolver from a drawer in his modest home. He shot himself in the chest, dropped the gun on the floor, and barely managed to push it under the couch with his foot. His son was upstairs, getting ready to go to the airport and return to Russia. He ran down to his father's side when he heard the shot. Alex immediately tried to stop the blood coming from his father's chest.

With difficultly, Andrei spoke to his son, "Alex, I have told you about Margrit Czermak before. Well, I accidently killed her, and I meant to kill her husband, John, who has ruined my life the past ten years. I had hoped that, after his death, she and I could have a life together. But instead, he just left here after shooting me. I have no reason to live now. Please do not call anyone. Pack your bag and return to Russian as soon as possible. Please make a promise to me that you will apply to Clemson University and study under Czermak." Then Andrei whispered another promise for Alex to keep before his heart stopped.

Chapter 5
Academic Life at
Clemson University

I

After an agonizing fortnight of final work in California, John accepted Tim's offer at government expense (via the Penny Group in San Francisco) to go on a mission to North Korea. John had always wanted to take the train across China to Tibet, and he planned on doing that after the dangerous CIA assignment. He also planned to meet Ying in Beijing to discuss her coming to Clemson as a postdoc in his research group. He had hoped that the travel would help him cope with his loss. He also wanted to start spreading Margrit's ashes around the world. Her desire was to have some of her ashes sprinkled around all the places she lived and loved as well as some of the places she always wanted to visit but ran out of human time. Before his departure, John sent out the following letter:

> Dear family,
>   I will leave for Beijing early next Tuesday morning and arrive there about 3:00 p.m. the next day. Our nine-member humanitarian group, sponsored by Global Exchange, will spend the first night at the Beijing Holiday Inn Express before flying to P'yŏngyang the next day. Our host has provided me the following information that he thought I should pass onto you all:

There is no U.S. embassy or consulate in North Korea. You can inform the U.S. Embassy in Beijing about your trip or notify the embassy of Sweden, U.S. protecting power, in P'yŏngyang.

Love,

Dad

After John returned to California, he sent the following copy of his diary concerning the North Korea trip to Tim along with a note asking him if he wanted any copies of the many photos he took:

On the flight from Los Angeles to San Francisco, the middle seat was vacant, and a lady from Pasadena (Linda) was in the aisle seat. Linda had a blind person's cane and said she was legally blind (from a brain tumor). Linda had glasses and could read all right. She was flying to Okinawa, Japan, to spend a few weeks with her son and his girlfriend, who both work for an international company. This was Linda's third visit to Japan. She was originally from Mississippi, and I asked her if she could spell it. She did. Then I asked her to spell it with one eye, and she could not. It was the first time she had heard that puzzle about spelling Mississippi with only one of her eyes open. She had a short connection with her flight to Japan on another airline and probably did not make it.

I arrived in Beijing the next day and was transported to the Holiday Inn for an overnight stay. I took a walk, had dinner at Burger King next to the hotel, and came back and had a great massage at the hotel.

After an early breakfast the next morning, I took another walk near the hotel, taking lots of pictures. I departed for the airport at ten. At the Beijing Airport, which is very big and modern, I met one of my fellow travelers, Phil. Phil took me to the Delta Air Lines lounge, where we got free food and drink. Phil, a lawyer, grew up in Westminster, Colorado, and now lives on seventy-five acres of farmland in Minnesota. He is a tall guy, balding, and great company. Later, Phil, I, and the other members of our group boarded our Air Koryo flight to P'yŏngyang.

The other members of the group are Tim and Wing, both from Buena Vista College in Iowa (they plan to bring ten students back here next year); Adam, a young Canadian artist; David, who brought his folks along; Joan and Chuck (who had brought lots of gifts for the schools); and good-looking Brittany.

On our Friday-the-thirteenth flight, all the passengers got a hot lunch; and as we approached the P'yŏngyang Airport, the sky was very overcast and smoggy, and one could not see anything until our landing at around five. There are lots of farmland, two lakes, and a couple of rivers near the airport. The area is surrounded by mountains, and the landing strip is rough; the plane had to taxi over a river.

The airport is small, and we made it through immigration and customs okay. They x-rayed my luggage, and the inspector asked to see the batteries in my pocket. There were no problems with my suitcase, which was checked.

Our small group of nine was herded aboard a big bus. We had two guides, Mr. Lee and Ms. Kim, plus the driver. The countryside from the airport has lots of rice fields and some orchards; we passed many small plots of land being farmed. It seemed like the whole country is utilizing all available open land for growing food. Indeed, the country is very beautiful, with lots of hills and mountains. Along the way, there were nice apartment buildings, and everything seemed to be in great shape. There were some bike riders and many people walking. In two places, there were many soldiers working on the train tracks that parallel the road.

Today is the same day that a long-range rocket was launched with the USA in strong objection; Mr. Lee said everyone is very proud of their rocket launch. During the ride, Ms. Kim gave us a talk about how the West profits from the war. It took about thirty minutes to get into the city with its wide streets, many tall apartment buildings, and several parks and monuments. After we arrived in the city, I noted that the people seem well off and were walking, riding bikes, or waiting for the bus or underground. They were well dressed and later very friendly since they let me take their picture. One thing I did not see were trains and fire trucks but lots of police and soldiers everywhere.

The Yanggakdo Hotel, where we would be staying, is surrounded by hills, shaped like a triangle, and forty-seven stories high with 1,001 rooms and a revolving restaurant on top. It did have a beautiful lobby, but the small dingy rooms are more like those in a twenty-year-old Motel 6. I did have a private bath, but there was only hot water two hours in the morning and two hours at night. One morning I got a hot bath, on another morning a cold one, and then a warm shower. The amenities are six small plastic bottles of shampoo and body wash, but they are about half empty, apparently partly used by the previous occupants. The bed is very hard and uncomfortable to sleep on. There is a small TV, but the only English language channel is a Japanese news station. That channel was our only source of news from the outside world, but even it, as we were told, is not available to ordinary citizens in their homes (if they even have a TV). There are five restaurants in the hotel: Japanese, Chinese, revolving, Restaurant no. 1, and the one where our group ate—Restaurant no. 2.

There were many official delegates at the hotel that were in the city for the one-hundredth anniversary celebration of the birth of the first president. The elevator was usually full coming from upper floors. Because of all the delegates, there was a long wait for the elevator.

That evening, my fellow travelers and I had a nice dinner with plenty of separate dishes brought to the table. After dinner, we got on the bus and planned to go to an amusement park, but we were held up at the Arch of Triumph by a caravan of army vehicles that had participated in a parade earlier. We waited about twenty minutes as truck after truck slowly went by, carrying what looked like rockets and dismantled planes. At that point, Mr. Lee told everyone we would try another night for the park visit.

The first morning, I was up early and had a walk around the outside of the hotel, taking lots of pictures. As usual, I did not pay any attention to what Mr. Lee had told us the night before: "Please do *not* leave the hotel on your own." I had asked why, and he said, "It is for your safety," but like other totalitarian dictatorships, there are no issues of personal safety in North Korea.

P'yŏngyang is a city of three million people, most from the upper stratum of North Korean society, that is, high-ranking Communist Party and army officials and their top functionaries. There are lots of tall buildings in the city, many under construction; the most distinctive structures are two hotels. P'yŏngyang has many broad avenues and boulevards, yet there is very little traffic as privately owned vehicles are forbidden to all but a few of the very top officials. Ms. Kim explained that not only are cars very expensive but they also would contribute to air pollution. Yet some of the army trucks have been converted to carbon-producing, wood-burning engines because of the lack of petroleum. One of the questions Mr. Lee asked us concerned the quality of air in our home city versus P'yŏngyang; he was visibly disappointed when we said our air is equally clean and fresh. There is also an extensive underground metro system that is the main means of transportation for people to get around the city. Later, we got to see the metro and the throngs of North Koreans trying to get on and off the trains.

The little traffic in the streets consisted of crowded public buses, army vehicles, lots of bicycles, a few motorbikes, a few taxis, vans making public announcements, and trucks holding twenty to thirty people crouching in back while being transported to their workplace. During the whole week, the only negative thought expressed by Ms. Kim was that the vans blaring patriotic songs, political propaganda, and uplifting thoughts were actually "noise pollution." Patriotic movies are also shown in the evening on huge screens in the large public squares. I wondered what happens during the cold winter season.

Ironically, despite the small number of vehicles, there are numerous pedestrian underpasses connecting all four corners of many intersections. Many baton-wielding young white-uniformed traffic ladies are stationed at these places and even at the intersections that had traffic lights. These young women directed the few vehicles with robotic arm movements and motioned pedestrians to use the pedestrian subways. One of the few disobedient acts performed by some citizens was crossing the street rather than using the underpass, but this only happened when the traffic lady was standing on the far corner of the intersection.

Citizens who work together are encouraged to do team games. It was not unusual to see small groups on the sidewalk jumping rope, singing, or exercising together. They appeared to be enjoyable activities. Every Friday afternoon, most of the workers in the city head out to toil on the collective farms. Mr. Lee said the office staffers "like to help the farmers," but we were a little skeptical of this claim.

Throughout P'yŏngyang, there are huge statues of Kim Il Sung, the founder of modern North Korea, and his son, Kim Jong Il, who ran the country from 1994 until his death late in 2011. One is referred to as the Great Leader, the other as the Dear Leader, along with many other laudatory phrases and titles. Every important building or landmark has a large picture or sculpture of one or both, depending on which one is credited with designing, building, or inaugurating the project. Virtually every North Korean wears a lapel pin with the picture of the Dear Leader.

According to their history books, Kim Il Sung spent World War II fighting against the Japanese who had occupied all Korea since 1905. He then led the newly independent country through the next forty years. The North Korean people, of course, never learned that Kim Il Sung actually spent most of

WW II in Moscow, learning from Joseph Stalin how to organize a Communist Party and set up a totalitarian dictatorship. Kim Il Sung even outdid Stalin, Mao, and other Communist leaders by continuing his legacy and setting up his own son as the next leader. Kim Jong Il followed his father's teachings by maintaining the million-man army (out of only twenty million inhabitants), concentration camps, informant networks, collective farms, and other accoutrements of a completely isolated socialist autocracy. In turn, after his death, Kim Jong Il has been succeeded as head of state and army by his number three son, Kim Jong Un.

Every North Korean business, from the largest power plant to the smallest food kiosk, from the smallest farm to the largest firm, is owned by the state. Every abode, from the smallest mud and straw hovel to the largest apartments in the city, is owned by the government. (They are all rent-free, but where you get to live depends on who you know more than what you know.) Each business is called a company, so when you meet someone who says they work for a restaurant, a store, or even a tourism concern, they are employed by the government.

We set out early on Saturday to visit the infamous demilitarized zone (DMZ), the area between North and South Korea that was set as the border in 1953 at the conclusion of the Korean War. The tree-lined highway from P'yŏngyang to the DMZ is seven to ten lanes wide with no median and good pavement, probably a result of no traffic. The only vehicles we saw were a few old intercity buses, army vehicles, and an occasional small tourist van. We saw no private vehicles. We passed many farms on the way with lots of rice fields and only one tractor but lots of farmers plowing behind cows. It was a two-hour drive with lots of tunnels on the highway through mountains. There were numerous checkpoints that we had to stop at. North Koreans must carry ID cards and are not allowed to travel from city to city without permission. However, the soldiers at most barriers—seeing the insignia of the Korean National Tourist Company on our van—just waved us through.

Wisely, we refrained from taking pictures of the soldiers at the checkpoints.

On the way to the DMZ, we stopped in Migok village to see a collective farm. This was a "show" farm, and there were almost no mechanical aids. The top administrator was not a farm manager but rather a Communist Party official. Some of the group asked to use the restrooms, and the manager had to get the key hidden on a tree branch. I and the other toilet seekers had a good laugh. After arriving at the buildings just outside the DMZ, we had to wait with an assortment of other foreign tourists while our guides submitted our documents for inspection.

The DMZ stretches from sea to sea across the middle of the Korean peninsula. North Korea controls 2½ miles on the northern side of the actual border and South Korea the southern half. The road leading from North Korea into the DMZ is hemmed in on both sides by large boulders. These huge rocks are balanced with a hair-trigger switch so that they will fall on the road on a moment's notice and block tanks should the North Koreans think the South Koreans are invading. Off the road are cornfields, but we also found out that the whole DMZ is full of land mines.

Our group was not supposed to take pictures while on the bus presumably so we could not show them to the South Koreans later. Most of the group, including me, did anyway, hoping the soldier on board wouldn't notice and confiscate the cameras.

After a short bumpy ride, we arrived at the complex of buildings where the armistice talks to end the Korean War were held. In touring the structures, our group was shown— in movies, photographs, and lectures—how the brave North Koreans held off the imperialist Americans and their South Korean lackeys. The only indication that there were other troops besides the aggressor Yankees was in the Armistice Hall. The two flags sitting on the desk where the truce was finally signed in 1953 were the North Korean and that of the United Nations. Before the group's arrival, Mr. Lee told us that the Americans kept delaying the peace talks for several years; and even now, the North Koreans do not know if they will be okay by South Korea and the U.S. They are hopeful for reunifications of the two countries.

There were many soldiers in the whole area of the DMZ, and I was astute enough to foresee this as I had placed a little of Margrit's ashes in my pants cuff at the hotel. At a place dividing the two countries, I bent down to retie my shoe and cautiously released the ashes from my pants cuff.

On the way back, we stopped at the Reunification Monument of the Three Charters for National Reunification at the east entrance to the city. Inside is a mausoleum of many dead. After we returned to our hotel, Mr. Lee told us officially that the rocket launch was successful, but we found out later that it had dropped into the sea shortly after its launch.

On Sunday, we briefly visited the subway, where there were long lines of people waiting for the train. Later, we drove north through a lot of fog on our way to Kim Il Sung's birthplace. To complete the anti-American day, upon our arrival back in P'yŏngyang, we were taken to the river berth of the ill-famed USS *Pueblo*. According to the North Koreans (again via film, photos, and local guide), in 1968, the *Pueblo* was engaged in aggression by spying on the North Korean army while in North Korean waters. The "heroic" North Korean military was able to subdue the American Navy ship and force it to shore. Of course, whether the *Pueblo* was actually in North Korean waters is debatable, and the ship was armed only with one small machine gun on the bow. In due course, the American captain and his crew "confessed" to spying and were returned alive to the USA. The North Koreans are very proud to have the only written formal apology ever given by American authorities to a foreign country. The *Pueblo* is kept docked in P'yŏngyang's river as a trophy.

The next day, we watched the parade and heard the speech by the son of Kim Jong Il, Kim Jong Un, marking the one-hundredth anniversary of the birth of his grandfather, Kim Il Sung. The young leader is twenty-seven years old. We were at the edge of the square near a statue of a hammer and sickle, an art studio and museum, and between lines of soldiers and where the dignitaries sat. Many ladies had tears in their eyes during the speech. After the speech, the parade started with lots of trucks carrying soldiers and rockets. The sides of the street were lined by many people, all dressed well and looking very happy. As all this was taking place, I was candidly and quickly taking lots of photos.

After the parade, we went shopping at the Paradise Store, which had lots of merchants. After shopping, we went to a bowling alley filled with bowlers and pool players and had pizza. Later, we boarded a cruise ship for dinner and had a short ride on the river to a bridge and back. During dinner, we saw a beautiful fireworks display. Afterward, everyone was tired, so we returned to the hotel.

The next morning, as usual, I waited five to ten minutes for the hotel elevator. The first elevator to arrive was loaded with North Korean delegates. I caught the second elevator, and it filled up fast. Most of these people ended up in our breakfast room. I avoided the hotel breakfast that morning because I had my own powdered coffee, chocolate cookie, and Kit Kat bar. At the time, none of my fellow travelers had arrived for breakfast; but later, I met them in the hotel lobby with all our luggage to change hotels for one night.

On the way to the spa hotel, we again passed a lot of farms that were not being used and then drove to Nampo to see a major feat of engineering—the wide outlet where the Taedong River meets the sea had been barraged so that salty ocean water could no longer flow up the river, thus helping fishing and irrigation along with a dam generating electrical power. We stopped for lunch at the last place we expected, the P'yǒngyang Golf Club. Originally set up by the Japanese, it is used sparingly today by foreign diplomats and a few members of the North Korean ultraprivileged class. There were actually a couple of people playing, but our group declined. We had lunch at the club's pagoda house. After arrival at the spa hotel, we found out that each room has a large tub that can be filled with natural spring water and also a shower with regular water. It is a great hotel.

On Wednesday, we first stopped at another hotel to buy water since the spa hotel was out of it. I asked for two bottles of water and one orange juice. She said there was no orange juice, but she had a can of peach juice. I said okay. On the bus, I opened the can to find out I got milk coffee. We went by some beautiful buildings and visited the cemetery for soldiers that died at Japanese hands in the 1932–35 war. North Koreans want the Japanese authorities to apologize and compensate them for all the atrocities they committed in past wars. The relationship of the two countries is still bad because of this.

Then we visited the zoo along with many families. The zoo visit was depressing since there were tigers and other animals in very small cages, and the poor dogs wanted to be petted by us, but it was not possible.

After lunch, we spent some time at a university and children's school. They had a film studio in the eighteen-thousand-student university, of which four thousand were graduate students. Our university guide showed us one classroom with a computer and electronic whiteboard and said that this is typical of every classroom. Maybe they just showed us the best classroom? He also showed us a great library.

Then we went to the children's school. The students looked of all ages. After a rushed tour of five classrooms, we went to the auditorium, where some of the young students put on a great one-hour program. It was very professional. At the end of the visit, Joan and Chuck handed out the gifts that they had brought to a small crowd of students. The soccer balls, first inflated, were the most popular. After fun and games, we went to dinner at a local restaurant; and as usual, we had vegetables, chicken, fish, and rice. And then we went back to our original hotel.

On Thursday, we took a thirty-minute ride to the airport. Check-in was good, but we had to wait first for immigration and then a brief security check. The plane was late for our 10:30 a.m. departure to Beijing. I was anxious to get out of North Korea because of the potential for arrest. However, the North Korean people were very nice and the children beautiful. We need to try to build bridges with the North Korean people, especially the young people, by shipping food, school goods, and so on all marked Made in the USA.

We landed at the Beijing Airport at noon and got to the hotel at two. I had a massage after checking in and later watched TV and had dinner at eight. Ying arrived at around nine and checked into her own room down the hall. The first thing she said was "Dear Professor, I am so sorry to hear about the passing of your wonderful wife. Please accept my sincere condolences for your loss."

The next day, we had breakfast together and then went for a walk around the palace. In the Forbidden City, with lots of people around, I left a little of Margrit's ashes to stay forever in such a beautiful and historic place. We then took a taxi back to the hotel, where we had some discussions of her planned research at Clemson over lunch, and later played a game of pool—she won. After the pool match, we went about a kilometer to a shopping center in the rain. Ying bought a lot of stuff, mainly clothes. We had dinner at McDonald's and then waited for a taxi to take us back to the hotel—what an experience. I thought we should go one way and Ying the other, but Ying was correct, and we finally got a taxi.

On Saturday, Ying was sick and could not join me on a bus tour to the Great Wall. On the tour, there were three retired ladies from Malaysia and two young ladies from Krakow, Poland. We visited the Mutianyu Great Wall, the Badaling Great Wall, Ming Tombs, a jade factory, and a tea and silk factory. I left some ashes on the Great Wall.

On Sunday afternoon, Ying flew back home after she said that she was looking forward to working with me at Clemson. Later, I had a massage to relax; the masseuse said she was only interested in money, and the North Koreans also said the same about the Chinese. Then I went on a long walk to find the shopping mall that Ying and I had found on Friday night since I was having a Big Mac attack. Instead, I found a different McDonald's in a long pedestrian mall. I slowly made my way back to the hotel a different way and ended up at the hotel very tired and missing beautiful and charming Ying. She was so much fun to be with. Of course, I was missing Margrit much, much more.

The next day, a young lady representing the tourist company that arranged my trip to Tibet came to the hotel and took me to the train station. I boarded a fairly nice train in the early afternoon and found my first-class sleeper compartment. The dining car is in front of my car, and in the rear of my car is a second-class car overflowing with people, some without seats. An older couple and a young lady were sharing the compartment with me. The young lady has a boyfriend who was staying in the second-class car. The first morning, he came and took a nap on her bed. Later, I went back to our compartment and tried to take a nap, but the girl's boyfriend had very smelly feet.

During the trip, I had a little entertainment. A very cute little boy was playing hide-and-seek with me, and I took some pictures that the boy enjoyed seeing. His parents were in the next compartment and played cards most of the way. It looked like I was the only Westerner on board. I spent most of the daylight hours watching the scenery go by and eating three meals in the dining car.

About halfway to Tibet, we stopped in a very large city, Lanzhou. I got some new company, a young man and an elderly teacher and his wife. The teacher woke me up with his loud snoring in the middle of the first night, even though there was an aisle between us. I reached over a couple of times to wake him without success. A little later, the young man below me received a call on his cell phone. It seemed like everyone in China had a cell phone, and there was even cell phone reception out here on the train. Anyway, the guy talked for the longest time until the teacher told him off.

On Tuesday afternoon, we arrived at Xining in Qinghai Province. There, we changed engines, from electric to diesel. The train started to go slower, and the countryside started getting fairly desolate, with lots of sand on one side and mountains on the other side of the train. I was surprised that there was not any farming here since, earlier, we went by a river with a dam. Along the way, it was very foggy. I saw lots of sheep and windmills, even a few deer and antelope but few cattle. At this part of the trip, we went through a lot of tunnels. At one stretch, we were parallel with a river, with lots of ice on it, and a highway. We passed a couple of small towns but had no stops. Later, the mountains were on the other side of the train and sometimes on both sides with lots of snow on them. I even saw a few glaciers.

On the last night, there was oxygen flowing on the train; but so far, I did not have any breathing problems. In the morning, I had two eggs and coffee for breakfast and later another coffee and cookies. During the forty-four-hour trip, a lot of the men were spitting on the floor and smoking in the aisles, which was disgusting.

We reached Lhasa on Wednesday afternoon. I was looking forward to the hotel room. At the station, my guide, Taysee, and driver, You, picked me up and took me to the hotel.

On Thursday morning at breakfast, I met a guy from Holland. He was with a tour group. I also spoke with a couple from Switzerland. The lady said she was working in Shanghai. Later that day, Taysee took me to the inspiring and beautiful Potala Palace and the garden in front of Jokhang Temple. I left ashes at both places without Taysee's knowledge.

On Friday, we went to Norbulingka Park to visit the Sera and Drepung Monasteries and see the monks performing. After arriving, I told Taysee that I was having trouble breathing. Lhasa is 10,800 feet in elevation. So we went back to the hotel. Later, a masseuse came to my room, where I got a wonderful Tibetan massage. Of course, I started feeling better, so I went for dinner at a nearby restaurant where I had yak stew with potatoes and rice on the side. The yak tasted a lot like beef.

On Saturday, I woke at six after a night full of dreams; and at first, I did not know where I was. I seemed to have slept well but was still having breathing problems. Later, Taysee and You took me to the train station to catch my train for Shanghai. On the way to the station, Taysee told me that Tibetans do not like the Chinese rule. She said that Tibet has mineral resources that the Chinese do not have, and she thinks that was one of the reasons they took over.

I boarded the train at around eleven, and the crowd was like a herd of sheep—everyone pushing, shoving, and crowding in line. Some people boarding the train were carrying large packages and other large boxes on their backs. In the crowd, I was next to a Polish couple working in Australia. They were put in separate cabins, she in my cabin and her husband in another. I traded with the man so they could be together.

On the way back, I was with a young Chinese couple. There was no one in the bunk above me. It seemed like my short-term memory had gotten worse during the stay in Lhasa. I found it funny that the Tibetans are required by the Chinese not to say "Lhasa" but "Ha-sa" or something like that. The return trip seemed shorter than going to Lhasa, but the travel time (forty-four hours) was about the same. We went through Xi'an, Zhengzhou, and Nanjing before arriving in Shanghai at about eleven on Monday morning. There was some kind of holiday there, which lasted a couple of days.

I checked into the hotel. During the night, I had two episodes of waking and not being able to breathe. I took an aspirin both times. In the morning, I went down and told the front desk clerk that I needed to see a doctor since I was having trouble breathing. The clerk said the international medical care hospital is a two minutes' walk away.

At the hospital, I was escorted by an English-speaking nurse for check-in. I filled out a simple one-page form and paid in yuan what amounted to about $50. Then another nurse took me to a blood-drawing center, where she put on a face mask but no gloves or hand washing. After the blood draw, I was escorted to another building for an X-ray and then to a very nice waiting room. The nurse said I should wait about an hour for the blood test results. I did not see any other patients, but it was a holiday. After the wait, I was escorted to see the doctor. She was a good-looking young gal, and her office contained a desk and sink but was not too big. She asked me about my symptoms and other medical problems. Then she took my temperature and blood pressure and reviewed the blood tests and X-ray. She said my blood pressure was normal, and she could not find any medical problems. She ended up saying that nothing was wrong with me and that I worry too much.

After spending the morning at the hospital, I took a taxi into the city to a Buddhist area where I left some ashes. I then jumped on a tour bus (double decker) where I got to see most of the city. I got off in a shopping area with pagoda-type buildings. I had a late lunch at McDonald's and then caught a taxi back to the hotel.

My general impression of the day was that everyone seems well off, dressed nicely, and doing a lot of shopping. It was very crowded in the shopping areas perhaps because of the holiday. Smog was very bad. The taxis were all VWs, but there were a lot of Audis, Mercedes, and even a Porsche parked in front of the hotel. There were a few people on the streets asking for money. I have never been in a city with so much horn honking, people walking in front of traffic, cars not obeying red lights, and bikes and motorbikes almost hitting people, including me.

The next morning, I went to Fudan University, where I gave a lecture on actinide chemistry to Dr. Wei's class. Professor Wei is an old friend, and I have known him for more than ten years. I had made several trips to Japan because of a joint project we had had together at IRI, a small research company near Tokyo. During that time, Dr. Wei had even obtained Japanese citizenship. Dr. Wei returned to his homeland about a year ago after an appointment at Fudan University. Later, I dropped a little of Margrit's ashes on campus and the next day returned to Los Angeles.

II

Upon John's return to California, he made a couple of more short trips before the movers came and transported his household belongings to the newly purchased home on Golden Pond in Pendleton, which Margrit loved. On the last night in Simi Valley, John slept in a sleeping bag in the town house's second-floor bedroom. He was awoken at four thirty by a 6.7 earthquake that had its epicenter in Northridge, about ten miles away. He thought the devil himself had come to call. After the shaking stopped, he got dressed, packed his remaining personal items, and headed to Denver in Margrit's car. After spending a few days visiting the kids and family, he continued his drive to South Carolina.

After the furniture arrived and the home arranged, he started his new job in Clemson's Research Park, about ten miles from the main campus. At the university, he started using his middle name, James, instead of his first name, one way to start a new life. At the time, James received many e-mails from family and friends and replied to some of them:

> Hello, Uncle John. Thank you so much for organizing Aunt Margrit's memorial and making it possible for all of us to come. I can only imagine how difficult all this has been for you. I am so glad that I accompanied Mom and Dad to lunch on Mother's Day and had the opportunity to enjoy Aunt Margrit one last time. I have many fond memories of both of you. I will forever remember her smile

and how her eyes would light up with happiness and life when she did smile. Margrit savored life and seemed to always find the good, the joy, and the fun in everything. I wish that I was more like her. I snuck away on the day of the memorial as I was having a very difficult time controlling my emotions. I did not want to embarrass myself or make anyone else uncomfortable. I guess I have too much of my mom's blood; we cry easily. I weep as I write you this note. Anyway, I wanted to let you know that I am thinking of you and that I love you. Margrit's loss will hurt for a long time, but I am comforted by the memory of her smile and the fun that she brought to us all. I feel fortunate to have been her niece and to have had her in my life for so many years. Let's get together the next time you are in Colorado. We can drink Shiraz and toast her memory at the little Italian restaurant in Arvada. I promise I will try not to cry—no guarantee on that.

Much love,
Martha

Dear Martha,

Thank you so much for your kind and dear note. How do you manage not to cry all the time on your difficult job as a nurse? Anyway, I am trying to keep busy. I just returned from a short trip to Canada, and if my visa arrives, I will be off to Iran in a couple of weeks to give an invited conference talk, followed by serving with a humanitarian mission to Afghanistan for ten days.

Love,
Uncle John

Dear John,

I am so sorry to hear about your loss. She was a remarkable lady, and I know there are a lot of your friends, including me, that will miss her very much. Now that you are closer to Florida State University, I hope we can get together more. I was thinking of you earlier this week as I was at Rocky Flats for an advisory committee meeting. They are completing the work on the site to turn it over to stewardship this fall. Many buildings are down, and the rest will be demolished in the next two to four months. There is still a lot of remediation and stabilization going on. The residual activity will be such that even the overseers for the contaminated areas will not be able to stay on site all day. I have been pushing hard that the stewardship have a requirement that DOE review new processes about every ten to twenty years and, if feasible, further clean up the soil so the site can be released for normal use and occupation in a few decades. There are now a number of houses very close to the fences, so the thought of keeping people off the site for several hundred years by stewardship seems completely impractical to me. I am mailing you three reprints of review talks on actinide separations. Hope you find some of them useful.

Take care,

Karl Chopen

Fred,

Thanks for your note and kind words about Margrit. I just got back from attending a mine water conference in Sydney, Nova Scotia. The landing there on Saturday night was very wild, thanks to Hurricane Earl. An earlier flight tried landing but had to go back to Halifax because of the wind and rain. Lots of trees were down in Sydney, but it is a very beautiful place. Wednesday, a Canadian colleague took me around the Cabot Trail and through Cape Breton Highlands National Park. It is a beautiful country, and we saw a mother moose and her baby. Thursday evening, we went over to an island by water taxi for the conference lobster party. There were many old friends there, and I made some new friends from Africa, Australia, Germany, and Sweden. Now back to work at Clemson.

Best wishes,
James

Ala,

I hope you and your family is doing well. Thank you again for your kind words about Margrit's passing. I asked you in past e-mails if you had any plans to attend the African Chemical Congress in Luxor. Do you? I plan to attend and give an invited paper. I will visit Cairo a day or two after the meeting and then go to Algiers. It would be great if you and your whole family could come to Egypt for a few days' holiday. Perhaps we could meet in Tunis before the meeting or in Cairo after the meeting. I wish it was easier to get a Libyan visa at your airport.

Best wishes to you all,
John

Dear John,

We are under siege by the rebels, and the militia has been fighting with them for four days now. Gunfire is everywhere, dead bodies are along the streets, and we are hiding inside the family house in Abu Salim with limited amount of food and water; bullets are flying all over from machine guns in the hands of young teens in the streets. My brothers are with us. So far, we are okay, and I hope in the next few days everything will settle dawn. God bless Libya and the Libyans.

Ala

Dear John,

I hope you all do well during the bad weather in South Carolina. We had a newborn baby girl. She looks like Mary. Mimara and baby are in a good health. We are all well. Please convey my greetings to your family. Last night, we were terrified by NATO bombs on military targets near our family house.

Best regards,
Ala

Dear, dear Ala,

Congratulations on the new addition to your lovely family. It is so great to hear from you and to know you all are surviving the terror of the NATO bombs. I am so sorry that this is happening. I wish I had a private jet so that I could come and take you all to Pendleton. I tried to phone you the other day as well as after the return from my trip, but there was no answer. Anyway, I am so pleased to receive your e-mail. Please be very careful and give your family my love; tell them I miss them and that you all are in my prayers.

Best wishes and love,
John and Uncle John

Dear John,

How are you? We are okay. Kids are still out of school because of the catch-up program for the other students who did not study during wartime. I am back at the Academy of Graduate Studies, but the classes may start after two weeks because of the students who are returning from the front, as well as students who did not want to pay the tuition fees. Now everyone has freedom of speech, and the people are asking for so many things that are impossible to fulfill. I was looking for Abdul's scholarship, still trying to find out the suitable one via the state department. Our politicians are busy with transitional government and so on. No one can give you an affirmative action regarding scholarship for undergraduate studies abroad. Banks restricted the amount of withdrawal; only LD 750 a month are available. Hopefully, it will change soon.

Kind regards to you and family,

Ala

Professor Czermak was to start teaching an environmental actinide chemistry course in the fall but had the spring and summer semesters to get his graduate students' research underway, attend a few conferences, and get more research funding. At the time, he was trying to expand his research group. One of the things he did was to arrange Ying to come and work for him as a postdoc. James was glad to have her in his research group since she was hardworking, extremely intelligent, and full of ideas. She was also very cooperative and pleasant to be around since she had a wonderful personality. She arrived about a month after James had started supervising the research of his three graduate students, Shana Sharp, Jerry Crow, and Chris Brown. When the fall semester started, James got a fourth graduate student, Alex Pushkov, who had received a bachelor's degree in chemistry at Moscow State University and master's in chemistry from the University of Toronto.

At the first meeting with his research group, James brought up the topic of them attending technical conferences. He emphasized that they were good learning events where they could give papers, interact with other researchers, and perhaps make some new friendships. Of course, he said, "There were limitations of time and money."

He went on to say, "I have been invited, all expenses paid by the Egyptian Atomic Energy Authority, to give the plenary lecture about our environmental nuclear studies next month. I would like one of you to participate. I suggest we put your names in a hat and see who gets to accompany me. For the next meeting, the person going this time would not be permitted to participate in that drawing. Does this seem fair?" Everyone agreed.

Then the professor added, "I am sorry, but next week, I head to Iran and Afghanistan. In Iran, I will attend a conference at their expense, followed by going on a humanitarian mission in Afghanistan for the government. I will return in about two weeks but will try and stay in touch via e-mail. I assume you all will continue to work hard on your coursework and do some reading on your planned research projects."

III

A letter to Tim from James was as follows:

I left Kabul yesterday morning at nine and got back home last night at six via London and Atlanta. The humanitarian mission to Afghanistan was very interesting (thanks for arranging the funding) as well as the three-day water conference at the University of Shahrood, about a six-hour bus ride north of Tehran and surrounded by beautiful mountains on three sides. The Iranian people were so wonderful and kind and want better relations with the USA. I sent the attached letter to our president on the matter:

Dear President Obama,

Two weeks ago, I attended an international conference on water resources at Shahrood Technical University, Iran. Shahrood is north of Tehran (six hours by bus) and has a population of about three hundred thousand. There were over three hundred participants at the meeting but only five foreign guests out of an expected thirty, two from India, one each from Brazil and Spain, and me. The mayor and university president hosted a dinner for the foreign guests the first night, and we were treated like celebrities. I urged the mayor to invite you to his beautiful and hospitable city. Three dear students from the University of Shahrood gave me a picture and a card that they had signed, and on the card, they wrote a Shakespeare quote. "This life is too short even to love ... I don't know how people find time to hate." I spent the last day of my trip in Tehran with two graduate students from the University of Tehran who showed me around the city, including the university, major museums, and parks.

The Iranian people I met were all very kind and helpful, and some of them expressed concern that most Americans thought badly of them. I returned from the trip knowing that we urgently need to normalize relations between our countries. Let them have their peaceful nuclear program as long as they allow IAEA safeguards. Inform the seventy-five million Iranian people that we trust their leaders' words that their nuclear program is for peaceful purposes only. Similarly, South Africa clandestinely built several nuclear weapons but gave them up once apartheid was over.

Sincerely,
Prof. John James Czermak, Clemson University

Tim, per your request, I have mailed to you a copy of my diary writings about my trip to Afghanistan. I assume the information above on Iran is sufficient. For your information, next Saturday, I will board a plane to London and then fly to Vishakhapatnam via Bangalore and Hyderabad. I will be attending a nuclear conference there for five days, and then I go to Casablanca via London. If my visa arrives, I will visit my god family for a few days in Tripoli. Otherwise, I plan to visit Marrakech and Tangier and then fly to Tombouctou via Bamako. There, I plan to join an excursion by camel caravan to visit a Tuareg camp on the dunes. (I hope I can stay on a camel for the two-hour journey.) They tell me it is too dangerous to go farther out into the desert because of al-Qaeda. If all works out, I will also fly to Mopti and sail on the Niger River and then onto Djenné and Ségou for short visits. I can send you a copy of my diary entries if you wish. I hope your work goes well in Denver. Let me know if you want to meet with me before I head back to South Carolina.

Best wishes,
James

The following was a copy of James's diary that he sent to Tim concerning his trip to Afghanistan:

A few days before our departure on a Global Exchange-sponsored trip to Afghanistan, I received an e-mail from Naib, director of Afghans4Tomorrow (A4T) and our host in Kabul. The e-mail described the car bombing that had just occurred at the Safi Landmark hotel where five police and civilians were killed and more than five injured. Naib wrote that the A4T guesthouse and his staff were fine, that the streets were closed in the area of the bombing, and that things were generally very quiet now. He advised us not to worry as attacks happen daily in Afghanistan, and this is a random thing. Guesthouse bombings are rare, but hotels and police station bombings are common.

On Saturday, I arrived at the Atlanta Airport for the fourteen-hour Delta Air Lines flight to Dubai. I met George from San Diego in the airport, who is also a member of our humanitarian group; he is a writer/teacher and hopes to write a story on Afghanistan from a new angle. George, a widower, taught journalism at San Diego State University and now writes periodically for newspapers.

We left Atlanta in a fully loaded Boeing 777. I had a window seat, and next to me was a Filipino who was going back home; he had flown from Miami and works on a cruise ship in the Caribbean. The fellow in the aisle seat was from Sri Lanka, a pilot who spent two weeks in the United States getting his FAA approval.

In Dubai, George and I met five other members of our group: Terry, who lives in San Francisco, thirty-six years old, single, served in the Peace Corps in Albania and Guinea, and now works in marketing; Dan, who lives in Seattle, thirty-two years old, single, has a BA in biology and a master's in environmental engineering, grows and sells food, and works for the forest service; Ada, who lives in San Francisco and does nonviolent political group work and poetry; Brenda, who lives in San Francisco, thirty years old, single, and studies international law; and Betty, who is twenty-five years old and single.

Dubai Airport is very nice with an English pub, McDonald's (I had a Big Mac), Dunkin' Donuts, spa, and lots of duty-free shops. The flight to Kabul was 2½ hours late in leaving since two of their pilots got hurt in the hotel attack on Friday. On our flight to Kabul, we went over some beautiful snowcapped mountain ranges.

In Kabul, we were met at the airport by Naib. The airport is not too big, and immigration and customs were easy. Outside the airport were several money changers and lots of guys with carts wanting to help us with our luggage. Our group was transported to the A4T guesthouse by a van driven by Abdil, but I rode in a car with Dan, Mohammed (one of our hosts), and Mike (who lives in Chicago, twenty-eight years old, studied BS political science, now in training in Pasadena to become a pastor, and desires to run for public office; he spent three months in Palestine and joined the marines right before 9/11 and served in Iraq and Afghanistan). Mike thinks I look like Richard Holbrooke, who played a key negotiation role in Yugoslavia during their war and was involved in Afghan problems until his death in early 2011.

We drove to the guesthouse over Kabul's muddy roads. In driving through the city, there were lots of people and traffic on the road and much reconstruction and new buildings going up. There were also many street vendors, especially young boys, who approached cars at intersections, trying to sell about anything under the sun. Kabul is surrounded by beautiful snowcapped mountains, and there was a lot of smog over the city and its five million inhabitants.

Upon arrival at the guesthouse, we met the manager, Ali; the financial manager, Elys; and one of two guards, Naceb. We also met the remaining members of our group, who consisted of the following: David, who lives in Kansas, forty-six years old, works for a nonprofit agency, single, and has a master's from Williams College; Mary, who lives in Dallas and is a lawyer/economist; and Ahned, forty years old, who is with the UN and a university lecturer.

The three-story A4T guesthouse is near a high school. When I and the others entered the house, we had to take our muddy shoes off in the basement entryway and put on some slippers. The basement and first floor are laid out about the same way. We are all staying on the first floor, which has four bedrooms with three single beds in each room and one bathroom with an open shower. (There was low flow of water in the shower that was not always warm.) I shared a bedroom with George. In the main room, there is a large table as well as a television, bookcases, and pictures on the walls.

During our first night at the guesthouse, we had the first of our nightly meetings to discuss the day's events and to tell everyone more about ourselves. Mary was nominated by me to be the victim in "Murder at the Kabul Guesthouse," a short story I considered writing. There are several lawyers on the trip, and she is also one—maybe I should be the victim of a nasty kidnapping. However, we are a friendly group, and we all got along well.

Our bedrooms are heated by wood stoves, and probably all the wood being burned along with all the cars made for the air pollution. I had slept well, only getting up once to use the bathroom. In the morning, the group was talking about the 2:00 a.m. earthquake. Apparently, everyone felt the tremor but me. I told them that we need not worry about an earthquake or a bomber but more about carbon monoxide poisoning during the night with all the wood burning in the house. There are no fire detectors, let alone carbon monoxide detectors, and every once and a while, a puff of smoke comes out of our stove in the bedroom.

A4T was founded in 1988. It is a nonprofit, nonpolitical group to assist students and disabled people mainly with agricultural waste and environment projects, such as how to plant trees. By the way, Kabul used to have lots of big trees lining the streets, but Russian soldiers cut them down because snipers used to hide there.

The waste project involves making briquettes for burning in stoves. Wastepaper, tree leaves, weeds, and other combustible waste materials are collected, mixed with water, and pressed together. Toilet paper is not flushed down the toilet but collected in wastebaskets and used in the briquettes. They have plastic bottle recycling, but most household waste is not recycled but collected and landfilled. The sewage goes to a septic tank that is periodically pumped out and landfilled; the overflow water goes directly into the river running through Kabul. Some people, especially in the south, have "kitchen gardens," and this program is being extended to northern Afghanistan. Some animal and human wastes are used for fertilizers. There is a lot of good land to cultivate, but it is not used.

Afghanistan has a population of about thirty-five million, and our host told us the country could easily handle one hundred million since other provinces are sparsely populated. The country needs dams to capture water going to Iran and Pakistan and hydropower for electricity. The country suffered a 33 percent death rate of children in their first year, and it needs better medical care, nutrition, and water. We were informed that sixty thousand people died in the recent civil war, worst of the past thirty years of wars, and that the people need jobs and for the U.S. military to get out.

On Tuesday, we visited the A4T Children's School. They accept only girl students, especially ones that could not, for some reason, get into school when they were of the right age. For example, in the first-grade class, we saw girls of all ages. They were just wonderful, introducing themselves one at a time. They typically said, "In the name of Allah, I am . . . My brother's name is . . . My sister's name is . . . My parents' names are . . ." So, so cute. We went to several other classes and then joined them all outside for recess and ball playing. Finally, we saw how they made the briquetting equipment (all constructed there) and briquettes. One of the older girls explained their methods of selling the briquettes.

Then we went to see the leader of the National Independence Peace and Reconciliation Commission Organization. He talked about them getting 3,500 Taliban to come back peacefully from Pakistan. He said the International Security of Pakistan (ISI) is making all the trouble; Pakistan wants to control Afghanistan and is causing all the problems. They would like to see the United States take out targets that the Afghans find and not the targets the ISI finds.

After lunch (I had pizza), a woman parliamentarian came to talk to us at the guesthouse. Mirsh was an educator in the past and ran as an independent candidate. She was voted Afghan Woman of the Year. In parliament, there are 228 parliamentarians with 68 women. She had brought her twelve-year old son and lovable handicapped six-year-old daughter, who went around the table and hugged everyone.

On Thursday, we met the program director for the Partnership for the Education of Children in Afghanistan over breakfast. The organization was founded in 2003 and supports girls' schools until eighth grade. They also support a boys' high school in Khost (in southeast Afghanistan near Pakistan) as well as a boys' primary school.

Then we visited Aschiana (meaning "street children") and met the manager of Afghanistan's Children—A New Approach.

After lunch, in front of a local restaurant, we watched some kids that had a gasoline fire going in a big tray, and then one of the youngsters kicked the tray and made the flames go higher, and then another kicked it over and almost caught one guy on fire. They put out the fire only to have another kid light a gallon plastic bottle with a little gasoline in it, and then he stepped on the bottle, shooting a flame out at two of the other eight boys.

After the fire show, we boarded the bus for a short visit at the deaf school. The deaf kids were of all ages and went to three classes a day, depending on their level of advancement on different subjects. When they graduate, most will know how to read and communicate in sign language. A lot of them were good artists, and I took some pictures of their artwork.

The last meeting of the day was with Ms. Senlika, who founded the All Afghan Women Union about twenty years ago.

In 1978, she was sent to jail for her women activism. She said she was tortured in jail, and the conditions were very bad.

Friday was a long day but very enjoyable. Omar met us at breakfast. He is part of A4T and works on the Afghanistan Higher Education Project. Omar also works with another university but said they are just starting an environmental program at Kabul University, where they could use my assistance. We then took a 40 km trip to a mountain village north of Kabul called Istalif. On the way, beautiful mountains were off to our left. After we pulled off the main highway, the road was dirt and rough. We went a long way on a winding road up toward the mountains to the village, and the road kept getting narrower, rougher, and muddier. At times, there were rock walls very near and on both sides of the bus. At the village on top of the mountain was a cemetery where I deposited a little of Margrit's ashes. We went into the village for some shopping and then returned by bus to the main road.

Then we went to an exhibition in a horse stadium. We saw some Turkish soldiers there along with an American soldier in charge of security. There was tight security, and we were checked twice. The performance in the stadium involved one horse rider trying to keep a dead sheep on his horse from the other horse riders, and the horsemen were beating their horses brutally to get at the horseman carrying the sheep corpse. This brutal horse game is a traditional sport in Afghanistan. There were children there selling various things such as gum, boiled and dyed eggs, soda, and others. They were very aggressive in their selling. I finally bought some packs of gum and started handing them out, but more boys joined us (eight to fourteen years), and some of them started grabbing the gum, so I started throwing the packs in different directions and almost caused a riot.

Our group then went into the city, stopping about halfway at outdoor toilets next to the highway and a large cemetery. After our arrival in the city, we went to the hill overlooking Kabul near where there is a large blimp that is remotely operated with security cameras aboard. The Nader Shah Tomb is there as well as lots of people, some of whom were flying kites, an old Afghan tradition. One thing they do is cut the kite string, and others try to catch the kite. I put more of Margrit's ashes near a large cemetery on the hill.

Finally, we went shopping in the city; and again, a gang of street kids wanted to sell us a variety of items. I bought a city map and two purses. There, I started handing out $1 bills and almost caused another riot. I recalled that during one of my trips to Bangladesh, I had mistakenly done the same thing with a group of youngsters.

The following day, we had breakfast with the head of children's education in Afghanistan. She came here five years ago from New Delhi as a volunteer for A4T. Last June, she became the expedition director of A4T. Her husband is a physician in Minnesota. At the A4T school, they need electricity and water. They do have clinics with female doctors and nurses to help the students.

Then we visited the Foundation of Sustainable Technologies. Their main project is briquetting education and teaching students how to become teachers. Management and leadership skills are included in the curriculum. For graduates, it takes $200 to get a briquetting operation set up, and they can make $200–$300 per month. This is cheaper than buying wood for heating and cooking. The project is 1½ years old, and funding for the school comes from the University of Massachusetts and USAID. Of course, the school has security guards and lots of fences surrounding it.

We were told that there used to be wineries in Kabul before the Taliban. Thirty years of war has destroyed so many infrastructures, including agriculture and education, and 60 percent of the population is depressed or has trauma. Of course, there is malnutrition and lack of medical care, and survival is only by strong extended family and communal support. There are about four psychologists in the country, so depression and trauma go untreated for most of the population. This is a vital need for international assistance. We were also told that bullying of kids is not that extensive; the elder brothers look after their younger siblings. Corruption is as big as it is in the USA and is more extensive at the higher levels of government, especially at the minister level. People are not paid enough, including the army.

Future A4T projects may be related to employment, bike repair, tailoring, wiring, plumbing, and training. Also, agriculture needs attention. The Afghans we spoke with are concerned about American occupation. Although the United States cannot afford to stay, $5 billion per week for development is needed. Most of the money goes for military action, but only 10 percent goes for development. However, warring and tribal factions could cause trouble if the U.S. military left.

Then we went to Kabul University to meet with a professor who told us about the university. Then we met with the director of a human rights group. After lunch, we went to Meg's house, who is managing director of Micro Finance Institute. She is Canadian and served in twenty other countries, Haiti being the worst as they are very violent people, she said. She has been in Kabul for ten months and likes it. She has an office in another part of the city and goes there by taxi.

On Sunday, we went to the Olympic stadium to see the women's basketball team practice; I told my colleagues that I was disappointed that the ladies in the group did not challenge the girls to a game. Then we went through a high-security area, having to walk two blocks down a street with high concrete walls on both sides with lots of razor wire on top, to the entrances of embassies, government houses, and so on with armed guards at each entrance. The purpose of the visit was to go to a high school to join a Women's Day celebration. The vice president came and made one of the speeches. There was also a craft fair next door. A ten-year-old boy came up to us who spoke perfect English. He said they had once lived in Washington DC; his mom worked, and his dad stayed home all the time because he had lost a leg in a land mine blast.

After leaving the fair, we went to lunch and then to the environmental office. Afterward, we returned to our bus and had to wait about ten minutes since all the government workers were leaving in their buses at 3:00 p.m. They left the high-security area at high speed, one bus after another. Then the police let us go, and we were near the rear of the pack; it was like a demolition derby, with all the cars and buses racing down the road until we finally ran into stopped traffic. We nearly had an accident, although I have not seen any accidents yet. Finally, we went to the Women's Maternity Hospital. The bus drove through a long passageway with people on both sides, sitting on benches, waiting for their loved ones in the hospital.

On Monday, our first visit was to the Kabul Museum, followed by looking over a destroyed mansion next door. There was another partially destroyed mansion a couple of blocks away. This is the second day of beautiful weather, but there is still much air pollution east of town. Then we went to the largest mosque in the city, which is fairly new and has a small university; it is very impressive. We had our lunch at the Rose Restaurant, which is next to KFC (Kabul Fried Chicken). We had kebab, rice, vegetable soup, and the usual bread. After lunch, we stopped at the post office. Then we went to the Women's Peace Garden, and the men had to stay outside (taking pictures and so on). We also went to the Kabul Golf Course (nine holes), where I played only the first couple of holes since the land is sandy, rocky, and full of weeds. Last, we visited the reservoir above the golf course.

Tuesday was our last full day where we visited the office of the Conservation Society and found out about their work. We also visited an animal shelter run by an American lady. The shelter has numerous animals, including a couple of horses, and is located on a citrus farm.

After departing Kabul, I stayed a few nights at the Al Jawhara Gardens Hotel in Dubai and took a city tour. I saw the man-made island, indoor ski area, and much more. I also left some ashes at the base of the world's tallest building, with many onlookers wondering what I was doing. I enjoyed walking around Dubai, which is so clean and modern, with no worries about security or being kidnapped, being free to enjoy the evening and see all the lights of modern businesses and so on. What a contrast to Kabul, where we were confined to our guesthouse.

At the last minute, I arranged a flight to Muscat, Oman, for a quick visit. At the Muscat Airport, I negotiated a city tour with a cabdriver and saw many beautiful buildings along the area where the Persian Gulf meets the Arabian Sea. I left some of Margrit's ashes at a beautiful mosque overlooking the sea. The next day, I returned to Atlanta via Dubai, a long Delta Air Lines flight.

The following were a few e-mails James received after his return from Afghanistan:

> Dear traveling companions,
>
> So hey, you all. I have been thinking a lot about our time together in Kabul. What an experience. I felt so lucky to have gotten to meet you all, to have such a thoughtful, interesting, well-informed, diverse group of people to share this exploration and adventure with. I want to send you all the wishes for wisdom and love and peace, which are, in our better moments, our focus in this season in which we look for light in the darkness, the birth of something new and miraculous. And God knows there's a lot of darkness. But I recently read an interview in the *Sun* magazine—can't remember the fine interviewee who said that optimism is a radical act. I think that's a great thing to focus on at the moment.
>
> I miss you all and think of the special things I learned and shared with you. I just got a book

that was mentioned in one of the e-mails, *War Is a Lie*. It is unbelievably good and upsetting and everything I suspected I knew and believed, but the facts are outlined. Sometimes I'm a little short on facts and long on intuition and passion, so I always appreciate a good fact-based outline. I have some new books to read on Afghanistan, but if you all have any to recommend, let me know. I'm working on a book of poetry about the trip and related issues, which I hope to use in more fund-raising (for A4T) slideshows in the new year. So blessings to you all.

Love,
Mary

Dear Dr. Czermak,

I was really thrilled to receive your e-mail. As I told you before, I like your writing. I think your mind is full of sentences about different topics. I admire you, my friend. The political situation in Iran has been very disturbed since the last presidential election about one year ago. You may know that most of the people were really mad at the government after the election, and they came into streets to show that they didn't accept the results, and they believed that, me included, some other things happened. Ahmadinejad (oh god, how much I hate him!) gave a speech after announcing the results on TV, and that made people angrier. After that, Khamenei, the leader (I can't stand him too), congratulated him and then on the next Friday (Friday prayer) stated that there was no cheating in the election and that no one had the right to object and disagree with the government. The next Saturday (after the leader's speech) was one the worst days because Neda was killed that day. She became a symbol of Iranian protesters, although there were hundreds of people who were killed or sent to jail.

Sometimes I think our leader and others are Muslims, and they strongly believe in heaven and hell. How could they do this to the innocent people? It's a sham. I hate politics. It was really bad those days. We watched BBC Persia and VOA, and we saw how people were hit and killed by cruel officers. We cried and grieved and hoped authorities in another side of the world would help us, but nothing happened. The government tried to keep people in a very restricted situation. Our cell phones were not working. Most of the Internet sites were filtered, especially Facebook and YouTube. We could not check our e-mails even. They sent some signals to prevent Iranians to watch news from foreign channels. Oh, I become upset when I remember those days. The only thing we could do was shout a phrase on the roofs from 10:00 till 10:30 p.m. that represents our religion, "God is great" (Allahu Akbar).

Let's talk about a pleasant subject. It's summer now; however, it's not lovely. As I told you before, I live in Shiraz, and I teach at universities in Būshehr. Both are in south of Iran. The weather in Būshehr is really hot because of the Persian Gulf. Shiraz is not as hot as the other one in summers, although it's somehow sunny and hot during days. As much as I remember, summers were not fun, except when we took a long trip around Iran till summer would be over. In answering your question, I must say yes, it's summer, a really hot one.

I love my country, but sometimes I wish I lived in another country with more freedom like some of the Arabian countries like Dubai. Don't worry, my friend. The government spy on those who are involved in politics and political oppositions. I haven't taken part in anything political yet because I hate it. Most Tehran residents were involved in demonstrations against the government.

I want to apologize for my mistake in the previous e-mail. The first semester begins on September 20 (Mehr month) and the second one on February 10 (Bahman month). I sent you a clip about days of protest against the election. I hope I could clarify that situation.

Best wishes,
Kadi

Dear Professor,

I received your e-mail a couple of days ago. Economic situation in Iran is about to change these days. Everyone talks about inflation in the country because of boycott of other countries. Almost all Iranians are sure that anything is going to be more expensive soon. I am so worried about poor people. I don't know what they are going to do. This week was the second week of my classes at the university. I went to Būshehr, and my classes started. Unfortunately, my Internet connection there had some problems, and I couldn't continue my plans well. I mean, I couldn't continue searching scholarships. This problem made me so disappointed because I didn't want to lose time. With this political situation in the world, I may not be able to go to another country to pursue my studies. That makes me disappointed. I am not hopeful and happy these days. I feel blue.

Kadi

IV

The following was a copy of James's diary regarding the Egyptian trip that he mailed to Tim:

My student Jerry Crow and I left Atlanta for Paris on Thursday night. The eight-hour flight went well, but as usual, I slept only about two hours. In Paris, we waited a couple of hours to board the plane for Egypt. Then we were told to change planes because of mechanical problems. We went from terminal 1 to terminal 3 by bus and found out we had to go back to terminal 1 to get our tickets changed at the Air France ticket counter. We went back to find their office closed. We returned to the EgyptAir office at terminal 3 and got them to give us boarding passes to Luxor. We finally departed Paris and got to Cairo a little before our flight to Luxor was to leave.

We landed in Luxor on Saturday morning. At the airport, we met a couple of conference attendees, one from Libya and two from Japan. Later, the conference bus came and collected us and several others. On the bus, I had a nice conversation with a lady from Brazil who was accompanied by her husband, also a chemist, and their two children.

At the hotel and after a long check-in process, Jerry and I went to our rooms. We had breakfast before the opening of the conference. After that, we returned to our rooms for a couple of hours of sleep. After our naps and lunch, we went to the conference room, where I gave my lecture. There were about thirty people in attendance out of about three hundred attendees at the conference. That night, we experienced a wonderful sunset over the Nile.

On Sunday morning, we had breakfast with Nati (an old friend of mine) and her roommate and then walked around the city and visited the Palace of Luxor. We then went for a visit to the Valley of the Kings. Our driver took us there in about thirty minutes. We walked around the tombs, and in Ramses V's tomb, I started to deposit some of Margrit's ashes, but the guard came over and asked what I was doing. I did not reply but had already released a little of the ashes. We then went to another tomb to complete my goal of depositing the ashes. The mountain area around the Valley of the Kings looks more like the surface of the moon. There is also a Valley of the Queens, but I thought Margrit would be much happier with the kings.

On Sunday night, there was another beautiful sunset over the Nile, with boats going up and down the river. After the sunset, we heard the calling for prayer from a couple of mosques. The next morning, we walked up to Luxor Palace, and then I had a TV interview about our research. In the evening, we watched a display of lights and narrative history of Karnak Temple, which was spectacular, just like in the James Bond movie. We returned to the hotel for dinner. After dinner, there were a great singer and lots of old folks dancing. An English lady asked me for the last dance of the night.

On Tuesday afternoon, we left Luxor for Cairo. From the hotel, we took a shuttle bus full of conference folks, including a couple with a baby, and everyone had lots of luggage. On the way, the driver got a call to return for more passengers. We went back to the hotel to find four others with lots of luggage, wanting to join our fully loaded van. They tried to get one guy and his luggage on but to no avail. This was an example of how the whole conference went—fairly unorganized, no refreshments except coffee and tea, no lunch, and all the sessions containing a vast mix of papers instead of them being in similar fields. Jerry seemed to have enjoyed every minute of our trip, even though we had not attended very many lectures.

In Cairo, Jerry left me and boarded a plane for Atlanta via Paris. During my first day in Cairo, Hesham took me to the Pyramids. (Hesham is an old friend of mine that I continue to see at conferences.) Just as we were entering the area, a guy in the street stopped us and convinced Hesham that he had to accompany us to the horse carriage—that was the only way up the hill to the Pyramids. The guy jumped in and took us to a car parking area where we got into a horse carriage. Then he asked Hesham for some money. After some arguing over the money, we proceeded up the hill about a block by horse carriage to find a large parking lot full of cars where we should have gone in the first place. We got off after the guy wanted more money. I knew it was a scam from the beginning. We walked over to the largest pyramid, where I left some ashes.

After walking around and taking pictures, we headed back to Hesham's flat. On the way, we traveled over a bridge and saw below several political rallies taking place. Nearby were about a hundred policemen ready to break up any demonstrations. Later, we found out on the news that several people were hurt in the demonstrations and in the fighting between different political groups. (This event and others eventually lead to the downing of Mubarak's government.)

That evening, I had some discussions with Hesham's daughter, Sue. She is working for UNIDO, trying to eliminate hazardous chemicals in Egypt, and had just returned from London, visiting her brother who works as a chef for Harold's. Hesham and his daughter will join Iva (Hesham's wife) in Norway on Monday for a family wedding.

We spent the next morning at the offices of Hesham's new business partner, who is working on a feldspar mine in Sudan. They are trying to get a mining company under contract to excavate the ore so they can sell it to a chemical company. The ore is 98 percent calcium fluoride, but they want us to perform some beneficiation studies on lower-grade ores to remove impurities. Afterward, we walked along the Nile and ate at an

Italian restaurant on the island. At lunch, one of the waiters at the restaurant looked thirteen years old (he told us he was eighteen) and just like a young President Obama. Hesham and I joked that the Secret Service could use him as a decoy.

I asked Hesham what he had to do next, and he said only wait to hear from the mining company. I said the only thing that both of us need to do is to take our next breath. Hesham has a wonderful loud laugh, and most of the time, he grabs your arm or hand with his hand as he laughs. Hesham's father was a landlord, renting out land north of Cairo to farmers. His father's real love was archeology, and he had many old relics, even a mummy. Two of Hesham's elder brothers died, as well as his parents, and now there are only six of them left.

Cairo is a very dirty city, and there is rubble, paper, plastic, bottles, cans, and other trash everywhere. Most sidewalks are blocked by parked cars and rubble, so people have to walk in the streets. There are also lots of air pollution, dust, and noise. However, the weather in Cairo was very pleasant. Later, back at the Cairo hotel, I thought that I could not manage to drive here since it is so chaotic. When I spent two weeks working as an IAEA consultant several years ago at their Nuclear Research Center, about an hour's drive outside Cairo, the van driver would sometimes drive down the sidewalk in Cairo to get around traffic.

On Friday, I woke at four. Hesham arrived shortly thereafter and took me to the Cairo Airport to catch my early morning flight to Paris. There had been a snowstorm the night before in Paris. I went from sunny 70°F weather to freezing snow. In Paris, I had to change terminals, from terminal 2E to 2F, and was worried I would miss my flight. But I got to the gate on time for the start of boarding. It was a two-hour flight. We flew over Barcelona, Spain, and I took pictures of snow-covered mountains. Then over the island of Corsica, the air turbulence was quite bad. Finally, we descended through three layers of picturesque clouds into Algiers.

At the Algiers Airport, a guy at the terminal kept nagging me if I needed a taxi or money exchange. Finally, I said no in several languages, and the guy left me alone. I found the Hilton Hotel booth and got a free shuttle ride to the hotel. After checking into the hotel, I had a sandwich in the bar area and a beer for 100 dinar, about $1.40. There was a cardiology conference going on, and two gals who were handing out bags gave me one and welcomed me with a kiss on both cheeks. She thought I was there for the conference. It appeared like the cardiology conference had only French and Arabs attending.

Saturday was cloudy with a little rain, so I took a car tour of the city for about two hours. The relatively quiet, clean, and beautiful city with green grass everywhere and modern painted buildings overlooking the Mediterranean Sea is a strong contrast to the shabby old buildings and barren, sandy surroundings of Cairo. There was no rubble in the streets as in Cairo and Luxor, and traffic was very orderly; everyone was staying in their own lanes, and even the drivers were courteous, maybe because there were lots of police everywhere. After the tour, I explored the beautiful church of Notre Dame on a hillside overlooking the harbor. I placed a little of Margrit's ashes there. The next day, I returned to Atlanta via Paris.

During James's travels, he had been preparing lectures for his actinide chemistry course for the fall semester as well as making proposals to the DOE, EPA, and IAEA for funding research projects. Tim had promised to find some research funds that would be part of a CIA mission. While on campus, James planned to continue having periodic meetings with his students to review their research. Shana, Jerry, and Chris were also taking a couple of classes and were financially supported by the department. Ying was serving as a laboratory assistant for her paycheck, Jerry had started his research on a uranium removal from drinking water, and Chris was examining methods to remove arsenic from drinking water.

James's first research grant came from the EPA to support Chris's research. At the first project meeting with Chris, James stated that arsenic poisoning was most prevalent in villages in South Asia, particularly Bangladesh and eastern India in the Ganges Delta. Traditional village life and farming in these areas were governed by the seasons (monsoons) and old agricultural practices. The social fabric was held together through strong family ties and religion. Houses were made of clay, locally produced bricks, and corrugated tin and may be arranged in a family-courtyard fashion. In most villages, no electricity was available. Extended families lived in proximity, often with half a dozen or more people in each house. Furnishings were typically sparse—wooden beds, floor mats, and clay stoves. People tended to live outdoors most of the year. Water was usually supplied by a hand pump at the center of the courtyard or close by, but in some cases, it was taken from local ponds, of which there were many. Sanitation practices varied widely, depending on the availability and effectiveness of public health efforts. This environment made for easy transmission of waterborne illnesses.

James explained to Chris, "Our approach has to be some process that is simple and inexpensive and hopefully uses materials available in these villages. I suggest that you start with using iron oxides since arsenic is known to adsorb on their surfaces. The water would first have to be made slightly basic, and this can perhaps be done using waste concrete ground to a fine powder. The iron oxide could just be rust from discarded iron. After the arsenic is removed, the water would have to be neutralized with perhaps lemon juice, filtered with sand, and some type of bacterial treatment method used such as boiling.

"Anyway, these are my initial thoughts, so map out some experiments you want to perform after you study the literature on arsenic separation methods. We can have another meeting after these tasks are completed. By the way, there is a three-day meeting on drinking water methods in Washington DC next month. I would like you to attend. I think it would be very useful, and there are funds in the grant for your expenses."

James had just returned from a Thursday afternoon chemistry seminar when he received a call from a Mr. Johnson in the U.S. Department of Homeland Security. Mr. Johnson stated that James had been recommended to him as one of the world's leading nuclear sleuths. He wanted to know if James was interested in coming to Boston for a few days of consulting to assist in a dirty bomb threat to the city. Mr. Johnson stated that they had received intelligence reports alleging that two Iraqis had smuggled dirty bomb material into the country from Canada and were heading to Boston. James told Mr. Johnson that he would be pleased to do what he could for his country.

James never had trouble accepting these types of government assignments when it would give him a chance to visit relatives, friends, or new places. He was also concerned about his younger daughter, who was now attending Boston University and residing in Waltham, a suburb of Boston. In fact, James had discussed the threat by phone with his daughter and advised her of appropriate measures.

Early the next morning, James left Pendleton for the two-hour drive to the Atlanta Airport. He had left behind very mild weather in South Carolina and was advised to dress warmly for Boston since there was a forecast of a big snowstorm on Saturday afternoon. As the plane started its descent into Boston, James could see previous snow on the ground through the partly sunny sky.

He was met at the airport by Mr. Johnson, who promptly took him to the state emergency center. The two joined a small group of nuclear and radiological experts in a secure conference room. They were asked to review an emergency plan and how to respond to the dirty bomb threat. The usual scenarios were discussed, mainly dealing with detonation of nuclear material in a strategic location to contaminate as much area and people as possible. It was James who brought up the possibility of terrorists just walking into the front entrances of airports, hospitals, public buildings, or schools and casually dropping a small amount of radioactive material on the floor, letting the building employees and public be the vectors to spread it around. For example, this could cause all the major hospitals in Boston to be evacuated and not usable for some time. With the approaching snowstorm, this would add to the problems of a nuclear incident.

After visiting his daughter and returning from Boston, James had the idea of writing his diary from the viewpoint of Ashley, his new name for Margrit's ashes. Most of the narratives would only be for Tim to read, but others not related to any CIA trips would be for family and friends. The new diary, titled "Ashley's Adventures," started as follows:

Hello, I am Ashley. I once was part of Margrit Czermak, whose soul and spirit are now in heaven in her new heavenly body. I was mainly her bone structure, and most of the other matter in her human body has already been distributed around the world in the form of water vapor, carbon dioxide, and other gases. Margrit's desire was to have me spread around all the places she lived and loved as well as some of the places she always wanted to visit but ran out of human time. Margrit's husband, James, a Clemson University professor of environmental engineering and science, was kind enough to take me to numerous places around the world and leave some of me at these wonderful locations to enjoy the view and goings-on. Parts of me are enjoying most of these places very much, but there were times I almost got the professor in trouble with guards and police since I could have been easily mistaken for anthrax powder, radioactive material, or some other deadly substance. I guess I really am a deadly material. Other times, I embarrassed him when I decided to go with the wind and ended up in the faces of some folks nearby. Some specific moments are described in the following pages. Please keep in mind that, in this literary masterpiece, I cannot see, hear, eat, walk, or talk, but the writing may suggest that I am a real, living person. Anyway, enjoy my ashy adventures.

V

About the time when newspaper headlines around the world were describing the exposure of Dr. Khan, father of the Pakistan nuclear program, exporting nuclear technology to Iran, Libya, and North Korea, James received an e-mail from Dave Phillips, head of the IAEA Seibersdorf's Safeguards Analytical Laboratory. Dave and James's friendship started when James was working for the IAEA. Dave's e-mail offered James a part-time consultancy to advise on the improvement of an analytical method used to detect uranium and plutonium in safeguards inspectors' samples from various nuclear facilities around the world. Dave said the assignment would entail three one-week trips to the laboratory.

James agreed to take the assignment and planned on using the three trips to Europe to visit some friends and relatives in Austria, Germany, and Switzerland. He also hoped to accept some speaking engagements from university colleagues in Romania and some countries arising out of the former Yugoslavia.

That evening, James reread the following article:

Seibersdorf Laboratory is just outside the village of Seibersdorf, about an hour southeast of Vienna, among beautiful rolling hills and tidy farms. There are fences around the laboratory that are topped with barbed wire, and the guard at the gate carefully lets only cleared employees and visitors into the world's top laboratory for nuclear sleuths. The laboratory, part of the IAEA, is an arm of the United Nations that helps monitor the nuclear ambitions of 145 nations. Its mission is to analyze clues of chemistry and physics to verify that states are meeting their peaceful atomic pledges and not secretly making deadly weapons.

Skeptics note that Iran, Iraq, and North Korea have embarked on secret arms programs under the nose of the agency's teams. But agency supporters say that, of late, investigators have gained major powers. They can now examine tiny particles invisible to the eye. It is a world of precision focused on wisps of evidence that inspectors have gathered from nuclear sites. The Clean Laboratory analyzes up to two thousand samples of nuclear materials and five hundred environmental samples a year. Its ultrasensitive machines can obtain vital information from particles one-hundredth the width of a human hair.

The inspectors run the swipes across surfaces where dust or other telltale particles may collect, like the corners or ventilation ducts of a nuclear plant. Then the inspector double-bags each swipe to make sure they remain uncontaminated. Swipes being analyzed are given unique identifiers.

The Clean Lab has some of the world's most advanced machines for disclosing the signatures of atomic materials. A signature may arise from a special mix of isotopes, atoms of the same element whose nuclei bear different numbers of neutrons. Detecting such nuances can shed light on a sample's history. And by matching distinctive samples, much as a detective matches up fingerprints, inspectors gain insights into the places they have originated.

Only thirty-eight nations have a nuclear agreement in force, and just about half of those have significant nuclear programs. Even so, Libya—long an outcast among nations—has this month signaled its willingness to sign the protocol so that the agency's inspectors can verify the elimination of its program for nuclear arms. And the agency has scored a significant victory on

December 18 when Iran, under intense international pressure, has signed the accord. The country has been accused of using its civilian nuclear program as a cover to develop nuclear arms, an accusation that it has fiercely denied. Free to conduct inquiries in Iran even before that signing, the atomic agency is trying to track down the origins of highly enriched uranium that its inspectors have found last spring and summer. Iran has told the agency that the suspicious uranium is contamination from centrifuge parts that it has imported. If the IAEA finds otherwise, gathering evidence that Iran has made the highly pure uranium 235 itself, the agency could judge the country in violation of antiproliferation accords and send the case to the United Nations Security Council, which could impose sanctions.

James started his work in the Clean Lab a few days after he got settled into a one-bedroom flat in Vienna's tenth district. He was transported to the site by agency bus along with other lab workers living in the area. James was excited about the work since he knew several of the chemists in the laboratory. He was also aware of the importance of improving the analytical methods.

During his first week advising on the methods, he suggested using a smaller more efficient ion-exchange resin to concentrate the uranium and plutonium from samples while impurities would be separated from the two elements. He also recommended using more washing cycles to remove the impurities from the resin. The resins were ordered, and after James's return from Europe, he received an e-mail from Dave that the new resin greatly improved the isolation of uranium and plutonium for mass spectroscopy analysis.

James had enjoyed the week in Vienna and Seibersdorf, even though he was missing Margrit more than ever with memories of them traveling around Europe. The second week before his return to Clemson, he was asked to go to Skopje, Macedonia, by Tim to observe and report what he had seen. Much ethnic unrest had taken place recently, which did not bring much news coverage in the United States. James assumed it was related to the recent ethnic troubles in neighboring Bosnia. He was asked in particular to interview troops in the city.

During the flight to Skopje, James read the following article about Macedonia:

International recognition of the Former Yugoslav Republic of Macedonia's (FYROM) independence from Yugoslavia in 1991 was delayed by Greece's objection to the new state's use of what it considered a Hellenic name and symbols. Greece finally lifted its trade blockade, and the two countries agreed to normalize relations, despite continued disagreement over FYROM's use of "Macedonia." FYROM's large Albanian minority, an ethnic Albanian armed insurgency in FYROM in 2001, and the status of neighboring Kosovo continued to be sources of ethnic tension.

This small country in the southern part of the Balkan Peninsula is a veritable treasury of cultural heritage; churches, monasteries, archaeological sites, mosques, valuable old icons, historic books, and other artifacts can be found in great number all over the country. The first Slav alphabet and literature also have their roots here. National folklore and traditional arts and crafts are still cherished. The "pearl of the Balkans" abounds in natural beauties and rarities. Because of the great variety of plant and animal species, three areas in the mountains have been proclaimed national parks: Mavrovo, Pelister, and Galichica. There are three tectonic lakes in Macedonia—Lake Ohrid, Lake Prespa, and Lake Doiran. Lake Ohrid, the biggest and most beautiful of them, enjoys UNESCO protection.

Skopje is the capital of the Republic of Macedonia and its political, economic, and cultural center. It lies on the upper course of the Vardar River and is located on a major north-south Balkan route between Belgrade and Athens. Skopje has been struck by two catastrophic earthquakes, the last one in 1963. The clock in the preserved ruins of the old railway station remains frozen at 5:17 a.m., the moment the earthquake turned Skopje into a landfill. Thanks to world solidarity, the city has been quickly renewed and reconstructed.

Today the first impression of a visitor to Skopje is invariably the same: it is a new and modern city. Among the many international architects who have participated in its reconstruction is the Japanese urban planner Tange Kenzō, who has given the center a city wall of high-rise buildings, while the banks of the Vardar have been laid out as a pleasant tree-lined promenade. The ancient trading quarter (Charshija) has been completely renovated with the notable features of its original architecture. Today the city is still spreading in all directions with a number of new developments.

Skopje is also the birthplace of Mother Teresa. There is a memorial plaque on the square where her house of birth has been located, which has been destroyed in the earthquake.

Upon James's arrival in Skopje, he found that it was a very nice city with a castle. Between two major hotels sat a long shopping mall that paralleled the river. In front of the mall were numerous outdoor restaurants. The Holiday Inn was on one end, where James received a wonderful twenty-five euro massage by a lovely young masseuse and her student. James found out that four hands were indeed heavenly. At the other end of the mall was the Best Western Hotel, where he stayed. The city was very lively on Saturday night, with crowds of young people and many families walking about. Nothing was threatening about the people out that night.

James made the rounds at the major hotels and public places, trying to bring up conversations with airline employees, taxi and bus drivers, hotel personnel, soldiers, and other locals about the current situation in Macedonia. He also visited the major university in Skopje, Saints Cyril and Methodius, and spoke with some faculty and students.

After leaving Skopje, there was a fierce rainstorm, and out came a beautiful huge rainbow. James thought of the dream he had earlier—or was it real?—with Margrit's face towering over the train and asking for help, yet she had a smile on her face. After that, James had a restless night on the train and could not get to sleep. As the train crossed the Alps at Simmering, he remembered the time he and his family took the train to Graz and almost froze in the snow. On that trip, the train windows were covered with hoarfrost, but they could make out the beautiful villages covered with snow. Later, they would return to Simmering many times by car for skiing.

After arriving back in Vienna, James flew back to Atlanta, got his car out of the parking lot, and drove back to Pendleton. The next day, he sent a report to Tim and resumed his duties at Clemson. Two weeks later, he returned to Vienna and continued his consulting job at Seibersdorf. That week, he supervised a technician performing tests of the new resins.

At the end of the week, James took the train from Vienna to Budapest at the last minute so as to get out of Vienna for the long weekend. He did not notify Tim of his plans since he decided to take a relaxing three-day trip and not worry about writing a report for Tim. He shared a train compartment with a nice-looking Hungarian lady and two young American girls who were teaching English in Sopron. They had been at the Lutheran school for almost a year and had learned Hungarian fairly fast from the students in grades 6 to 12. One young lady was from California and the other from Minnesota. They were headed for Santorini for a long weekend.

They related to James a nice story of their travels through Hungary by train and how they were told to get off the train by the conductor on one trip to find that he really wanted them to move to another car that was going to their destination. They had quite a time where they were stranded since there was not another train until morning. They had to find a place to stay. James told them that he almost had the same experience on his return from his last trip to Budapest since one-half of the train was remaining in Budapest and the other going onto Gyor. He said that he finally figured it out and moved to the front car that was later connected to some cars going to Venice, and he had to change again in Gyor and just made his connection to Vienna since the train was late in arriving.

James wrote the following in his diary:

The trip across Hungary was very interesting. Between Gyor and Budapest, the mountains and hills are very lovely. Then between Budapest and Békéscsaba, the landscape is flat with field after field of farmland. Many beautiful flowers dominate the landscape, especially the red California poppies. At the Austrian-Hungarian border, immigration and customs from both countries came aboard to check passports and ask if I had anything to declare. It was the same procedure at the Hungarian-Romanian boarder, but the Romanian immigration asked me where I was going and why. I had a wild eight-minute train change in Arad, having to cross over several tracks in back of a couple of waiting trains to get to my train to Radna. In Radna, I had my last train change. It was a milk run with many stops in small villages, but the scenery was very pleasant with rolling hills and the Transylvania mountains in the background.

I arrived at Timişoara North Station at seven and took a taxi to the Best Western Ambassador Hotel. The hotel is fairly new, with wonderful old paintings and antique furniture everywhere. It had a workout room, spa, and small pool. I had a one-hour massage scheduled for nine. The masseuse was a very attractive blonde who knew some English. She was a medical student at the Polytechnic University. She told me a little about herself and how her boyfriend of three years is so immature. I told her to give him time and be patient; he will grow up. Joanna said that she had an anatomy exam on Monday morning and would not be working Sunday night for my second appointment, but I would have one of her other colleagues.

I usually do not talk much during my massages so that I can concentrate on the wonderful therapeutic work. Joanna was good and very interesting. She wanted to practice her English, and then I said, "Let me help you for your exam. Recite the body part you touch during the massage in Romanian and English, and then I will correct your English if necessary." So that is how the massage went while I was on my stomach. Then I had turned over under a big towel, and she proceeded to start with my toes, feet, ankles, knees, and so on. Then she put her hand on my groin area and stated, "Penis and pesticles."

I said, "Joanna, it is testicles."

As her hand remained on my private parts, she said, "You wanna."

I said, "Excuse me?"

"You wanna."

I said, "You wanna what?"

She then said, "You wanna—that is how my name is pronounced in Romanian." Then she proceeded to my stomach. I told her after the massage that she would have no trouble with her exam and that she had wonderful, caring hands and would someday make a fine doctor.

The next morning, I awoke early, said my prayers, exercised, showered, and went down for a delightful breakfast at seven. No one was about, and later, I was to find out there were only sixteen guests, but I saw only a couple of couples during my stay at the hotel. After breakfast, I walked into the city center, about a twenty-minute walk. Sunday mornings are so nice and quiet with few people about. The city is very lovely with a river running through, many university buildings, churches, and others. At one end of the long city square is a church, and opposite it is the opera house. On one side of the opera is the Polytechnic University's main building, and on the other side is a lovely old building housing McDonald's. The first thing I did was to get a cup of coffee and sit outside, watching the number of people grow, and a few beggars and Gypsies come by for change.

Later, I caught the train for my return to Vienna via Budapest. After a night in Vienna, I returned to South Carolina.

Back in his office, James received an e-mail from Dave that he was satisfied with the improved process that James developed and that there was no need for him to return for another week's work. He did ask James if he would draft a paper regarding the work for journal publication.

Chapter 6
The Final Bear Hug

I

Near the end of the fall semester, James received word that he had been awarded a grant from the National Science Foundation to study radioactivity in Antarctic ice layers formed since 1930. Tim also notified the professor that the CIA was providing additional funds through the Penny Group. Tim described his assignment for James and informed him that this was their last communication because he was retiring. He thanked James for all his time in assisting the CIA and ended the call by saying his replacement would be in touch with him after the trip to Antarctica.

The grant and Penny money would cover the entire trip cost for him, two graduate students, and a postdoc. Chris and Jerry had already been on trips, and in addition, they cannot come because of family matters and the fact that the trip would start after Christmas. James planned on spending Christmas in Colorado with all his family.

Several days after Christmas, Shana, Alex, and Ying came to James's office for a meeting on the trip. James gave each of them a list of things to buy for the expedition. "Be sure and bring me the receipts so the university can reimburse you from project funds. The most important things on the list are motion sickness pills, sunglasses, sunscreen, knee-high waterproof boots, a warm parka with waterproof poncho, waterproof gloves with separate liners, and waterproof pants that would go over long underwear and regular pants. Buy a sweater and stocking hat, if you do not have one. I will take the ice-coring tool with me and am sure I can borrow a hammer aboard the ship."

James asked Ying to stay after the meeting. He told her how much he had enjoyed working with her in Australia and the past year and thanked her for all her hard work. He said he admired her very much for her cooperation, intelligence, and good work. Then he concluded, "How about having dinner with me tonight at the old plantation house in the Pendleton Town Square?"

"Thank you. That sounds wonderful and romantic, Yim. Please excuse the Yim, but that is your new nickname with your students."

The evening was so nice for James that he asked Ying to accompany him the next evening to a concert at Clemson with dinner afterward. One could tell they were in love.

II

A few days later, James, Shana, Alex, and Ying waited in the Atlanta Airport for their flight to Ushuaia via Buenos Aires. During their wait for their flight, they watched on TV a program reviewing the news on the exposure of Dr. Khan, father of the Pakistan nuclear program, for exporting nuclear technology to Iran, Libya, and North Korea. After the broadcast, James told the group that even though a country may not use a weapon, they may sell it to another country or group. Of course, terrorist groups would like the bomb, nuclear materials to make one, or radioactive materials or waste to make a dirty bomb.

James then thought about the assignment Tim had given him. He was requested to keep his eyes and ears open on a small group of scientists from the Argentinean Nuclear Energy Agency, located near Buenos Aires. James was to find out if nuclear weapons information, the type that Dr. Khan was selling around the world, would be passed to the Argentinean nuclear scientists during the trip. He was not told any more as had been typical of his previous assignments.

James recalled meeting two Argentineans working at the nuclear center during his last trip to Egypt. They were trying to get Egypt to buy their reactor for power. One guy, the boss, was born in Argentina and had worked in Toronto for some time. The other fellow had emigrated from Iraq to Spain, spent ten years there, and then went to Argentina. They both had PhDs in nuclear physics and were going to attend a radiation conference the following week in Cairo. James had asked them about Argentina wanting to build a bomb. The boss said there was no way it could happen today, but twenty years ago, it was considered. Argentina did have a uranium-enrichment plant but for low-level enrichment. They were also reprocessing fuel now and making mixed uranium and plutonium fuel, so indeed, they could make a bomb, but why? If they did, other South American countries would follow.

James thought that Brazil would be the first South American country that would consider wanting the bomb, not Argentina. As an IAEA expert a decade ago, he had spent a couple of weeks at the Brazilian atomic energy site in São Paulo, advising on recovering americium from smoke detectors and lightning rods, developing a solvent extraction process, and related activities. He remembered seeing a highly secure area where uranium enrichment was taking place when his host, Dr. Cecee Corona, took him on a tour of the site.

And then there was Venezuela; they certainly had the money and were not that friendly with the United States. That triggered him recalling his trip to Caracas and onward to Angel Falls. He made the trip as part of his goal to visit all the major waterfalls, mountains, national parks, and natural and man-made wonders of the world. He recalled trying to sleep in a hammock with mosquito net and, the next day, flying with the pilot in a single-engine biplane around the spectacular falls.

On the group's flight from Atlanta to Ushuaia (most southerly "city" in the world) via Buenos Aires, James could not sleep as Alex, Shana, and Ying. He thought of Margrit and the last time they had been in Buenos Aires. He remembered how excited Margrit became upon hearing the news that he had been invited to a chemical conference there. She said it was the answer to a long-held dream and how great it would be to enjoy some of their old international friends again, including Cecee. He was also looking forward to seeing old friends and making new ones with some Argentinean nuclear scientists and to visit their facilities.

James recalled that one of the highlights of Margrit's first visit to Argentina included a conference-sponsored trip to Iguaçú Falls. Iguaçú Falls was 237 feet high, about two miles wide, and 14 miles above its union with the Paraná River. The area around the falls was where Brazil, Argentina, and Paraguay met. He remembered climbing around the rocks and the terror of falling into the falls as there were no handrails to protect him. They also had a side visit to Paraguay, attended a concert at the magnificent Teatro Colón and a most exciting tango party, and took a cruise on the Tigre River and a hydrofoil trip across the Paraná River to Colonia, Uruguay, for a bite to eat. Their last adventure was a flight over the breathtaking Andes to Santiago, Chile, where they rented a car and drove to a ski resort one day and to Valparaiso and Viña del Mar the next day, just making it back in time to catch their return flight to Buenos Aires.

At the invitation of Cecee, Margrit and James went onto Rio and enjoyed meeting other colleagues who, with Cecee, were there for the Brazilian nuclear conference and to see the impressive sites of the city. From Rio, they flew to São Paulo; there, Cecee and her husband, Walt, graciously wined and dined them and escorted them around their interesting city. The next day, James lectured at her institute and met several interesting people.

James's three traveling companions woke on the descent into Buenos Aires. After immigration and customs, the foursome went to the gate for their flight to Ushuaia via a short stop in Río Gallegos. On the flight, there were two beautiful young children sitting next to James with their mother across the aisle. He started talking to the mother, who was fairly fluent in English. James had to refrain from speaking with her in Spanish in spite of understanding the children's Spanish. He did not want anyone on the plane to know he was fairly fluent in the language since there might be someone going on the same vessel to Antarctica. Aboard ship, he was planning on eavesdropping on conversations of the Russian crew and the Argentinean scientists. James almost slipped a couple of times in trying to talk with the two children.

The mother let James practice his favorite hobby, photography. The children would laugh when they saw their images in James's digital camera. He was also trying to take some pictures from the plane window of the snowcapped mountains and seashore below, but these were not of high quality. On the short stop in Río Gallegos, the family got off.

The plane arrived in Ushuaia less than an hour later. The foursome took a taxi to the hotel, and after check-in and a meal in the hotel restaurant, they all went to their individual rooms very tired. At breakfast the next morning, James summarized his past two trips on the *Akademik Abraham* for his students. He did not mention the encounters with Felex. Then the foursome had a walk around the beautiful city, which was surrounded on three sides by beautiful snowcapped mountains; did some shopping; and enjoyed a meal and drink. In the afternoon, they joined some of their future ship mates, as well as some who had just returned from the Antarctic, on a short tour of the national park. It had been a beautiful and relaxing day.

III

The passengers were transferred to the *Akademik Abraham* at around four, and everyone went to their assigned cabins.

James and Alex were cabinmates as were Ying and Shana. After unpacking their luggage, many of the passengers explored the ship's facilities and enjoyed the scenery and wildlife as the ship moved down the Beagle Channel. James also took a walk around the ship and met several of his ship mates, including the group of Argentinean nuclear scientists. The Argentineans were only a small part of a much larger group of Australian adventurers, naturalists, and scientists who sponsored and contracted the trip. Later, James met Ying, Shana, and Alex, and they all went to one of the uppermost places on the ship to take some pictures and to have a last look at Ushuaia. It was a beautiful sight, a glacier off to the west and a high mountain range to the north.

At around six, everyone assembled in the dining room, where the expedition leader, Phil Daily, gave a safety briefing and overview on traveling aboard the ship. After Phil's presentation and dinner, there was a mandatory lifeboat drill. About that time, the ship passed the southernmost town in the world, Puerto Williams, on the Chilean side of the Beagle Channel. At midnight, the Argentinean pilot left the ship via a small speedboat. It was where the Beagle Channel ended and the Drake Passage of the Atlantic and Southern Oceans began.

In contrast to the trip to Greenland and the High Arctic, which turned out to be quite dangerous with an attempt on his life, James thought that this trip would be a vacation since he was not asked to take sensitive radiometric equipment along to detect nuclear materials or radioactive contamination on the ship or to collect water samples. Instead, his only duties were to supervise Alex, Shana, and Ying on the ice sampling and observe six Argentinean scientists who might be receiving nuclear weapons technology from someone else aboard the ship, especially a Russian crew member from Kaliningrad. He did recognize several of the crew members from the last trip on the ship and exchanged greetings with each of them in Russian. He was more acquainted with friendly Swetlana, who worked in the kitchen and dining room. Felex, the Russian who had shot at him during the last trip on the *Abraham*, did not exchange any greetings with James.

That night, James was reading some articles that he had printed from the CIA website. One article in particular was the following:

Speculation over the existence of a "southern land" was not confirmed until the early 1820s when British and American commercial operators and British and Russian national expeditions began exploring the Antarctic Peninsula region and other areas south of the Antarctic Circle. Not until 1840 was it established that Antarctica was indeed a continent and not just a group of islands. Several exploration "firsts" were achieved in the early twentieth century. After World War II, there was an upsurge in scientific research on the continent.

A number of countries have set up year-round research stations on Antarctica. Seven have made territorial claims, but no other country recognizes these claims. To form a legal framework for the activities of nations on the continent, an Antarctic treaty has been negotiated that neither denies nor gives recognition to existing territorial claims; signed in 1959, it has entered into force in 1961.

Another article stated the following quotation:

To anyone who goes to the Antarctic, there is a tremendous appeal, an unparalleled combination of grandeur, beauty, vastness, loneliness, and malevolence—all of which sound terribly melodramatic but which truly convey the actual feeling of Antarctica. Where else in the world are all these descriptions really true? (Capt. T. L. M. Sunter)

The next morning, the passengers woke to the motion of the surrounding seas as the ship made its way steadily south. Sunrise was a little after six. Crossing the Drake Passage was unusually calm, and several of the crew referred to it as crossing the "Drake Lake." After breakfast, the educational presentations began with a talk from Rinie, one of the technical staff members, who gave an introduction to the Antarctic Convergence.

Robert, another expert, presented a summary of the history of the Antarctic Peninsula and an interesting and informative talk about Ernest Shackleton's *Endurance* expedition and the lengths that Shackleton went to ensuring his men made it back alive. In the afternoon, the presentations continued, with Sean giving an introduction to the marine mammals that everyone may encounter on the voyage. He also gave an introduction to seabirds that were flying around the ship. Graham gave a few tips on photography that he knew would come in handy over the next week or so as the passengers tried to capture the great white continent on film or with digital images.

After these excellent presentations, everyone made their way into the dining room for another fabulous *Akademik Abraham* meal. After dinner, Robert gave a lecture on climate change; he discussed the significance of Antarctica as a barometer for the rest of the world. After Robert's talk, Scott hosted a wine-tasting party in the library for interested passengers. Some of the group adjourned to the bar immediately afterward to join Graham for the liars' club—a fun competition among Rinie, Robert, and Sean. The drinkers returned to their cabins at sunset and were all rocked to sleep once again on the Drake Passage.

The sunrise the next morning was a little before seven, and after breakfast, everyone attended a mandatory talk from Phil and Robert on the International Association of Antarctica Tour Operators' regulations and how to stay safe in Zodiacs, which everyone would be doing a lot of very soon. Phil also presented the trip's itinerary, and Sean explained the plight of the graceful albatross and the effects that longline fishing was having on this majestic bird. Everyone knew they were in Antarctic territory when the first iceberg was spotted at latitude 63° south before lunch. Another spectacular sight was a pod of humpback whales feeding just off the port bow. They also observed the first Adélie penguins on an ice float and some fur seals and minke whales. The crowd on the bridge was very excited to be seeing the first real evidence of the continent.

Captain Putan announced at lunch that, due to our smooth crossing of the Drake, the ship was going to head farther south and cross the Antarctic Circle. The educational presentations continued while waiting for the crossing of the circle. Toni gave a great talk on the life of her father, Frank Hurley, and Sean talked more about humpback whales. After the talks, all the passengers and most of the crew went to the bow deck to celebrate the ship's arrival at 66°33'—the Antarctic Circle. Although visibility was low and the air temperature was zero degrees Fahrenheit, excitement was high among everyone. South of this line of latitude was where there were periods of twenty-four-hour daylight or darkness, depending on the season.

As everyone on deck was assembled in front of Captain Putan, James asked Ying to accompany him to join the captain. There, James got on his knees and said, "Dear Ying, I love you so much. Will you marry me?"

A surprised Ying said, "Yes, yes," with a big smile and tears in her eyes.

"Ying, the captain was aware that I was going to ask your hand in marriage, and he agreed to marry us if you accepted my proposal."

The captain then conducted a short marriage ceremony. With music playing, everyone had a toast to the couple with special hot chocolate. Then most of the attendees gave them hardy congratulations with handshakes and hugs. Shana had tears in her eyes, and she and Alex gave them their best wishes. Both told the newlyweds that they were surprised that they got married on the ship but knew they were in love with each other and that eventually they would marry. Later, James made a short speech, thanking the captain and everyone for traveling this long distance from their homes to attend his and Ying's marriage. The crowd laughed and applauded.

Then James said, "Ying and I must now depart for our honeymoon at the five-star resort on nearby Detaille Island in our speedboat with cans attached to the back as you all throw rice over our heads." There was more laughter. In the evening, the newlyweds had a special dinner with the captain and his officers.

James was an early riser, and with coffee cup in hand, he made his way back to his usual spot, the middle rear of the lower deck near the flimsy cargo gate. There, he had watched a spectacular sunrise over Detaille Island. James then went back to his cabin and woke Ying. Shana had agreed to let Alex move into her cabin since there were separate beds. Later, the four of them went to the dining hall for breakfast and sat at their usual table within earshot of the Argentineans so James could overhear their conversations.

There was an exciting start to most of the passengers' adventures after breakfast as the backdrop of the Antarctic Peninsula was getting clearer. The brave ones first cruised in Zodiacs with some humpback whales alongside. Later, they went ashore at Detaille Island, where they visited the abandoned British Base N. It was a great opportunity to stretch their legs after being on the ship for several days. James and his threesome took some samples of ice on the island. On the way back to the ship, everyone saw more Adélie penguins, skuas, and sheathbills. They also spotted more humpback whales and some seals.

There was an excellent presentation after lunch about kayaking along the Antarctic coast by Graham. The *Akademik Abraham* then started going north along the Antarctic Peninsula. The weather was pleasant as the ship crossed Waddington Bay, passing through lots of brash ice and some beautiful icebergs.

After lunch, most of the passengers went ashore on the mainland and visited Vernadsky Station, a Ukrainian research center once owned by the British and called Faraday Station. The group toured the station and was informed that it was mainly performing upper atmosphere studies and that the Ukrainian scientists were instrumental in discovering the ozone hole. The station was quite colorful, with a bar and homemade vodka, pool table, dartboard, and souvenir shop. Later, James gave a short talk on his environmental radioactivity studies at Clemson to a small group of Ukrainian scientists. They also visited Wordie House, a small museum preserving part of the early British base, and ended the visit with a walk to the top of a nearby snow hill to enjoy the view, followed by sledding down the hill on their bottoms. The foursome took some ice cores before they joined the others to go back to the ship via Zodiac for dinner.

Over a delicious dinner, the captain had studied the weather conditions and charts and concluded that it was a good night for anyone wanting to spend sleeping on the snow and ice. After dinner, they were treated to a superdisplay in the Lemaire Channel by a pod of eight killer whales, including a mother and calf.

James and Alex decided to join the campers. As James was packing the necessary clothing for the campout, Ying said, "Do you really want to camp on the freezing ice and snow on the coldest and harshest continent in the world?

"Yes, it will be one of the most unique experiences of my life besides making love to you."

The Zodiacs were loaded with supplies and the anticipation was ripe among those who had chosen to camp. As the fifteen campers, Phil, and three Russian crew members were being transported to Hovgaard Island, there were sightings of several humpback whales. Once on the island, James, Alex, and the other campers prepared their camp spots by digging a level place in the snow for their sleeping bags. James had selected a secluded spot near the top of the hill overlooking the entrance to the Lemaire Channel and a beautiful glacial mountain range on the mainland that reminded him of the Grand Tetons in Wyoming. Phil had suggested that James put a big rock at the foot of his camping equipment to prevent him from accidentally sliding down the hill. The equipment consisted of a cocoon waterproof outer cover with an inside sleeping bag and foam pad.

After watching a beautiful slow sunset at about ten o'clock over the sea, James turned his attention in the opposite direction toward the red glow on the mountains with a perfect reflection in the channel containing numerous ice floats, a few icebergs, and the *Akademik Abraham*. The stars were starting to come out as James took off his boots, waterproof pants, and jacket before getting into the sleeping gear. He then crawled into the gear and zipped himself in the outer cocoon and then the sleeping bag. As he watched the number of stars increase around the Southern Cross, he spotted a satellite slowly crossing the sky. Then he saw a falling star and made a wish. The last time he had come close to seeing this many stars was camping out at Yellowstone National Park in Wyoming or perhaps on his property in Nederland, Colorado.

James was pleased that he had the night off from his surveillance of the Argentinean nuclear scientists and whoever was suspected of trying to pass nuclear weapons technology to them. Only one of the Argentineans had opted for the campout, and so far on the voyage, he had not overheard any talk among the Argentineans or observed them having conversations with any of the crew members about nuclear materials. James was not going to pass an experience of a lifetime by and stay aboard ship to continue his covert government assignment. At least this way, he would not have to worry about an attempt on his life and could hopefully get a good night's sleep.

But James was wrong as he was awoken in the middle of the night by a sharp jar to his sleeping bag and found himself sledding fast down the hill, cocooned in his sleeping equipment, and heading for a high ledge over the icy channel. As he was frantically trying to unzip the bag and cocoon, all he could think about was *Is this the same feeling Margrit had experienced when she lost control of his car going down Black Canyon in the Santa Susana mountains in California?* It had been no accident as the brakes of the car had been tampered with, and someone had intended to take his life, not Margrit's.

As James was about to go over the high ledge of the ice-covered hill into the freezing waters of the Lemaire Channel, he managed to roll over and got stopped by grabbing onto a large rock and hitting a snowbank. A few seconds later, Alex and then Felex and the Argentinean arrived and asked James if he was okay. They got James up, and he asked, "What happened?"

Felex did not say anything, but the Argentinean said, "You must have turned over in your sleep and off the rock holding you in place."

James knew that was not the case as he always slept on his back.

"It is a good thing you got stopped by the snowbank you hit," said Alex.

James told them he was okay, and the four returned to their camp spots to try to get some sleep.

Of course, James was unable to sleep the rest of the night. He suspected the Argentinean or Felex of wanting to kill him by removing the rock holding his sleeping bag in place. During the night, he recalled that, in his youth, he and his friends would sled down a snowy hill on an air mattress that was tied to them. If they needed to stop, they would just flip the mattress over. Luckily, the rocks in James's path ripped open the outer cocoon cover, allowing his arms free so he could flip over and get to stop, just like he had done in his youth.

The campers all came back onboard at seven for breakfast. Most of the campers said they had a great night with spectacular views of stars, albeit a little chilly. When James got back to his cabin, Ying asked, "How was the camping on the freezing snow last night?"

James responded, "Well, it had its bad aspects." Then he told Ying the whole story of his near-death experience and who he suspected of removing the rock.

Ying asked, "What are you going to do now?"

"I am not sure since there is no proof of the Argentinean or Felex trying to kill me. I will just have to be very cautious for the rest of the trip."

There was just enough time for the campers to warm up over breakfast before their next excursion to the iceberg alley behind Pleneau Island in Zodiacs. The visitors again had picture-perfect conditions as they wandered and drifted among icebergs of all shapes, sizes, and colors. They had good views of leopard, crabeater, and Weddell seals.

In the afternoon, most of the visitors went ashore at Petermann Island. A greeting party of penguins was there, and everyone had plenty of time to watch them and get to know their ways. Sean and Rinie led a hike over to a big ice/snow bank and then headed to an Adélie penguin colony to find that all the chicks had left for the winter, and only the molting adults remained. The nearby gentoo colony, however, was full of playful fluffy chicks. The skuas were still trying to take their chance on the chicks for food. Rinie continued on and took several people over to the blue-eyed shag colony.

Later, after the foursome collected ice samples, everyone went back on board to enjoy a summer BBQ on the stern deck while the ship continued its passage north through the Lemaire Channel. That night was relatively quiet on board, and Robert and Sean kept everyone entertained after dinner.

By breakfast time, the ship was nestled in Andvord Bay, just off Neko Harbor. This was the visitors' second chance to put their feet on the Antarctic continent. The weather was starting to get a little gray and windy. The brave ones made an excursion to Cuverville Island, home to one of the biggest gentoo colonies on the peninsula. The visitors walked among the penguins and saw the gentoo colony at a slightly earlier stage, with the chicks still small, fluffy, and in their crèche. They also found two leucistic penguins—James named them Louie and Louise. Rinie explained that the rare light pigment color of the feathers was what made them really stand out in the crowd. After a good look at the antics of chicks chasing parents for food and even one penguin still with two very small chicks on a nest, the group made their way back to the Zodiacs and went for a short cruise.

On the way back to the ship, they saw a leopard seal on an ice float as well as a large calving of a glacier that created a wave set big enough to swamp the beach; luckily, the Zodiacs were far enough to be out of harm's way. Back on board after a spectacular morning, the ship headed a little farther north during lunchtime. Everyone had a great Chinese buffet.

After lunch, a Zodiac cruise was offered that provided a fantastic opportunity for the passengers to have close encounters with minke whales, the small baleen whales that usually moved together in pods. The pod observed earlier in the morning seemed highly curious and kept coming past the Zodiacs and the kayakers; some were even spy-hopping (which was when they put their heads straight up in the air just to have a look). The Zodiac cruise was in very calm conditions, so passengers could even see penguins as they swam underwater.

Back at the ship, the adventurers dried off and warmed up before a toast to Antarctica just before dinner. Robert kept everyone entertained in the bar, and Rinie gave a special presentation after dinner. The ship also briefly met up with the sister ship, the *Vavilov*, as it loomed nearby in the fog. There was some gear transferred by Zodiac as well as one new crew member who came aboard with several packages. James wondered if he was the one the Argentineans were to meet and, if so, what were in the packages. After the quick transfers, the *Abraham* was on its way again, this time across the Bransfield Strait.

The landing the next morning was on a black volcanic beach on Deception Island in bad weather that later turned into a real blizzard. The visitors split into several groups for different walks. The group that included James and his students headed along the beach to Neptune's Window to look at all the old water boats and remnants of whale oil barrels. When they reached the gap, they could see a little into the distance, but the snow kept falling. They also walked past some fur seals and marveled at their ability to move along on land. Then they had a tour of the historic British Antarctic Survey buildings with large metal tanks and processing equipment from the whaling era. The last stop was the hangar, where there was still a single Otter plane on site. Before the group headed back to the ship, several of the brave ones, including James and Alex, went for a "swim" in the relatively warm plunge pool created with volcanic sand by Robert.

The sea was choppy as the visitors left the island. They enjoyed the lively Zodiac ride along the way since they managed to see many chinstraps and a lone macaroni penguin, which were both new species seen on the trip. The macaroni was a lone molting bird that was in the middle of all the chinstraps. They were characterized by their black face and yellow feather crests. This was the southernmost place that the macaroni was found, and every year six or seven pairs established a nest and tried to breed. Giant petrels were also nesting high on the ridgelines all the way along the mountains. The elephant seals were plentiful and noisy all the way along the black sandy beach that was littered with the bones of whales from a past era.

After returning to the ship and going out of the harbor, the ship made its way to Livingstone Island, where most of the group went ashore for more walking and penguin watching at Hannah Point. Later, the ship went to the Bulgarian Research Station, where some scientists boarded for their journey home. After dinner, some of the passengers attended a special poetry reading by Robert in the library. At the same time, most of the other passengers attended a presentation in the dining room by Rinie on the Arctic.

The passengers awoke the next morning to discover that the ship was going north across a calm Drake Passage. The day's program was busy. The staff gathered a very helpful team of passengers, including James and Alex, to assist with the packing up of the camping gear. During the morning in the dining room, Phil made a presentation titled "Living and Working on Cuverville Island" while Sean spoke on his experiences with killer whales. The passengers were treated by another great lunch and, afterward, a chance to get into the gift shop for some last-minute shopping. During the afternoon, Robert spoke about aspects of the Australian Antarctic program; he outlined the medical research on the expeditions that consisted in spending lengthy periods in remote stations and field camps.

That night at dinner, as usual, the foursome sat together. Shana told Ying and the professor that Alex would join them in a few minutes. She said, "I'm so happy to be sharing the cabin with him. He is such a gentleman and so interesting to talk to since he has lived in Russia, Austria, and Canada. He has many stories to tell, and some are so funny. I like him so much."

Ying stated, "I also like my roommate and that we also have a lot of fun together."

James said, "The only annoying thing is sometimes I get up in the middle of the night and find that our Australian friends in the next cabin have locked us out of the bathroom we share. I must then go out in the hallway in my pajamas, knock on their door, and ask them to go and unlock the bathroom door on our side."

Everyone laughed as Alex came to the table. After dinner, Sean gave a special presentation in the library about cleaning up disused Antarctic stations. Scott challenged a small group with trivia in the bar.

The Drake Passage was getting rough but rocked James and Ying to sleep. The next morning after breakfast, Phil recapped the journey. James had skipped the talk to write his report to Tim's replacement concerning the Argentinean scientists. He ended the report by stating,

> Some contractors and government employees dealing with espionage could have easily concluded that some type of nuclear weapon information is being provided to certain Argentinean nuclear scientists to develop a nuclear weapon in Argentina. I think that Brazil would be a more likely country, but of course, Argentina was having

economic problems and might be starting down the road to nuclear blackmail similar to what the North Koreans now have underway.

Later, he and the passengers settled their accounts with Phil. Then another delicious lunch was enjoyed by all. Ship tours followed in the afternoon, and everyone learned a lot more about the vessel that they had been traveling on from Scott, Sean, and Robert. The tour even included going into a room where the sonar instrumentation was located.

In the evening with rough seas, everyone carefully headed to the dining room for a special captain's dinner that included a magnificent array of appetizers and a special dessert buffet. As usual, James and Alex were seated together with their ladies and four others whom they had befriended during the expedition.

In a soft voice so as not to let the others overhear, James asked Alex, "What were you doing on the campout just before my accident since you were the first one to arrive where I had rolled over and stopped? Do you know why the Argentinean and Felex immediately followed you down the hill?"

Alex replied, "I think they must have heard my yelling and came running after me. Can we meet after dinner at the stern, where you always have your after-dinner cigar?"

"Certainly," James said.

After the captain's dinner and drinking and dancing and in spite of the weather changing and the sea getting very rough, most of the passengers headed out on the decks to see if the mainland was starting to appear. Although it was overcast, one could make out the outline of the landmass and Cape Horn.

Instead of joining James and Ying on deck, Alex and Shana went to their cabin. Alex told Shana that he was in love with her. After exchanging loving emotions, Alex told Shana all about his past, his father, and the promise he had made to him. He told Shana that he now planned to someday be a professor just like James and wanted to marry her when they arrived back in South

Carolina. He promised to change his life and make amends. She said that he should go down and tell James everything he had told her and ask his forgiveness.

IV

Later, James was on the bottom deck at the stern, where he usually went to relax, looking at the stars and smoking a cigar since usually there was never anyone about. It was a grand night as it just had gotten dark at around eleven, but the sea was very angry. The ship was being tossed back and forth, and large waves were hitting the ship as it was starting to go around Cape Horn. They would be disembarking the next morning. James was not feeling any pain since the dinner with lots to drink. Ying was not feeling well and went to their cabin. Shana quietly went to the second deck, above where Alex would be talking with James, to overhear what they both discussed.

Alex joined James, who said, "You had better hold on to the railing as the sea is really getting rough."

After some discussions on the joyous evening, Alex started a conversation about how much he had enjoyed his graduate studies, how great an adviser James was, and how he wanted to follow in his footsteps. He also stated that he was so lucky to have found Shana and that someday soon they would marry. James smiled as Alex spoke.

However, as Alex continued to talk, James's smile turned to the opposite with a look of surprise and astonishment. Alex said that his real name was Alex Pushkin and that his father was the one who had a love affair with Margrit in Vienna. He related to James that his father had faked his death, tracked him and Margrit down in California, and tried to renew his love affair with Margrit by killing him. "Professor, it was my father who caused Margrit's death. He told me that it was meant for you to die in the car crash, not his love."

The conversation continued with Alex telling James the rest of the story. As James stood in disbelief, in silence, and getting an angry red face, Shana was overhearing everything. Then she was shocked beyond belief as Alex quickly moved to strain James in a bear hug. Shana cried out, "No, no!"

Epilogue
Yim and Ying

I

In the living room of her home on Golden Pond in Pendleton, South Carolina, a middle-aged lady was seen sitting on a rocker in the company of her three grandchildren. The eldest, a girl of twelve years, was sitting on a couch next to the rocker; and the other two children, a ten-year-old boy and a girl of eight, were sitting on the floor. The eldest spoke first. "Grandma Ying, please tell us again how you and Grandpapaw met."

"Well, Milana, are you sure you want me to tell that story again, or would you rather like to hear more about our adventures before we were married?"

Milana, Edward, and Anabella all shouted out, "Yes!"

Edward said, "But please tell us the whole story from your first meeting in Hong Kong and then going to Australia and then here."

"Well, I will start the story, but I will have to stop when your mother and father return from the theater at Clemson University. I know they will want you to start packing your clothes and Christmas gifts for your flight back to Vancouver in the morning.

"As you know, my best friend, Suzie, brought me and your grandpa together. Suzie, along with Wally, her husband and a friend of your grandpa, met her at a conference banquet in Santiago, Chile. After their return to the United States, Suzie sent your grandpa an e-mail with my résumé attached stating that I wanted to come to the University of New South Wales and get a degree in industrial chemistry and that I would like to meet him in Hong Kong to discuss the matter. Suzie and Wally had planned their annual trip there to see her parents and brother, and it coincided with a Chinese chemical conference. Both Wally and your grandpa were invited speakers at the conference.

"Anyway, your grandpa was interested in meeting me. Thus, we started exchanging several e-mails up to our meeting in Hong Kong. At the Hong Kong Airport, I was holding a sign up that read 'MAK' per Grandpa's instructions. As you can easily guess, MAK was the last three letters of his name, Czermak. I waited awhile and was surprised when he tapped me on the shoulder and said, 'Hi, I'm John.' He then introduced me to his wife, Margrit, and we sat for quite a while and talked about various things, including my desire to attend the University of New South Wales. I also told them about my divorce from your other grandfather and having a daughter. Later, Wally and Suzie joined us since they had been on a later flight. We then proceeded to travel to Shenzhen together. Upon arrival, we checked Grandpa and Margrit into the Panglin Hotel. I planned on meeting them the next day to show them the city.

"The next morning, I arrived at their hotel, and we had breakfast together. After breakfast, I first showed your grandfather and Margrit around the city near the hotel. Then we took the metro to the Lianhua, which means 'lotus,' Mountain Park. At the park, we walked to the top of the hill, where there is a wonderful view of part of the city. After lunch and more touring, we returned to the hotel for an early dinner with Suzie and Wally.

"The next day, Suzie's brother drove the four of us to the OCT East Park. We had a grand time walking around the park and riding a few rides. Later in the afternoon, Suzie's brother took Grandpa, Margrit, and Wally to Hong Kong so the men could attend the conference the next day. After the conference, Grandpapaw and Margrit had a two-day visit to Singapore to see a friend, followed by going to Tokyo so Grandpa could assist in the Fukushima nuclear disaster. As you know, he was a nuclear scientist. He wrote me later that, after his business in Japan, he and Margrit had gone to Disneyland in Tokyo.

"Our second meeting was in Sydney when I started my university studies. During my first full day after arriving in Australia, Grandpa showed me around the university and introduced me to some of the faculty and his graduate students. Then we met Margrit and went into the city for a walk and took the ferry across the harbor to Manly. After seeing a lot of the two cities, we took the bus to Coogee Bay to see the beautiful ocean, followed by my return to the apartment I was sharing with another graduate student.

"Well, I started my studies the following week and worked for your grandfather on a research project for a year until he returned to the United States. He had been offered a job with his old employer, Rockwell International, since his three-year leave of absence was to end. Instead of Colorado, the job was in Simi Valley, California. He really wanted to remain in Australia but mainly took the job to resume his years of service with Rockwell, which meant he would receive more money after retirement. For the next three years, I was supervised by another professor with assistance from Grandpapaw via e-mails and several visits. During this time, I was falling in love with him. Three years later, I received my doctoral degree. It was about this time Margrit met her tragic death, and Grandpapaw moved to Clemson. Naturally, I wanted to continue working with him, so I applied to Clemson University and got accepted as a postdoctoral student under his supervision.

"Our last time together before I went to Clemson was in Beijing after Grandpapaw's trip to North Korea. The first day in Beijing, we went around the city, seeing all the major attractions, including the Imperial Palace. We had arranged to take a tour the next day to see the Great Wall, which I had never seen before. Sadly, I was sick, and your grandpa had to go on the trip alone. On the third day, I returned to Shenzhen for work, and Grandpa got on a train for Tibet. His return on the train took him to Shanghai, where he gave a lecture to a group of graduate students that his friend was supervising at Fudan University.

"As you sadly know, God took him from me a year ago. There is not a day that goes by that I shed some tears of his death. I miss him so much, and I know you do too."

Edward sadly said, "Yes, I really miss Grandpapaw and the pranks and funny things he would do and say. Just like his name, he preferred us to call him Grandpapaw instead of Grandpa, with the paw being associated with the Clemson Tigers football team. Halloween was special for him, and he told us some funny stories about the Halloween pranks he had pulled on his children many years ago. I only witnessed his last Halloween prank when you both came to our house on Halloween eve with us not expecting you, and Grandpapaw left you in the car and came to the door to fool us. He had hidden in a big box with a scary mask on, and Mom told us there was a box outside that had just been delivered and was for us. Of course, she was in cahoots with him. When we went outside to look, he suddenly pushed his head out of the folded box top with a scream. He sure scared us. That visit was the last time I saw him."

"Yes, your grandfather was quite a joker and always full of the devil. By the way, your grandpa believed that we have had previous lives, and he knew somehow that he was a Japanese sailor on a large sailing ship in his last lifetime. On his last voyage, they were coming into Tokyo Harbor, and someone pushed him overboard on the sailing ship. He said that he was killed by a shark. What do you all think of that?"

"I am not sure of his previous lives," Milana interjected. "But I think it was so clever what you told us about when Grandpapaw first introduced you to students and friends, and they would ask you what kind of work you did back in China. Sometimes Grandpapaw would quickly pipe up and say that Ying worked for the Chinese government in intelligence, with them thinking you were a spy, and then after a short pause, he would say, 'Indeed, she worked for the government but tested the intelligence of high school students to go onto the university.'"

"It took some time for me to get the American visa to attend Clemson University, but a month after your grandfather started work at Clemson, I left for the United States. Upon my arrival in Los Angeles, Grandpa met me at the airport, and we went to Uncle Eric and Aunt Ann's home in Thousand Oaks for three days. We had a grand time with Uncle Eric, Aunt Ann, Mark, and Joe at their house. We spent a lot of time at their swimming pool, and your grandpa took me to the beach, Universal Studios, and where he had worked for three years at the east end of Simi Valley in the Santa Susana mountains. The road to his old workplace goes up Black Canyon, which is very narrow, curvy, and steep.

"This is the first time I had told you this, but it was on this road where Margrit had her fatal accident. That tragic day, Grandpa and Margrit went up the canyon together as she was going to take his car to run errands since her car was in the shop for repairs. At the site, after Grandpapaw had parked the Toyota MR2 in the usual place, he and Margrit went into the nearby company restaurant and had breakfast together. Afterward, Grandpapaw walked to his building to work, and Margrit drove down the canyon.

"A few minutes later, a guard saw some smoke coming from the canyon and phoned the fire department. By the time assistance had arrived at the accident site, they saw that the car had gone off a cliff, overturned, and was on fire. Margrit was lying dead some distance from the road on some rocks. Investigators later found that the rear brake line had been cut, and the roadway had a thin stain from the leaking brake fluid from the top of the hill to the accident site. Foul play was suggested at the time, but no suspects were questioned except Grandpa. At the beginning of our trip to Antarctica over a year ago, your grandfather told me that the deadly accident was meant for him and not Margrit.

"After our stay in California, we flew to Denver. There, we spent almost a week together, and I got to meet his two daughters and their families, a few relatives, and some of his friends. He also took me to see the sites around the city and in the mountains. We even went skiing one day at Breckenridge after your grandpa gave me some lessons.

"At the end of our stay there, we flew to South Carolina for me to see his Pendleton home, where I would be staying in one of three bedrooms upstairs. The other two bedrooms were occupied by two other Clemson students. He was living in the walkout basement that had two bedrooms, living room, kitchen, bathroom, and its own entrance. He also took me to meet his graduate students and to see the area around Clemson. The following week, your grandfather resumed his teaching duties, and I started my postdoctoral studies."

"Grandma," smiling Milana asked, "was it about the time that Grandpapaw's students started calling him Dr. Yim?"

"It started a few months later when his students saw us together a lot, and the name stuck."

Edward spoke up and said, "Grandma, please tell us more about your life in China, from your youth up to meeting Grandpapaw."

"I know your grandfather is looking down from heaven with a smile on his face as I summarize my life story. I was born and raised in Chengdu, the capital of Sichuan Province. There are many provinces in China just like states in the United States. Guangzhou is the capital of Guangdong Province. Shenzhen is well known in the world, and it is also located in Guangdong Province, near Hong Kong.

"I started my studies at Sichuan University. It is located in Chengdu and is the best university in Sichuan Province and very famous in China. I graduated from the Chemistry Department with a degree in physical chemistry. I do not want to brag, but I was the best in my class. Then I went to Zhongshan University, known as Sun Yat-sen University abroad. It is famous abroad and in China, and it is located in Guangzhou. I was in the Physics Department as a postgraduate student and studied image progressing and learned how to teach. I taught there for several years, and at that time, I had a short marriage to your Chinese grandfather, whom, as you know, you have only seen once.

"After leaving Zhongshan University, I started working at the Office of Enrollment and Examination of Shenzhen. Our job was to administer tests for high school students to get into college. I worked myself up to the position of vice director. After several years in that position, I met your grandfather.

"As you know, my departed father, or your great-grandfather, was a professor of chemistry, and my departed mother was a retired high school teacher. She had been recognized for her outstanding teaching of chemistry. You all have met my brother and his wife and son. He teaches high school chemistry in Shenzhen.

"My life drastically changed when I met Yim, your grandfather. My life with him has been a dream, and I woke up when he left me to join Margrit, his parents, and his other loved ones and friends in heaven."

They all thanked Grandma for telling them again about her life but with more detail this time. Both Milana and Edward asked, "What about Grandpapaw's life? We have only heard a little of it."

"Well, Grandpapaw told me that he was born in Denver, and the family lived in a two-bedroom house. Your grandpa and your two great-aunts and two great-uncles had to share one bedroom. The house was within walking distance of two of his schools, Irving Elementary School and Kepner Junior High. He had to get a ride for his first year at West High, but later, he started to drive his own car.

"Your grandpa went to St. Francis Catholic School for third grade and was always getting into trouble. He told me one time, at the Catholic school before classes started, that he went to a nearby busy street and acted like a policeman, making cars stop so his fellow classmates could cross the street in the middle of the block instead of going to the corner with a crosswalk.

The head nun found out about it and gave him some discipline, including whacks on the hand with a yardstick.

"He told me about some other episodes at Irving School. In fourth grade, he continued to get into trouble. For example, his teacher wrote on his report card, 'Johnny always finishes his work before the students around him and then bothers them.' However, in junior high, he told me that he was a good student and a lab assistant in his science class. He would even perform experiments in front of the class. He had a love of chemistry, which started when he received a chemistry set on his tenth birthday. He was also an admirer of Thomas Edison. A couple of years later, he and Great-Uncle Larry built a small shed in the backyard, where he would carry out numerous experiments. One time, he had made nitroglycerin and left it in his lab while he went into the house. Later, he discovered that the liquid had exploded all over his laboratory."

Anabella asked, "What is nitroglycerin?"

"It is a chemical that goes into the making of dynamite. He also told me that he made some gun cotton by soaking cotton in a mixture of sulfuric and nitric acids, followed by washing and drying it. He would take it to school and ask some girls to hold it in their hands. Then he would light the cotton, and it flashed and disappeared without burning the startled girl's hand.

"In high school, he only had hot rods and girls on his mind and not schoolwork. He also worked at a supermarket as a sacker and later became a checker. When he was sixteen, he bought a 1929 Ford Model A roadster. He told me that he ruined the car by making it into a hot rod. Later, he traded the hot rod for a 1932 Ford coupe. He put a V-8 engine in it and took it to drag races. A couple of years later, he sold this car and bought a new Chevrolet Impala. At the time, he belonged to the Sabers Hot Rod Club. He jokingly told me that because of work and his goofing off at school, he dropped out and did not graduate with his class. However, he went back after summer break and finished his high school education a year behind his schoolmates. At this time, he got a job as a janitor at the Rocky Flats Plant, which made nuclear weapon parts out of plutonium, a very radioactive element."

Milana said, "I have heard about plutonium in my science class."

"After your grandfather was a janitor for a couple of months, he was promoted to laboratory technician. At the time, young men were getting drafted into the army and sent to Vietnam to fight. To avoid the draft, he joined the army reserve and served six months of training and another five and a half years going to weekend meetings and two weeks a year at summer camp. He went from private to sergeant to second lieutenant. During this time, he met Margrit, and they got married three months later. Up to then, he had been going to the University of Colorado in Denver part time. A few months after he married Margrit, he received a Dow Chemical scholarship to attend school full time at the University of Colorado in Boulder. There, he received his bachelor's degree in chemistry."

Annabella asked, "What is a bachelor's degree?"

"Well, it is what you get for completing four years of study at a university. I have one in chemistry. The next two degrees are the master's and doctorate. Your grandpa received both of them in chemistry while he had worked full time at Rocky Flats and went to school full time. During this time, Uncle Eric and Aunts Amy and Lorrie were born. Your grandpa says that was the best time of his and Margrit's life, just like it was for me when your mother was young.

"After a couple of years of working at Rocky Flats as a manager instead of a chemist, your grandpa accepted a three-year assignment with the International Atomic Energy Agency in Vienna. His family really liked living in Vienna, and Margrit had a hard time returning to Colorado. Grandpapaw then continued to work as manager of Plutonium Chemistry Research and Development at Rocky Flats for three years until he had some security problems. He has never shared the details of the loss of his security clearance with me. However, your grandpa always wanted a change in jobs about every three or four years, so he was happy to accept a professorship at the University of New South Wales in Australia. As you all know, I started my doctoral studies under his supervision at the beginning of his last year at the university. We became good friends since I was his best student. Of course, a year later, he resigned from the university, and another professor started supervising my research for three years."

"Is that when Grandpapaw went to California to work?" Eric asked.

"Yes, after three years in Australia, your grandpa went back to work for Rockwell International at the Santa Susana site. He was there for three years until Margrit was killed in the car accident. He then accepted a job offer as professor of environmental engineering and science at Clemson University. Shortly after he joined the university, I was accepted to the university as a postdoc student under his supervision. Now let me tell you about our trips and adventures together, and with Ashley, to attend conferences."

"Who is Ashley?" asked Annabella.

"She is Margrit's ashes. A long time before her death, she told Yim that she wanted him to spread her ashes around the world on his trips if she should die before he does. Your grandfather had been writing in his diary about his trips and depositing her ashes.

"I have already told you about our first memorable trip when your grandpa met me in Los Angeles after my flight from Hong Kong so I could start my postdoctoral studies under his direction. Before going to Uncle Eric and Aunt Ann's home in Thousand Oaks, Grandpapaw took me to visit the Reagan Library. The library was a very special place for Margrit and Grandpapaw since they were at the opening ceremony and got to see the five presidents, together with many other dignitaries, celebrities, and Hollywood stars, including Bob Hope and Arnold Schwarzenegger. After our tour of the library, your grandpa wanted to place a little of

Margrit's ashes in a rose garden behind the library. We did not notice a security guard watching us as your grandfather placed a little of Ashley under a rose bush. The guard came over, looked down at the ashes with an inquisitive glare, and then turned and walked away without saying anything. I thought for sure Dr. Czermak would get detained for questioning.

"Your grandfather had to go to Vienna for an International Atomic Energy Agency meeting, and I got to go along. The first thing we did was to have breakfast at an anchor shop with their wonderful pastries. Then we walked over to Kärntner Strasse, past the opera, and then down to St. Stephen's Church, where your daring grandpa left some of Ashley in a large planter next to the church while many tourists were walking around. After strolling around the middle of Vienna, we had lunch at a *Würstelstand*. In the afternoon, we went swimming at the hotel. That evening, we ate at Figlmüller's with the Princes, some old friends of Grandpa. We had a great time, but I ate too much Wiener schnitzel.

"Wait, I know Edward and Annabella have a lot of questions, especially about what we ate, but let me continue, and I will tell you later when I finish with some more stories. On that same trip, we took the train to Prague. Your grandfather wanted to be brave again and deposited some of Ashely in a flower bed in front of a church in the middle of the town square next to the old city hall. He was even more daring at St. Vitus Cathedral at Prague Castle. He left some ashes there under the watchful eye of police and in the presence of many tourists. I sure hope each of you get to Prague and Vienna when you grow up. They are two of my favorite cities.

"Some other trips your grandpa told me about where Ashley could have gotten him into trouble were on Easter Island and in Berlin, Rio, and Moscow. After attending a conference in Santiago, where Grandpa gave an invited paper, he took a flight to Easter Island at his own expense. There, he had to do a lot of walking up and down many trails while being careful not to trip on volcanic rocks. He continued his tour after lunch, and a strange thing happened next. Your grandpa had deposited some of Ashley inside of the Rano Raraku volcano between two flowering trees, next to a small lake or caldera. A few minutes later, a dozen wild horses came over the ridge of the volcano, running over the ashes on their way to the other side of the lake. Maria, his guide, told him that all the horses on the island have owners according to the law and should be corralled, but most of the owners let their horses run wild because they cannot afford to feed them.

"In the Berlin TV tower, your crazy grandfather went to the men's room, put a little of Ashley in his hand, and then went over to the glass window ledge in the tower and released part of her with many tourists around him. In Rio at Christ the Redeemer statue, there were four guards at each corner of the statue. Your sly grandpa went to the statue, knelt down to tie his shoe, and let a little of Ashley out of his pants cuff that he had placed there before his visit. In Moscow, he did the same thing in front of St. Basil's Cathedral in Red Square with the Moscow police and soldiers about and at the DMZ during his visit to North Korea with lots of soldiers there as well.

"His trip to Paramaribo, Suriname, and Georgetown, Guyana, was also very interesting. Paramaribo was built by the Dutch and mainly consists of two-story old wooden houses. Dutch is still the official language there. They became independent from the Netherlands in 1975, and it is the smallest South American country in land area. The main landmarks in the city are the bridge over the river Suriname, the Cathedral of Saints Peter and Paul that is about 120 years old, and a mosque next to a synagogue. As you can guess, a little of Ashley stayed behind between the mosque and the synagogue.

"After two nights in Paramaribo at the new Marriott Hotel, he caught a Caribbean Airlines flight back to Port of Spain, Trinidad, and then lucked out and caught a much earlier flight to Georgetown. Upon arrival, he got a cab, and the first thing the driver asked was your grandpa's name and what he wanted to see in Guyana. He told the driver that his name was Jim, and the driver immediately said, 'Jim Jones?'"

"Who was Jim Jones?" piped up Edward.

"He was the founder and leader of a religious temple group and is best known for being responsible for the murder in 1978 of his temple members in Jonestown, Guyana. However, I think you and Anabella should wait until you are a little older to know more about Jim Jones.

"Now back to the cab ride. Grandpa told the driver that he wanted to see Kaieteur Falls, so the driver got on his cell phone and made the arrangements. He told Grandpapaw that he raced cars on weekends, and Grandpapaw told me it seemed like the driver was in another race on the way to town. He was told that the ride normally takes forty-five minutes, but he did it in half that time. Anyway, instead of taking him to the Hotel Pegasus, he took him directly to the city airport, where he joined two others who were waiting for one more person so they would not have to cancel the flight. It turned out that this would have been his only opportunity to see the falls.

"Grandpapaw said he sat next to the pilot for the one-hour flight to Kaieteur National Park. The other passengers were a young American lady serving in the Peace Corps and her visiting mother. They ran into a bad rainstorm about halfway there, and indeed, it was a bit wild and scary, Grandpa told me, being tossed about in the rain without being able to see a thing but the driving rain hitting the windshield. The rain stopped as they got closer to the falls and landed okay after flying right by the falls for a terrific view. They had lunch and then walked about a half mile through the jungle to the falls. Grandpapaw says they were spectacular and are billed as the largest single-drop falls in the world. They spent about two hours there, and a little of Ashley stayed behind to enjoy the wonderful sites. Grandpa says the return flight was much calmer than the flight there."

II

"I am so sorry, dear children, but I hear your parents coming, so I will have to stop my storytelling now."

"Grandma, please don't stop," pleaded Anabella.

After Helen and Larry got settled, Ying announced to her family that she had a new teaching job with Clemson University but still planned to spend time volunteering, helping the disadvantaged, and with friends. "I will also try to come and visit you all in Vancouver more often and join you in skiing at Whistler each spring. I do love to ski, and Yim taught me how to be a good and safe skier. He also taught me many other things like playing pool, tennis, golf, and bowling and speaking better English. Of course, I taught him some Chinese games and some of the Chinese language."

A little time later, the kids went to their rooms to pack, and Larry left to do some shopping at Walmart in Anderson.

"Helen, I am so sorry that we did not talk more at your stepfather's memorial and your last visit here. I was still too distraught to tell you about what took place before James and Alex's accident. Please let me tell you more now that we are alone.

"I did not witness the accident since I was in my cabin, sick. We were crossing the Drake Passage and heading past Cape Horn. The sea was very rough that night, and large waves were coming over the front of the ship. I woke up late the next morning and found that James had not been in our cabin overnight. I went to Alex and Shana's cabin, and no one was there.

"I finally caught up with Shana in the breakfast room, where she looked very distraught and like she had been crying a lot. She ran over to me and started hysterically sobbing. I took her in my arms, and she told me she was so sorry, but Alex and James accidently fell overboard last night. The crew had been searching for them all night. They notified the Argentinean Coast Guard for assistance, and they even used a helicopter without success.

The captain did not give any hope for their survival in the cold and rough waters since they did not have life jackets on. Then I started to cry, and we both went back to my cabin to try to console each other.

"We arrived back in Ushuaia that evening and went to a hotel for one night. At dinner, Shana told me what had happened before James and Alex fell overboard. She said with difficulty, 'Alex related to me that his real name was Alex Pushkin, and during the voyage, you probably observed that our intimate relationship grew. Alex told me a lot about his life and his father's love for James's wife, Margrit. His father was responsible for Margrit getting killed at a rocket engine testing site in California where James worked. Alex told me that, of course, his father did not know about Margrit being at the rocket testing site and her plans to take the car that morning. Alex's father, Andrei, had intended for James to be driving the car, with the brake line cut, after work. Alex also said that his father told him that he and a friend had arranged his fake death in Russia to get away from Margrit since he was ruining her life and marriage in Vienna. He also wanted to get away from his terrible cheating wife and start a new life. Thus, he had immigrated to Canada and got a job as a factory representative for rocket engine parts. I was very scared, Ying, and did not tell anyone about my conversations with Alex.'"

Ying said to Helen, "One upsetting thing for Shana to hear was when Andrei contacted Alex to come to Toronto for a visit. Of course, Alex had believed his father was deceased all this time. Anyway, Alex went to Canada, and he enrolled in the university for his master's degree. After graduation, Andrei told his son about his relationship with Margrit, which had started in Vienna; how James was responsible for him losing his job at UNIDO; his faked death; and visiting Margrit in California, trying to renew their affair. When she rejected him, he was determined to kill James. Instead, he had killed Margrit by accident. Alex was, of course, very shocked by these stories his father told him.

"The day Alex was packing to return to Moscow, he heard a gunshot below in the living room. He ran down from the bedroom to find his father shot in the chest. There was no gun around, and as he tried to stop the bleeding, his father told him in his dying breath not to call the police or to get help. Andrei told Alex that he knew that James had just accepted a professorship at Clemson University and asked Alex to enroll in their graduate program with James as his research adviser. He also said that Czermak had shot him and that he should go to Clemson and kill him.

"Shana said, 'Ying, I am very, very sorry to tell you this. But the night of the accident, James and Alex were at the stern talking, and I was on the deck directly above them where I could overhear their conversation without them seeing me. Alex joined James, who said, 'You had better hold on to the railing as the sea is really getting rough.' After some discussions on the joyous evening, Alex started a conversation about how much he had enjoyed his graduate studies so far and how great an adviser James was. Alex told James that he loved his work at the university and wanted to be a professor just like him. He said he also wanted to eventually marry me and, with difficulty, admitted that his real name was Alexander Pushkin, that his father was the one who had a love affair with Margrit in Vienna, and that he had cut the brake lines on his car with the intention of killing him and not Margrit.

"'James was shocked as Alex admitted that, on the camping night, it was he who had kicked the rock that was holding him in place. As James started to slide down the hill toward the ocean, Alex told James that he was immediately sorry for what he had done and then ran after him, trying to stop him, but that James had managed to stop himself at the edge of the hill by turning over and grabbing some rocks. Alex says, 'My father told me in his dying breath that you had shot him and that I should kill you.' James sternly told Alex that he did not kill his father and has an alibi. 'Yes, Professor, yesterday I received word that my father had actually committed suicide as the police found his gun under the couch where he was sitting, and it had only his fingerprints on it.' Alex told James that he was extremely sorry that he had tried to kill him.

"'At the end of the conversation, James said, 'Under the circumstances, I forgive you and know that you will turn out to be a great professor and husband to Shana. Come here, big guy, and give me a bear hug.' Alex happily jumped over to give James a bear hug, but they both fell against the unlocked, fragile cargo gate. It opened, and they accidently went over the back of the ship into the rough, freezing ocean.

"Shana told me that she was shocked and ran into the dining room, screaming, and yelled that Alex and James accidently fell overboard. The captain was notified and had the ship turn around and cruise the area, with searchlights trying to find the two in the wild sea. The captain said it was too dangerous to put Zodiacs in the rough waters to aid in the search. The patrolling around this area of ocean continued until morning, when the captain put the ship back on course after a couple of helicopters continued patrolling. At the end of the day, the authorities called off the search and declared the two were lost at sea."

Ying, with tears in her eyes, told her daughter, "Now you know how your stepfather and my beloved husband met his death."

Acknowledgments

The authors wish to thank their daughters, Mrs. Julie Kornman and Ms. Nicole Navratil, for their suggestions on improving the first draft of the book. They also acknowledge the valuable comments and editing provided by Mr. Ed Vjvoda and Dr. Gary Thompson, both former managers of Research and Development at Rocky Flats. Finally, they are very grateful for the kind assistance of Dr. Cinda Kochen and Ms. Micah Springer, author of *Keepers of the Story*.

Summary

The Final Bear Hug is a continuation of the story in *The Bear Hug*. The story begins with John James Czermak and his wife, Margrit, returning to their home in Arvada, Colorado, after spending almost three years in Vienna, Austria, where John has worked for the International Atomic Energy Agency. John is a world-renowned scientist and contributor to the development of the neutron bomb and returns to his job as manager of Plutonium Chemistry Research and Development at the Rocky Flats Plant, where triggers for nuclear weapons are made.

In Vienna, Margrit has been romantically involved with Andrei Pushkin, thought by the CIA to be a KGB agent. Realizing the futility of their relationship, Andrei and Margrit have, on several occasions, unsuccessfully attempted to terminate it. But Andrei has suffered agonizing continual self-debasement and eventually left Vienna for Canada after faking his suicide.

After their return to Colorado, John and Margrit resume a close, loving relationship that has been badly damaged in Vienna. About this time, John is recruited by Tim Smith of the CIA since John travels to conferences around the world, including Vienna and Moscow to have meetings with his Russian coauthors on a series of books they are writing. After more contacts with his Russian colleagues, John is informed that a background investigation has been conducted by the Department of Energy and the FBI. This investigation results in John losing his security clearance.

John is then granted a three-year leave of absence to teach in Australia. Tim keeps in contact with John and requests him to visit certain countries and find out if they might be producing nuclear weapons. During his travels, there are several attempts on his life.

After his return from his leave of absence, he starts work in California. There, Andrei surprisingly contacts Margrit, trying to renew their love affair. Margrit rejects him since she has a good relationship with John and tells Andrei she might go with him if she is a widow or a divorcée. This statement prompts Andrei to try to kill John, but instead, he accidentally kills Margrit. Upon hearing the news of her death, he commits suicide and tells his son, Alex, in his dying breath that John has shot him.

John wants to start a new life and leaves California for a teaching job at Clemson University in South Carolina and even starts using his middle name, James. Andrei's son, Alex, joins James's research group using a different last name. The story concludes during an expedition in Antarctica that Tim supports to see if one of the Russian crew members is passing nuclear weapon information to a group of Argentinean scientists.

On the expedition, Alex tries to kill James but later finds out that James has not killed his father. On the last night of the voyage, he meets James at the stern of the ship and makes amends to him, which ends by Alex giving James a big bear hug that causes both of them to accidentally fall into the rough and freezing ocean.

The book will especially be enjoyed by globe-trotters since a lot of the story is about Czermak's travels around the world.